Lavender and Lies

Lavender and Lies

Pamela Rivron

authorHOUSE®

AuthorHouse™
1663 Liberty Drive
Bloomington, IN 47403
www.authorhouse.com
Phone: 1-800-839-8640

First published by AuthorHouse   06/03/2011

ISBN: 978-1-4567-8347-1 (sc)
ISBN: 978-1-4567-8348-8 (ebk)

CHAPTER ONE

After positioning her car with exquisite precision between the ungenerous white lines of Woolchester town car park, paying and displaying, changing from driving shoes into black, shiny courts, checking for lipstick on her teeth and straightening her skirt, she gave a little hum of satisfaction. The clickety clack beat of her heels would register the number of paces to her destination in confirmation of the dummy run executed the previous day. She had chosen not to park outside the place for fear of recognition,—it would be just her luck, she thought, for her red Honda to be spotted by some busybody village acquaintance who would ask intrusive questions. No shame attached, of course, but she had no wish to advertise her visit. Two more click-clacks and there she was.

Lavender House was not easily missed with its faded, Victorian grandeur enlivened by the mauve brick frontage that pained the town planners who had approved the change of use and saw no point in arguing about the loss of old, yellow mellow or the insensitive treatment of the front door, now a rather alarming purple.

She hesitated for only a moment before pushing it open and stepping into a wide hall where she was unsurprised to find all the fresh paintwork was mauve, with pretty-pretty flower prints arranged in threes. There was a row of unoccupied cane chairs opposite an unhelpfully unmanned reception desk displaying pots and bottles of variously coloured lotions from which she selected one offering patchouli and ylang-ylang and popped it into her handbag. A fan of leaflets detailed the eye-watering prices of the many services on offer. On the wall above the chairs, a large board daintily edged with hand-painted lavender listed the therapists and their room numbers. The sound of pan pipes oozing from the nearest door was one she had always disliked, linked in her mind with whale music and causing an urge to smash the irritating source. Another area of unease was any allegedly therapeutic procedure involving physical contact. She did not wish to be aromatherapeutically massaged and certainly did not want to have needles stuck into her or endure hot stones applied to sensitive areas, and as for having lit Hopi candles poked in her ears she did not think so, thanks all the same.

Talking treatment was what she sought and, after scanning through Reiki, Indian Head Massage, Aromatherapy, Acupuncture, Hypnotherapy, Reflexology, Cranio-sacral Therapy and such, there it was:

LOIS PALMER, COUNSELLOR/THERAPIST Room number 5, Second Floor.

She checked her watch against the clock on the wall to confirm that she was, typically, exactly on time. The whole place smelled overwhelmingly sweet, and she thought as she climbed the stairs that just sitting in the hall and inhaling might be quite effective for minor ills. She tapped on the door which was opened immediately by a woman of the same height, age and build as herself, with similarly-styled shoulder-length blonde hair. As their blue eyes met the women gazed at each other warily for a few seconds, slightly unnerved by the doppelganger effect.

Lois Palmer recovered, smiled with well-glossed lips and held out her hand.

"Hi!" she said. "You must be Mrs. Durmer? Come on in," and she led the way into a square room with four easy chairs and a pine table overburdened with artificial flowers; there was an alcove leading off with a sink, a fridge, a kettle and cups and saucers. Lois indicated a low, green velvet chair. Refusing her offer of camomile tea or decaf coffee, her client watched as Lois took a pad and pen from the table and sat opposite on a significantly higher chair.

"May I call you Sarah? I'm Lois, as you've gathered. First of all, Sarah, how did you hear about me?"

"I'm afraid I picked you from Yellow Pages. All those letters after people's names didn't mean a lot to me, but you had more than most, so I chose you."

Lois, freshly qualified from her latest correspondence course, nodded modestly.

"You can't always judge by that but let's see whether I can help. Would you like to tell me a bit about yourself to start with, Sarah, just general information. In your own time."

Sarah settled back into the very comfortable chair and began, her hands tightly clasped in her lap. It had already occurred to her that they should have exchanged clothes, believing her own well-tailored grey suit and white shirt looked more professional and appropriate for a counsellor than Lois's yellow tee shirt, jeans and trainers. Perhaps dressing down was a deliberate ploy to make clients feel relaxed, but in her view it was too casual for the important job in hand. She took a deep breath.

"I'm thirty-nine," she began. "I used to work in advertising, but I've recently begun working from home as a technical writer. I've no children. I'm an only child. My parents live in Spain so I don't see much of them. I was widowed nearly two years ago."

Lois recognised happily that this was well within her bailiwick: a client bereaved, still grieving, childless, only child of absent parents, pushing forty, new, lonely job. Wonderful!

She adjusted her expression to show sympathetic concern mixed with an air of confidence. "And you've come to see me because . . . .?"

"Because I killed him. My husband, James. I killed him."

Suddenly Lois had palpitations and a very dry throat. After swallowing twice she coughed, took a deep breath and tried an encouraging smile.

"You don't mean that literally, I'm sure." Silence. "Perhaps you're carrying guilt about something you said? Or did?"

Sarah's expression of absolute composure did not change, adding to Lois's unease.

"I do mean it literally. It was nothing I said. It was certainly something I did."

Lois did not care for the way this interview was going.

"What do you mean, Sarah? What did you do that you think led to his death?"

There was an uncomfortably long pause during which Sarah examined her nails.

"Did you leave him?" pressed Lois.

It was Sarah's turn for the deep breath. "No," she said. "I stayed. He suffered from angina, had done for years. It was controlled, you know, healthy diet, regular exercise plus tablets when necessary, check-ups with his consultant. He didn't like people knowing he had a physical flaw. I suppose it was a macho thing."

Lois waited, but this time the pause lasted so long that she felt obliged to ask, "Was he stressed? Work problems?" Sarah's enigmatic half-smile persisted.

"Personal problems?" Lois asked hopefully.

Sarah gave a little sniff and again Lois waited for the expected outpouring of grief or guilt or blame or anything suitable for long, expensive treatment.

"Personal problems?" echoed Sarah, and Lois did not like the unsettling little snort from her client, who went on, "He didn't recognise a personal problem but, yes, having an affair with some common little tramp could count as personal and was certainly a problem to me, which would count as normal, wouldn't you say?"

Lois allowed herself a silent 'Aha!' but simply nodded gravely. "Yes, I can understand that. But his death, Sarah? Why do you insist that you killed him?" She smiled archly at the now tight-lipped Sarah. "I don't recall reading of a domestic murder in this region in the last few years."

"No," responded Sarah tartly, "You wouldn't. Not all murders are recognised as such. The perfect murder is the undiscovered one."

"Look, I guarantee confidentiality on most things," said Lois nervously, "but murder? I'd really rather not . . . .why are you telling *me*? If it's murder, and frankly, Sarah, I'm finding that very hard to believe, it's a police matter and I don't think I should continue listening to you."

She half rose from her chair but sank back. "Did you really kill him?"

Sarah crossed her legs, rested her head on the back of the chair and gripped its arms.

"He needed his tablets during an attack. I refused to fetch them and he died. Just like that. Over in seconds. I told the police I found him dead and nobody queried it. Everybody was awfully kind. Even the coroner offered his condolences."

"I see." Lois tapped her lower teeth with her pen. "Look, obviously it was a massive heart attack and he'd have died even if you . . . whatever happened." She looked hard at Sarah. "But from what I gather, you're saying it was your intention to let him die, and I suppose quite understandably your guilt has persisted until now it's consuming you?"

Rather proud of this assessment, Lois watched as her client not only relaxed again, but smiled as if they were discussing what to have for dinner.

"No. I don't feel any guilt. As you've observed, I intended to let him die and die he did. I didn't fetch his medication or call a doctor or an ambulance in time, and he obligingly died and I'm glad he's dead. He deserved it, as I explained."

The room became chillingly quiet while Lois struggled for an appropriate comment, but Sarah suddenly leaned forward before saying softly, "I'm aware, well, I went to a lot of trouble to find out, that you've got a husband and a child, Lois, and that you've suffered bereavement yourself, isn't that so?"

The therapist nodded uneasily and checked the position of her mobile phone before agreeing, "Yes, my dear mother died some years ago . . . ." but Sarah interrupted, "I didn't know about your mother. My condolences. It's not quite true that I picked you at random. You were very specially selected. And my name isn't Sarah Durmer and my husband's name wasn't James. A friend of mine knew you when you were a hairdresser, Lois. She was having her highlights done when my husband walked in. She overheard your conversation and soon knew that he wasn't there to book a short back and sides. Kindly, she told me, as best friends do, and I had him followed. Wednesday afternoons and Friday evenings, wasn't it, regular as clockwork and about as exciting, I imagine. Yes! It's Lucas we're talking about. Our Lucas!

You're the little tramp, Lois, and I'm the deceived wife, or, as it happens, the merry widow with the house and his pension and insurance money and freedom. I didn't want a divorce. I didn't want a confrontation, either, in case I liked you, which fortunately I don't.

My friend with the highlights said you seemed nice, so I haven't wanted to meet you until recently, when suddenly I wanted you to know how I managed to put the kibosh on your sordid little affair without all of us being exposed as pathetic losers—you in particular Lois, a mother with a presumably loving husband and a reputation of sorts.

Did you really love Lucas? Were you even aware that he was dead? Another friend,—does overweight, Scottish, black extensions ring a bell?—told me rumours at the salon had it that you'd also had a thing going with at least one sales rep. Did poor old Lucas know? It's academic now, Lois, except that if there is any guilt entailed I think it should be spread around a bit. Shall we ever know whether you might actually have been relieved when he left the scene."

She leaned forward, head on one side with an expression of honest enquiry.

"Also, I'd genuinely like to know, Lois, whenever did you get your housework done, or supervise your son's homework, or fill in your VAT returns? I admire that kind of superwoman organisation tremendously, I really do. Oh, dear, you're looking quite pale. Let me get you a glass of water."

As she moved toward the sink she was followed by a shaking Lois who was fearful of the knife drawer, but Sarah simply poured a glass of water, prodded Lois gently back into the lower, green chair, handed her the water and seated herself in the higher, therapist's chair.

"Now, dear, I saw you eyeing your mobile, but let's forget about the police. We don't want all this nasty business on the front page of the local paper, do we? Not good for the therapy trade. I imagine. Of course, you were still a hairdresser back when I used to go into Lemford with a friend each Saturday for aromatherapy. Lucas had a joke about Aroma the rapist. He told it before I went every week for a year. Did he tell you any jokes, Lois? Perhaps you'd like to think of a few for my next visit. I thought we could reminisce in a therapeutic sort of way. I'll tell you how I came to think of Lucas as a deeply boring, faithless waste of space and you can dispute my viewpoint if you want to. Let it all out, Lois, don't hang back!. I must say I was surprised he chose another slim blonde. Why not a dark, voluptuous type for a change? Perhaps he tried and failed. Who knows? Look at us! We're a matching pair apart from your spectacular fingernails and our clothes, of course, and I'm sure we can soon improve on yours."

While Lois sat frozen-faced in shock, 'Sarah' stroked the green velvet gently.

"I *do* like this chair! Good choice! It feels most satisfying to be able to look down on your client from a superior position, so perhaps I'll claim this one. I've made out a cheque for ten sessions and I've used my real name which you must know by now is Angela Smith, that is if Lucas ever mentioned me in passing. Don't you think that 'Drumer' was a rather clever pseudonym? No idea? I thought you might spot the anagram, but obviously you're not a crossword addict, and then you'd hardly have time what with all your other activities. No! Don't get up! I'll see myself out. I honestly feel so much better already and I'm sure that after a few more sessions you'll cheer up, too. Try not to cry so, Lois, it's not flattering and you must think of your other patients, if you have any. See you next week, dear."

The Reflexologist on the floor below who had heard the clatter of footsteps and what sounded like someone chanting, stepped out in time to see a woman she at first mistook for Lois, making her way out. Puzzlingly, the person seemed to be saying, "And the week after that, and the week after that, and the week after that . . ."

But even more disturbing was the sound of quiet sobbing coming from Room Number Five.

CHAPTER TWO

Trixie Callender, owner of Lavender House, arrived at the steps just in time to see and hear Angela Smith, a.k.a. Sarah Durmer making her conspicuous exit. Lips pursed, Trixie stepped quickly inside and found Juliet, the Reflexologist, standing in the hall looking anxious.

"The general idea of an establishment like ours is that people who come in here twitching and muttering, walk out smiling and calmed, not vice versa, "she hissed. "What was all that?"

"She wasn't mine! She was Lois's two o'clock, I suppose. My next lady's not due until three thirty."

Juliet, as pink as her tunic, looked affronted until Trixie patted her shoulder and apologized before asking, "Where's Boot? He was supposed to be looking after Reception while I slipped out."

Juliet shrugged. "I saw him leave soon after you."

Trixie rolled her eyes and headed for the stairs. "I'd better check that Lois is okay. Do you mind manning Reception for ten minutes or so?"

Visibly shaken, Lois had stopped weeping but was scrunching tissues into small balls.

Trixie moved to the kettle. "Talk to me while I make some tea," she said.

Lois had been thinking fast in the short time since Angela Smith's departure and had reached the conclusion that she had no choice but to admit the truth, or most of it. She needed Trixie's support and suspected, rightly, that she might be more tolerant of past adultery than present lies.

Trixie listened in silence but with eyebrows in constant movement as the tale was told.

"Well," she said, sipping the camomile brew. "Things tend to come back to bite us on the bum. Since she's left a cheque it looks as though she really means to come back, like the Terminator. Pay it into your account, Lois, and wait to see whether she cancels it or it bounces. Don't spend the money yet. I suspect she'll want to carry on with this game for a while and it'll be as well to let her. Tell her that I know everything. Don't involve your husband but try to give the impression that he knows all about it and its history. She's playing out some fantasy revenge, but you've got the upper hand. She's confessed to murder, for heaven's sake, which seems unlikely and I doubt the police would investigate; they'd write her off as a nutcase, if you'll pardon the technical expression. Now, I'll be on hand for the next session. Try to think of her impersonally as a patient imagining she's a therapist. She probably needs a psychiatrist, but I strongly suspect she just wants to talk. She's living alone and been bottling things up for years. She won't want exposure, any more than you do. Ride it out, sweetie! Practise your trade. Now, splash your eyes and prepare for the next mixed-up lady with an hour to spare."

Lois, reassured and impressed, impulsively kissed Trixie on the cheek by way of thanks.

"Now," sighed Trixie, "I need to find Boot, the little bastard."

She could have mentioned that she remembered the late Lucas Smith, the IT consultant who had set up and maintained the computer systems in all her hairdressing salons and, presumably, the one where Lois had previously been employed. An unlikely Lothario, she thought, a pale, slightly overweight man but obviously with enough charm to seduce, or be seduced by, the unfortunate Lois. His death had been greeted with surprise at the time because of his relative youth, but not with any displays of great loss.

Seeing an opportunity to return Trixie's kindness, Lois asked solicitously, "Trixie, have you ever wondered whether Boot might be gay?"

The older woman gave her a long, hard look during which she pondered on the IQ levels in the therapy trade.

"I think his large collection of Barbie dolls, the makeover of the playschool Wendy House, the ballet classes, his great interest in choosing my clothes and his fascination with musical theatre all gave us teeny clues since he was aged three. So yes, since you ask, we have wondered. That was largely why my late husband chose to work abroad, but that was his problem, not Boot's. He's a lovely, kind, clever man and I love him dearly just as he is which is not to say that I shall not strangle him for deserting his post. Now I must go and relieve poor Juliet before her client arrives. Don't worry about anything. We'll fix Angela Smith."

"Trixie, do you know an anagram of 'Drumer'?"

"Red Rum," replied Trixie without pause. "I backed him once."

Trixie Callender would have been unembarrassed to learn that her nickname was 'Matron', a job she believed she could have carried off as successfully as any of her enterprises so far. Built for a position of authority, she was tall with an impressively hoisted, brooch-bearing bosom, an unmoving helmet of platinum blonde hair and make-up that highlighted her sharp, blue eyes. Three weeks earlier when she was wearing a long, velvet purple skirt with matching sequinned top, her new colleagues—and she preferred that name to tenants, which was what they truly were—felt confident that they were embarking on a sure-fire venture with Trixie at the helm. Sometimes she referred to them as The Group which she believed implied professionalism and a common cause.

They were enjoying a champagne buffet in her spacious flat that, together with Boot's, comprised the whole top floor of Lavender House. The occasion was the launch of the Therapy Centre. For their inclusive rents they considered they were getting good value with generously sized, light and airy rooms with plenty of cupboard space, a kitchen bar with fridge, a cloakroom and an abundance of sockets. They had chosen their own furnishings, and of course, provided the essentials for their varied trades, such as treatment couches and electronic equipment. It had not gone unremarked that Lois escaped heavy expenditure, needing only a pencil and paper and chairs, and one or two unkind people had whispered about the rather unconvincing nature of Lois's qualifications.

Trixie had made it clear that she would have no truck with what she described as the tacky end of the market, and laughingly told of how she had given short shrift to an application from a lady who read Tarot cards and crystals. The credentials of the perfectly respectable sports masseur, Jason, had been carefully scrutinized; she advised them to display their diplomas and certificates prominently and warned them to make sure they had comprehensive insurance to guard against a litigious public. She asked that music, if absolutely necessary, should not be intrusive and was strict about opening and closing hours as she intended to be personally responsible for the security of the premises with the occasional assistance of Boot and the cleaner.

Boot would also assist at Reception, or, as later transpired, not.

There was general disappointment that the elusive Boot did not appear at the celebratory buffet which he was said to have organised. At that time only two of the therapists had met him and described him as a rather wispy, willowy, blonde young man. So far, the reasons for his name had not been revealed. According to Trixie he was a writer who had had an unfortunate, but unexplained, incident while at university studying for an M.A. in Creative Writing. Theories spread in Chinese whispers, but Trixie was keener to speak sorrowfully of her daughter, Lexie, who was in New Zealand as part of her veterinary training and had wilfully become engaged to a sheep farmer.

Somebody remarked that it was a coincidence that so many of The Group had come from hairdressing backgrounds, but Trixie countered loudly that it was not a coincidence at all. "There's a profession that gives you real insight into people's lives and characters and problems. We've all been therapists and counsellors while doing someone's hair extensions! The fact that you've all gone on to qualify for a different caring profession is no surprise. You've all had an excellent grounding."

She beamed round at them all, her gaze settling on Lawrence, her prize attraction. When a sixth-former he had had worked briefly as a dogsbody in one of her salons. Spotting potential, and already plotting her Therapy Centre, she had encouraged him, with his mother's permission, to train to become a chiropractor, and had part-funded him. She foresaw that, properly qualified, he would demonstrate respectability and gravitas in addition to his dark good looks. Her other less noble motive was to capture him for Lexie, sure that he would make a personable, malleable and deeply grateful son-in-law. Hence her frustration at the silly girl's absurd engagement.

Trixie made no secret that her ability to buy the well-situated former hotel now transformed into Lavender House, was the result of luck in the form of unexpectedly large and premature inheritances during the previous three years from her own parents and grandparents, in-laws and an aunt, not to mention the sizeable compensation awarded when her husband Andrew was killed in a car crash in Saudi Arabia where he was working as an engineer. It was for her a happy release from a miserable marriage. She was, she said, truly blessed and sitting pretty. She need not have worked again, but Trixie enjoyed a project and, as she piously told friends, she felt she should give something back to society. Her piety did not exclude the real likelihood of raising the rents substantially after the first year's leases expired.

There was still a vacant ground floor room which she hoped might be taken shortly by a homeopath who had made tentative enquiries.

In the cupboards of the therapists' rooms were packets of camomile, peppermint and green tea and varieties of spa water. At the party Trixie noted that devotees of the above were not constrained from drinking copious quantities of alcohol, but benevolently considered they had earned a jolly time, and knew from experience how a few drinks might lead to bonding. Certainly they had all generously helped each other to carry in boxes, equipment and potted plants in a pleasantly co-operative way, while admiring each other's rooms and examining their framed qualifications. It all, she thought, boded well. She raised her glass, tapped it with a fork and proposed a toast.

"To Lavender House, and all who work in her. God bless us, every one!"

On cue, though hardly Tiny Tim, a greenish Boot put his head round the door to tell his mother he wasn't feeling very well.

CHAPTER THREE

The incident with Lois and the muttering client, perceived by Trixie to be a potential blackmailer, though of the emotional rather than the financial kind, left her feeling more uneasy than she showed. Having promised not to say anything to the others, she told the anxious Juliet that Angela Smith was mildly eccentric, but one posing no danger, Lois confirmed this and declared herself happy to continue with her treatment.

"We are bound," said Trixie," to get the occasional oddball but we're here to help in our various ways."

Privately she cursed the bad luck that had attached itself to Lois. While in no position to criticize, having herself had a selection of lovers while Andrew was working abroad, she had not attracted the attention of irate wives or girlfriends threatening vengeance. Admittedly as it seemed to be taking the form of therapeutic duelling at five paces, it might prove harmless, but it was at best a nuisance and at worst rather frightening. She did not confide in Boot.

Confirmation of Angela's intention to keep her Wednesday booking soon came. Trixie promised to be standing by, and watched as the brightly smiling Angela checked in and climbed the stairs.

Lois stood when she entered the room and in spite of a personal resolve to take command of the higher chair, she was edged out of the way by her determined client and sat apparently submissively in the lower seat. Clearly Angela was set on dominating the proceedings, producing her own notepad and pen and weighing straight in before Lois could speak.

"Now, Lois, tell me, in your own time, why your own marriage is so deeply unsatisfactory that you felt obliged to steal my husband?"

Lois gritted her teeth. "It's not at all unsatisfactory, Angela. Not now. We went through a bad patch a few years ago when he was working away and I was lonely. I'm sorry about it, of course I am. I had no idea Lucas was married until it was too late. He told me he was unhappy. It was a comfort thing for us both, not a great love affair. He didn't blame you. In fact he didn't talk about you at all. I didn't know your name or where you lived. I was relieved when he broke it off. I'd no idea about his heart problem and when I read in the paper he'd died I was really shocked."

"And even more relieved? Freed from guilt?"

"Freed from guilt? No, Angela, you'll know yourself that that never happens. You learn to accept and accommodate the experience. Life goes on regardless."

"Except for poor Lucas."

"Except for poor Lucas. Exactly." Lois saw an opportunity to capture the high ground and possibly by the next consultation, the high chair. "I was guilty of adultery. I confess it. You are, so you say, guilty of murder which is in a different league altogether. You will have to forgive Lucas and me before you can forgive yourself."

Angela frowned as if considering the logic of that proposition.

"No," she said. "I don't think that makes sense on any level. You're still assuming my guilt. You admit you and Lucas were to blame. I can't accept I should feel guilty about anything: you told me I shouldn't blame myself as he'd have died anyway and I'm convinced by your persuasive argument. I'm plainly not guilty at all while you're feeling very guilty indeed. We're sitting in the right chairs here, Lois. Now, let's forget about Lucas for a minute. What else have you got to get out of your system? Any more illicit affairs you'd care to talk about? I'm here to help."

From being initially frightened, Lois was growing increasingly cross and combative. "I don't understand why you want to do this," she said. "It has been two years since Lucas died. You're a clever, attractive woman, Angela, and I'm sure you can make a new life, and easily find happiness with a new partner."

"Oh, you're sure, are you? Don't you ever consider that Lucas and you may have permanently destroyed my trust in my fellow man? How am I to know that this hypothetical bringer of delight won't also sneak out on Wednesday afternoons and Friday evenings in search of a little extra-marital excitement? Answer me that, Miss Diploma in Therapy and Counselling from the Internet University of Kidology!"

Lois stood, trembling and red in the face.

"I can't guarantee you a trouble-free life, Angela. But I do know you'll destroy any hope of contentment by continuing to harass me."

She opened the door and almost shouted, "I had an affair with your husband. You allowed him to die. GET OVER IT! . . . See you next week. Same time!"

Angela hesitated before slowly and deliberately putting away her pad and pen. Red-faced but unbowed, she walked out.

"You certainly will," she called back, and repeated, "You most certainly will," apparently oblivious of Trixie's beady gaze following her as she clomped downstairs.

"Shall I book you in for the same time next week?" asked Trixie loudly and with exaggerated sweetness.

"You bet," replied Angela, smiling. "Eight to go."

Juliet firmly believed that a trouble shared was a trouble halved, a maxim that had mildly irritated her husband Simon when she worked in a hairdressing salon and related every evening the many titbits of customers' personal traumas ranging from chipped nails to brain tumours. He nourished hopes that the tranquillity of reflexology treatments might deter people from determinedly spilling the beans to his wife who equally determinedly spilled them on to him. "Keep out of it," was his advice.

"That's what Trixie said, which is all very well but you didn't hear the woman ranting last week about 'See you again and again and again.' Then this week it's Lois shouting through the open door about adultery and murder!"

Now she had his full attention. "Lois was shouting what?"

"I didn't catch all the details. It was lucky I didn't have a client at the time." (This was also a worry to Simon who hadn't reckoned on unfilled hours.) "I don't know what kind of therapy she's supposed to be practising but it's bloody noisy."

"I know Lois's husband vaguely, from the gym club. Do you want me to have a word with him?"

Simon really had no wish to engage in socializing with the Lavender House Mob as he called them and had been grateful that Mrs. Callender had not invited spouses or partners to the opening party. They were not, he guessed, his sort of people.

"No! Of course not Simon, get a grip! It's all strictly confidential. They're patients, remember."

Privately, Simon regarded his wife's treatments as so much harmless pixie-dust, taking place in pleasant surroundings at inflated prices. He had remained uncritical and supportive while she trained, had helped her to move into what appeared to be a cosy set-up and was not going to rock the boat now.

"Of course, but if you're worried . . ."

"I'm not worried exactly. There are plenty of us on call but it seems so out of place. It's not a psychiatric unit. That sort of thing creates a bad impression."

Simon nodded. "It would. I can see that. It sounds jolly interesting, though. Keep your ears open, Jools." He grinned, inappropriately thought Juliet, now wishing that she hadn't mentioned anything. Now she had to worry that he might bump into Matthew Palmer, Lois's husband, and start gossiping so that Lois would know she had heard the incident and then been indiscreet. Then there would be a big row and they would have to endure the wrath of Trixie, who was neither their employer nor their boss but behaved like a scary head teacher, unnerving Juliet who had wanted only a nice, stress-free job in a scented atmosphere. She scowled at Simon.

"Trust you to spoil everything," she said.

It took the customary ten minutes for Boot, lying effortlessly after years of practice, to persuade his mother that she was the one at fault for having forgotten that he had an important appointment at the Wig and Pen at one forty-five with his literary agent.

Apart from which, what, he wanted to know, was so frightfully difficult about people finding their own way to and from the appropriate doors at the appropriate time. Hardly rocket science. Did anyone die, for heaven's sake?

Inwardly Trixie worried that someone might well have done, given the circumstances, and that Boot would have been as useful as a chocolate fireguard in preventing such an occurrence. She said merely,

"An unmanned desk just looks so unprofessional."

Boot shrugged. "Well, I'm sorry. Would you like a drink? I want you to forget all that because I have some good news. Wait for it! Carl loves my work and would like to publish a limited edition."

Boot's talents were surprisingly dispassionately regarded by his mother who considered his work to be pretentious rubbish. But there, she loved him and was willing to pay for this piece of vanity publishing simply to boost his self-esteem which to most other people seemed quite high enough. Boot wrote verse in a visual arrangement to form trees of various shapes. The words made no sense to Trixie in spite of his patient explanation that his work was a kinaesthetic experience that she needed to allow to feed her senses. Her unspoken opinion was that it was the kind of endeavour encouraged in infant school. Still, he would have some expensively formatted volumes with **TREES, AN EXPLORATION BY FELIX CALLENDER** on the cover and quite possibly a dedication inside to MY MOTHER, although this could not be guaranteed. She raised her vodka and tonic. "Congratulations. That's lovely." Questions regarding the substantial upfront payment were for another day.

In spite of Juliet's promise to Trixie and her protestations to Simon regarding confidentiality, she could not resist describing what she had seen and heard to Jason the sports masseur and to Beverly the aromatherapist whose rooms were on the floor above and who had heard nothing. Since they already regarded Juliet herself as a suitable case for treatment, they disregarded her version of events and checked with Lois who laughed and shrugged it off, remarking only that her excitable client needed a few more sessions and that she'd yell for Jason if problems arose.

It was an unfortunate coincidence that the following Wednesday Angela arrived at Reception just as Beverly was checking her next booking. Trixie paused to say, "Good afternoon. Go on up, Mrs. Smith."

Her query settled, Beverly lingered and nodded in the direction of Lois's room.

"That the noisy customer?" she asked.

Trixie presented a blank face. "How do you mean?"

"We heard there was a bit of a kerfuffle in number five. Jason's on standby in case of a punch-up."

"Jason? How on earth is he involved?" Trixie's eyes became steely slits of ice.

"He's not really. It was just something Juliet said."

"Is it now," said Trixie coldly. "I can't imagine what it's got to do with her. Lois is bound to have problematic patients from time to time. She's a therapist. It's no-one else's business."

"Actually, I recognise that particular patient," said Beverly, cheerfully undeterred. "It's Angela Smith, isn't it? Her late husband did the IT repairs at my Daniel's office. Lucas. He had an affair with a secretary and she committed suicide—drowned herself. Pregnant was the rumour, though it was all speculation. I'm not surprised she needs therapy but it was a long time ago. Lucas died of a heart attack; been overdoing it they all said. He wasn't too popular, but there. Fancy his wife turning up here."

Trixie's lips reduced to a purple line of disapproval.

"Yes, fancy. I'd be obliged if you'd keep all this to yourself, Beverly. This sort of gossip is very unprofessional."

"Well, of course," Beverly replied, big brown eyes opened wide. "I wasn't the one to start it. Jason's an absolute clam so no worries there. We were just anxious for Lois, but she seems fine."

"Yes, she is. Nothing to worry about. Ah, good. Here comes your Reiki lady"

Upstairs, Lois called. "Come in!" but this time did not rise from the higher chair when Angela entered, smiling sweetly.

"I see possession is nine-tenths of the law. That's okay. I feel tall today. Do you like my shoes?"

Lois looked obediently at the four-inch heels.

"Very nice," she said. "Do sit down.".

"Well now," began Angela immediately, "What shall we talk about today. Your marriage to Matthew still going strong? And how's your lovely son? You know, ignorance really is bliss. I was far happier before I found out that my Lucas, well, they used to say, 'had an eye for the ladies', but that doesn't altogether cover it. It was both eyes and his entire hairy body. Did you hear about the girl who committed suicide over him? That girl at the desk would have known her. Before your time but a nasty occurrence. He was upset for oh, a week at least before he started looking for a replacement. Then you came along, sad and lonely you. Have a word with Beverly Whatsername: she can fill you in on a few details."

Feeling extremely sick, Lois breathed deeply, composed herself enough to say,

"Angela, I really do want to help you. It's what I'm trained to do," and ignored the look of disdain on Angela's face. "Lucas treated you very badly and I really regret getting involved with him. His death was tragic but you must draw a line under it now. Start again. Remember all the happy times you had together and concentrate on them until the bad experiences fade away. You can do it, Angela. You can achieve closure. Anything else is self-destructive."

Angela had been gazing into Lois's face earnestly. With exaggerated enthusiasm she declared, "I do get it. I really do. Is it Frankel or Freud? You want me to ac-centuate the positive and e-liminate the negative, Latch on to . . . ."

Aware that her voice was becoming rather shrill, while wondering whether there had ever been a case of a therapist giving her client a hard slap, Lois cut across with,

"If you feel like singing, sing! Join a choir! Just make sure you have a full social life. You've very clearly spent too much time on your own. You need to mix with people. Join a club! What are your interests?"

Angela put a finger to her chin as if in reflection. "Oh, I used to belong to a gym. I could do that again. The Hightown Gym has a good reputation: your sports masseur Jason works there on Sunday mornings and Beverly Chaplin's husband's a member, I believe. Oh, and Juliet's husband. And yours."

Lois felt as though she had been dipped in a deep vat of icy cold water. The wretched woman knew everybody and everything, their relationships, their hobbies, everything. With admirable control she smiled tightly. "The only snag with gyms is that they offer lonely pursuits with no real interaction. How about a drama group?"

"Oh, good idea," replied Angela, keen as mustard, blue eyes shining brightly.

"I could audition for 'Guys and Dolls'. I love that! WOADS are advertising for singers. Boot's a member! I could try for Miss Adelaide. What a lovely suggestion! Thank you! Isn't it funny, I hardly ever came into Woolchester before I started seeing you, and now I'm here every day, exploring, researching, getting to know what's going on. That's what you're advising, isn't it, that I should get out more, talk to more people?

Look, I'm awfully sorry, Lois, but I must cut short this session, enjoyable as it is. I'm afraid I haven't helped you one little bit, which is what I aim to do. I'll make up for it next week. See you!"

"See you," responded Lois, dead-eyed and despairing.

Later, Trixie and Lois sat sipping tea and wondering what to do. The mention of Boot had immediately alarmed his mother, fearful of exposure of she knew not what.

Plainly, Mrs. Angela Smith was very efficiently mapping connections between Lavender House practitioners and their partners, but the reason, other than the obvious Lois one, was opaque.

"Why Boot?" asked Trixie fretfully. "He's nothing to do with her or her wretched husband. Oh, sorry, Lois, but you know what I mean. Boot has problems, God knows, but they don't concern her. What's she up to? Blackmail? For you, perhaps, but that's all. Jason's a decent family man, Juliet's nice, if a bit of a flutterwit, Beverly's a gossip queen but the others are open books. As far as we know. I don't see what's driving her. Is she trying to close us down?"

Nobly displaying spirit, Lois said, "She can't do that. If necessary I'll tell Matthew everything, and everybody else, and risk the consequences. When Lucas was alive he was a lousy lover and serial adulterer and he's not going to spoil things now he's dead. It's my fault and I'll have to sort it and suffer the consequences. I'm really sorry, Trixie."

"Steady now, you're jumping the gun. Let's see how the sessions progress. You never know, you might even cure her." Lois recognised the slight slur but was beyond hypersensitivity. Trixie went on, "We shan't give in. If she's stalking or threatening I'll call the police. If she turns out to be as mad as a box of frogs, which I half suspect, then we shall have to seek other help. I said we'd fix her and we shall."

Lois sighed and nodded. "Let's see what next Wednesday brings." She perked up and enquired, "I hope you don't my asking but how did Boot get his name?"

"He's Felix, actually. My mother-in-law used always to refer to him as a little beaut and he started calling himself Boot. It just stuck. We've all got x in our real names. Andrew's second name was Rex and even the dog's called Max. It seemed amusing at the time."

Lois smiled at the unexpected simplicity of it all and went upstairs to wait for her four o'clock mother and wayward, obnoxious daughter, trying to convince herself that this was an improvement on hairdressing. The chilling thought came to her that wherever she was and whatever she was doing, Angela Smith would be on to her. She made another cup of camomile tea.

Boot, a young man with many interests, was untalented in most of them. He had demonstrated with the WOADS that he could neither sing nor act and had not acquitted himself well as prompter, but at last he had displayed a much valued skill at running up stage costumes. Immersed in feathers, sequins, satins and silks, velvets, ribbons and brocade, he was excited to be able to create an outfit from a drawing—not his, for he had no flair for that either, but one true to the designer's intention. The local paper's review of their production of 'Kiss Me Kate' mentioned the costumes rather more warmly than the singing, which made him very proud. There was no real need for him to attend all rehearsals, but he enjoyed the company and atmosphere and the visit to the pub afterwards. Tonight there were auditions for 'Guys and Dolls', an added attraction. The chorus, hard to recruit, were accepted simply by turning up, no matter how old or lacking in talent they were, but there was competition for leading roles which provided very satisfactory entertainment. The usual suspects were surprised by the arrival of an unknown, attractive blonde declaring she'd like to try for Adelaide. She was given an artificially warm welcome, questioned about previous experience which was, she said, playing one of the three little maids from school when she was at school herself. Apparently unfazed after hearing two competent contenders, she showed no signs of nerves when her turn came. Her voice, though in tune, was thin and squeaky. The producer thought, and questioned her whether, she might be assuming the voice for comic effect, but no, that was it. Angela, for of course it was she, was undismayed by rejection and graciously accepted a chance to join the chorus.

At the end of the evening she also accepted the chance to go to the pub with many of the others, and was first at the bar to buy a drink for the bemused Boot, who found her to be a very nice person, so interested in his writing achievements and someone with whom he could have a real heart to heart.

CHAPTER FOUR

The following morning promptly at eight-thirty the new, much heralded homeopath arrived to examine the vacant rooms to decide whether they would be suitable for him. Trixie, who had had only 'phone conversations with him was greatly impressed by Jack Kent, a tall, well-built man of about forty with fair, curly hair, clear blue eyes and manicured hands. His tan was shown to advantage by his cream linen suit; there was the slightest whiff of expensive aftershave and even his leather briefcase pleased, stuffed as it was with the appropriate paperwork to convince Trixie of his all-round excellence as tenant of Room Two, the largest on the ground floor, and adjoining that of the acupuncturist, Lily Ho.

Impressed by the space and facilities, he soon decided he would like to start his practice as soon as possible. He explained that he was divorced, without children and had left his native York for a fresh start. His new flat was a short drive away and he had a good feeling about the direction his life was about to take. Lavender House had, he said, a wonderful ambience. Deal done.

Spirits raised, Trixie took him quickly to meet the other therapists before their clients arrived. All were welcoming and warm until she came to Lily Ho who remained unsmiling and distant, much to Trixie's surprise.

After the necessary details were sorted, and a moving—in date agreed, Jack shook hands and left and Trixie returned to question the acupuncturist.

Lily was the thirty-six year old daughter of Charlie Ho, owner of a string of language schools in the county. He also owned three restaurants and had a thriving import/export business. The Hos lived in an imposing detached house on the edge of town. Lily was his only child, greatly loved and indulged. She was brought to and collected from work in a huge Mercedes, usually driven by her father who was a small, pixie-faced, merry-looking man with large sparkling brown eyes and dainty hands and feet. Mrs. Marilyn Ho was English, tall, overweight, with a large and placid face with small, dull brown eyes. Unfortunately, Lily took after her mother, her face flat and beady-eyed and her movements slow. Academically bright she had a B.A.(Hons.) in politics and economics, which subjects she had lectured in unhappily for a few years before deciding to qualify in acupuncture, a decision both parents approved. She worked hard, her casebook was full, her patients convinced of relief from various ailments.

Homeothapy, though, was anathema to her. She derided its principles and practice, an opinion not as yet shared with Trixie and her colleagues.

When Jack Kent left and Trixie again knocked on the door, Lily was armed with research papers and statistics and a recent book debunking homeothapy; Lily believed its practitioners to be taking money under false pretences and said so, very firmly.

Much taken aback, Trixie pointed out that most of the treatments on offer at Lavender House asked for a certain amount of suspension of disbelief, including Lily's own speciality, at which Lily began to cry copiously and Trixie felt like screaming.

There seemed to be, thought Trixie, some underlying, unexplored baggage here which Lily declined to reveal, merely offering the aforementioned debunking books.

Patiently, Trixie explained that although she, personally, would not engage in several, or indeed any, of the therapies on offer, if the patients believed in them then they were worth every penny. Most people need time to talk and a bit of stroking, said Trixie, philosophically. She confessed that her own preferred therapy was a large vodka and tonic at the end of the working day, followed by a good DVD and if absolutely necessary a couple of paracetamol.

Lily looked so plain and woebegone that Trixie made the inevitable camomile tea.

"He's a charming man, Lily. Single," she said, encouragingly. "I'm sure two intelligent people like you can get along well enough to discuss the pros and cons of his calling in an informed and civilized way."

Lily looked at her with her little brown button eyes expressing real doubt.

"We'll see," she said.

At the back of Trixie's mind was a nagging fear of upsetting the Ho family to the extent that Lily might not only leave, but be set up by Daddy in a lavishly endowed rival establishment. She dismissed as a silly over-reaction the possibility of a Triad connection, but still returned to the Reception desk a worried woman.

*　　*　　*

It might be expected that rivalry,—enmity even, might exist between Boot and Lawrence, the blue-eyed chiropractor protégé. He had, after all, been expensively nurtured by Trixie and had developed as she anticipated into an engaging, handsome, hard-working man who enjoyed his place at Lavender House. With fingers crossed it had been emphasised to him that although Trixie would like him, when qualified, to work in one of her establishments, he must not feel obligated financially or morally. As luck had it, a fortunate family windfall had in fact enabled him to repay almost all of the borrowed fees, but this did not lessen his debt of gratitude and he insisted that he was entirely happy working where he did.

The disappointment to Trixie was that Lexie had shown nothing but polite interest in him and vice versa. Boot considered him to be an all round good egg, so there was no family tension. They had accepted their mother's sponsorship of him as one of her many unexplained, but usually profitable, business opportunities from which they preferred to distance themselves. Their own education had been funded without apparent difficulty, they had no interest in hairdressing or therapy and were glad that neither career had been foisted on them.

Boot enjoyed remaining on the periphery at Lavender House. Apart from Lawrence he tried to ignore the rest of The Group and was a reluctant first reserve on Reception. Having deliberately kept him in the dark about Lois's problems, Trixie was now in a bit of a quandary over Angela Smith and the drama group connection. With commendable self-restraint she did not even ask Boot how the auditions had gone, but the following evening he voluntarily regaled her with one of his exaggerated and comic versions of events. Mostly he was amused by the few new aged chorus applicants fresh, he said, from Homes for the Bewildered. According to him, the choreographer would have to take into account replaced hips, wonky knees and short-term memory loss, ruling out any thoughts of high octane dance moves. Trixie guessed that Boot's perception of senility was probably attached to anyone over forty.

"No others?" she asked innocently.

"There was a quite nice new woman with a squeaky voice hoping for a lead role, poor thing. She'll be the youngest member of the chorus instead."

"What was her name?"

"Can't remember. Anne, I think. Why?"

"Oh, somebody mentioned they were interested."

Boot then resumed his monologue having been greatly diverted by the Brummie accent of the man chosen to play Nicely Nicely Johnson.

Trixie relaxed, by then on the right side of her reward of a couple of vodkas, and counted her blessings: all the rooms were now leased, clients were filling their time slots nicely and so far Angela Smith hadn't turned up brandishing an axe.

CHAPTER FIVE

It did not go unnoticed by Matthew Palmer that his wife was edgy and pre-occupied for the entire weekend. They were not a couple who explored feelings beyond an occasional, "You all right?" query. Lois kept her therapeutic interests at Lavender House, to her husband's relief. Pressed, he would probably have replied that they rubbed along nicely. He had no expectations of overwhelming happiness and was content with his situation : pretty wife, healthy son nearly old enough to go to football matches, pleasant house, the car he wanted, a job that left his weekends free, an amiable and uncritical mother-in-law to cover the child care until he or Lois came home.

He had suspected a few years ago that Lois might be bored with him. She had shown the same kind of pre-occupation then and he had convinced himself that she might be having an affair. He would not have blamed her, really. It had surprised him that a pretty, smart girl like her had agreed to marry him. He could not bring himself to question her about it and eventually she lightened up and they seemed to be closer.

The therapy qualification had boosted her self-esteem, so she said and he had been surprised that she needed that kind of boost. Anyway, he was proud of her and wanted her to be happy at Lavender House.

"You all right?" he asked.

Lois thought for a moment.

"I'm afraid I might sometimes bring a few of my patients' problems home with me. I'm sorry, love. I'm still learning."

Matthew smiled, sympathetically, and offered to make a cup of tea.

Actually, she was hatching a plan which she outlined to Trixie on Monday morning.

She was going to suggest to Angela that she should try some of the other treatments on offer at Lavender House. As she explained, she would say that she was afraid she was not getting through to Angela who might like to consider the chance of finding inner peace with Reiki or a holistic massage or acupuncture or something. She was still unaware of the woman's aversion to being touched.

"I'd gladly transfer money to whoever took her on," said Lois hopefully. "Very gladly."

"You run the risk," Trixie pointed out, "that she's highly likely to reveal your little secret while she's being treated. So far, at least, she's kept quiet. Just imagine Beverly with that piece of information, never mind the murder confession. I don't think that'll work, dear."

Lois decided to ignore this advice and when Angela booked in, prompt as ever, on the following Wednesday, was keen to give her plan a try.

Hanging on to the high chair, Lois immediately made the suggestion and, hearing Angela's sharp and immediate dismissal of the possibility of any hands-on treatment, almost whooped with delight. She contented herself with a smugly triumphant smile.

"So-oo, you don't like being touched? Perhaps we're getting to the root of your problem. Lucas must have."

"Forget it, Lois. I'm talking about being touched by strangers. That's not natural. In fact it's perverse unless it's sex or surgery or something like that. There are those," she said, looking directly into Lois's eyes, "who enjoy being touched by any Tom, Dick or Harry. I'm not one of them. My idea of hell is a group hug. No, Lois, I'm still all yours, not likely to be the patient of some needle sticker or suspect massage peddler. You're stuck with me. Or, in fact, I'm stuck with you, because I thought we'd more or less agreed that you're the lady with the problem"

"No!" cried Lois. "We agreed nothing of the sort! You're not qualified!"

"Funny you should say that. I've been seriously considering undertaking a course of training. The government want everybody to have, what is it? behavioural cognitive therapy or something like that, more or less on demand. There'll be marvellous career opportunities for ambitious young women like us. Excellent prospects. You must admit, Lois, that your qualifications are, forgive me, on the flimsy side. Good enough for the average housewife wanting some ME time, but somewhat inadequate for deep analysis and treatment. You know quite well by now that my purpose in seeing you is not driven by uncertainty about my psyche. I know exactly what I want and what I'm doing. You've helped me to confirm I shouldn't feel badly about Lucas's death and you've encouraged me to improve my social life. I'm honestly grateful for that. Now it's my turn to get your house in order. I want to help you and Matthew and dear little Oliver to live in harmony, without guilt eating away at the foundation of your marriage."

"If you're trying to ruin my marriage you're barking up the wrong tree." Lois tightened her grip on her pen and furiously flexed her toes. "I can assure you Matthew and I have no secrets. What's past is past. I'm very sorry that you're not in a contented relationship yourself but you won't be helped by destroying other people's happiness."

Angela beamed.

"Now that's where you're wrong, Lois. I thrive on schadenfreude. It helps me enormously."

Lois's puzzled expression allowed Angela to prepare for departure on a high note.

"I know our sessions aren't lasting as long as they should, Lois dear, but I'm happy to pay because of the intensity of our exchanges. Give my love to Trixie. Such a nice woman. And dear Boot, of course. See you!"

Jack Kent had not shown great surprise when Trixie revealed that Lily was not exactly 'on side', as she put it. He nodded, agreed that there had been a spate of adverse criticism about homeopathy, but that results spoke for themselves. Of his many grateful patients in York, some were even prepared to travel to Woolchester to maintain their treatments. He smiled, allowing Trixie to make a swift estimation of the cost of his dental work. "I see," he said, "that Beverly offers cranio-sacral therapy to help when the body's tissue fields contract. Now you and I know that's ridiculous, but some people will say they feel all the better for it. Are we all quacks, charlatans, modern day witches and shamen?" He spread his arms in a wide, all-embracing gesture. "These are all benevolent practices and if they incidentally provide us with a reasonable standard of living, so be it."

For just a second Trixie believed she saw a second-hand car salesman shining through but thought none the less of him for that.

When he promised, still smiling, that he would woo Lily, Trixie did not realize how seriously he would take on that task, but later in the day Lily took delivery of a huge pot of lavender in an expensive zinc container with a card saying, 'Can we talk over a drink? Jack.'

Lily decided that they could and joined him that evening for a meal at the Wig and Pen, which clearly went well as from then on they seemed to be popping in and out of each other's consulting rooms whenever there was a gap between appointments.

Trixie pondered this as she re-assessed Lily's physical attributes. It had been an absolutely non-PC disappointment when Lily had turned out to be not the slim and pretty, wide-eyed Chinese girl in a cheongsam they had all expected, but a plain, half-English, lumbering young woman. Trixie wondered whether Jack Kent knew what he was doing, and rather feared that he did.

Later, Lois revealed to her that she had, against advice, tried to interest Angela in some alternative alternatives and had discovered she hated being touched.

"Quite a breakthrough!" she declared.

Trixie nodded, thoughtfully. "A Eureka moment, most certainly. Homeothapy doesn't involve touching, does it? It's not hands-on?"

"Not as far as I'm aware. From what I've read it has to do with prescribing tiny drops of water that have developed a memory."

They both laughed.

"It's a shame that a nice-looking chap like Jack should have opted for a non-contact specialty like homeopathy. Such a waste."

"What are you suggesting, Trixie?"

"I'm suggesting Angela Smith is many things, but she's not foolish enough to pass up a chance of spending a few hours with a handsome, charming, divorced man of appropriate age. With or without physical contact."

Two pairs of blue eyes twinkled at each other.

"How do you suggest we go about that? Angela reacts badly when I suggest anything. She's determined that she's treating me, and she's determined to hang on in there."

"Leave it with me. I shall arrange a happenchance meeting."

"You're an angel, Trixie."

"Yes, I rather think I am."

Jack Kent had been truthful about his patients, as Trixie realized as she booked in several York ladies eager for continuing courses of treatment in spite of the journey entailed. As it happened she had no need to struggle to manoeuvre a meeting between Angela and Jack since an offhand remark to Trixie regretting having to leave the York Amateur Opera Players was passed on to Boot who invited Jack to accompany him to the next rehearsal of WOADS.

"You'll reduce the geriatric representation no end," he said enthusiastically.

After a brief and successful audition, Jack was introduced to the assembled company and Boot spread the word that Jack was the new homeopath at Lavender House.

Angela pounced immediately, confessing to them that she was receiving counselling from Lois Palmer. Jack immediately remarked that they looked alike, but courteously refrained from asking the obvious question about the need for therapy.

Angela agreed that they were aware of their similar appearance but added archly that when you've seen one blue-eyed blonde you've seen them all.

"You must know that's not true," said Jack, flirting from habit. "There's a unique light in your eyes. A glint of silver."

Angela was hooked. For the first time since Lucas died she felt herself blushing and hoping this delightful man was single. Heart thumping, she made a deservedly self-deprecating remark about her own singing and a flattering one regarding this.

The rehearsal puttered along with Jack realising that standards at Woolchester were not what he was used to, but amused by this young woman with the terrible singing voice.

Bypassed, Boot was also amused and left the pair alone when they eventually moved on to the pub. From what he overheard, Handsome Jack was outlining the principles of homeopathy to a ready listener. Previously he had not realised she was a customer, or client as his mother insisted they were called, and prophesied to himself that she'd be signing up for some of Mr. Kent's peculiar practices as well as, or instead of, Lois's counselling sessions.

He was not wrong.

CHAPTER SIX

Lois could not help noticing when Angela settled down for her Wednesday fix that she was different. There was no tussle for the higher chair, no interruptions; her manner was calmer and less confrontational. She politely hoped that Lois and her family were well and was assured that they were. Lois braced herself.

"I hope you won't take this amiss, Lois," Angela began and Lois tried to look surprised in spite of having already been briefed by Trixie, "but I'm going to try some additional therapy, as you suggested, in fact. As you know I don't care for being handled, but I've had the homeopathy method explained to me and I'm going to try it on Friday."

"With Mr. Kent?"

"With Mr.Kent."

"Well, that's fine, Angela. There's no reason for you to continue our sessions if you're not finding them helpful. I understand Mr. Kent is highly regarded in homeopathic circles."

"Oh, I shan't stop our Wednesday consultations, Lois. Not until I'm satisfied you're ready to go it alone."

"Well, I assure you I am perfectly ready. And you must consider the expense . . ."

Angela raised a hand. "No worries there. The late and lovely Lucas left me very comfortable, as they say. You'll be able to monitor whether you think Mr. Kent is doing me any good."

"I feel very confident that he will manage that," said Lois, straight-faced but unable to conceal a slightly acid tone that crept into her voice, in spite of a feeling of potential relief. "Now, it sounds as though your social life is still broadening. Joined anything else? Townswomen's Guild?"

"Now, now, Lois. Let's not be sarcastic. Yes, thank you. The drama group in particular is great fun. Boot is a card, isn't he? His mother must be so proud."

Uncertain whether Angela was being ironic, Lois said, supportively,

"He's a gifted writer, you know."

"He told me, yes. And he sews really beautifully. Such an asset to the WOADS."

Eyes slightly narrowed, Lois asked, "How about the gym club? Are you weight-lifting or anything? Or are you merely there as an observer?"

"I use the pool occasionally. I understand you go to the Family Splash on Sunday mornings. That must be such fun. Personally, I like plenty of elbow room when I swim."

"Who told you we went on Sunday mornings?"

"I saw you there while I was on the viewing balcony having a cup of coffee. You in your nice periwinkle blue costume and Matthew in his red Speedos and dear little Oliver in his yellow trunks. I'd had a little chat with Jason Rugg who's very busy with all those people straining their backs and pulling muscles on the fitness machines. Nice man. His wife Pippa was there with their three boys. Quite a handful."

"I've never come across Jason there. His clinic is nowhere near the pool. I've never met his wife and children. Why are you stalking us all? What on earth are you up to, Angela? These people were strangers to you and their families are still strangers to me. What kind of perverted pleasure are you getting out of this?"

"*Stalking*? *Perverted pleasure*? Watch your tongue, Mrs. Palmer. Those are slanderous statements. I take a healthy interest in my friends' friends and their activities. You never know when that kind of networking will come in useful."

"For what? Blackmail?"

"Have I asked for money? Remember I'm in credit with my fees."

"Not money. Emotional blackmail. Playing with people's minds, unsettling them . . . threatening to ruin their lives."

Angela looked with pleasure at Lois's anxious face. "When you say 'they' you mean yourself. Not people in general, just one person. One life, Lois, just one. Just yours."

"What do you want me to do, send an e-mail to everyone I know to tell them I once had a fling with a man who's been dead for two years now? And that his wife didn't lift a finger to prevent him from dying? Is that the game plan?"

Angela studied the carpet for a few seconds. "It was something like that, yes. But in fact, nobody would care very much. You don't mean anything to them. Only Matthew. Poor old cuckolded Matthew. Shall we tell him? Clear the air? I can't make up my mind."

"You don't mean anything to them either, Angela. You might become a local hate figure for killing Lucas and ruining my life and Matthew's and Oliver's but nobody would actually care about you."

Angela raised her head. "Actually, Lois, I'm beginning to think somebody does care. Things are a bit different now."

Surprised, Lois looked at her intently and decided she was telling what she believed to be the truth.

"Do you mean Jack Kent? Your new homeopath?"

Angela shrugged.

"Oh, this is sad, Angela, but someone needs to tell you. I heard he joined WOADS and you went with him for a drink, but his interest lies elsewhere. I shouldn't say this, but confidentially he's a professional charmer, can't help himself. Don't raise your hopes there. You've only known him for five minutes."

"What interest elsewhere? You don't know anything, you've only known him for five minutes yourself."

It was the first time Lois had seen Angela rattled and she paused for a moment to consider. "You're a sophisticated woman, Angela, but out of practice. It's marvellous news that you're ready for a new relationship, but don't lose your head. God knows you're aware every time anyone so much as draws breath, so keep your eyes and ears open and your brain engaged."

Angela gave a short laugh. "If you're referring to that large, Oriental needle-sticker, I know he had dinner with her but really, Lois! You're confusing business with pleasure."

For once, Lois knew when to keep quiet. She had undergone a sudden flash of perception. Lily was from a seriously wealthy family. Unattractive she might be, but Handsome Jack might tolerate that in return for entrance to an appealingly cushioned lifestyle not achieved by homeothapy alone. Gently she said,

"I don't want you to be hurt. Believe me, I really don't. Play it cool."

Angela, however, was no fool. "You think I don't know about the needle-sticker's family connections and how attractive they make her? Better than anybody, Lois, you must know the advantages of settling for being a mistress, a bit-on-the side. No sock-washing, hardly any cooking, no nursing when they've got man-flu, no unwanted meetings. I watched and learned."

Shocked, Lois tried not to show her feelings. "Well, plainly I'm not in a position to lecture you or anyone else, Angela, nor would I. Just be careful. Don't get hurt again."

To her own great surprise she found herself almost in tears, which Angela quickly spotted.

"Are those unprofessional emotions I see before me? Are you really beginning to care for me rather than your own delicate skin? Under the circumstances, it's unkind to call you the tart with a heart, so I won't. But I am touched, Lois. I'd better go before you arrange a group hug. See you next week."

Lois nodded. "Next week."

*   *   *

Lawrence had a girlfriend. He wanted Trixie to be the second to know, after his mother, and couldn't wait to introduce Helen, a Primary schoolteacher. Severely irked and still hoping for Lexie to fall out with the wretched sheep farmer, Trixie invited them to join her and Boot for dinner on Saturday evening.

The girl was a green-eyed, red-haired, pointed chinned delight, dressed becomingly in black silk trousers and jacket, graceful and elegant. Dammit, thought Trixie, forced to acknowledge that she had more going for her than Lexie, even disregarding the New Zealand fiancé. Boot behaved beautifully, the meal was excellent and, as they relaxed afterwards, Trixie was asked to describe all the therapies and their practitioners, since Lawrence, Helen alleged, was totally unobservant and uncommunicative, at which news Trixie breathed a heartfelt 'Thank God.'

Truly dedicated and focussed on his patients, Lawrence had not deliberately avoided the others, but was unaware of much outside his clinic. Away from the building he concentrated on improvements to his new flat, visits to his now widowed mother and meetings with Helen for pleasant evenings in or out. She still lived with her parents who considered him suitable in every particular after some confusion with chiropody, and jokes about dyslexics thinking it was choir practice. All Helen's mother's friends seemed to be in need of alignment requiring his services, helping to fill his appointment book. When Helen revealed that her mother had her hair done at the salon where Beverly once worked, Trixie cursed the parochial connections of small town life. Lawrence and his mother had told Helen of Trixie's patronage and she wondered at the kindness and motivation, coming to the wrong conclusion that Boot was destined to be a disappointment and Lawrence might be a substitute son. Whatever the situation, she admired Trixie and found Boot entertaining, feigning interest in TREES: AN EXPLORATION and putting in an order for a signed copy upon publication.

After they left and Boot had cleared away they both agreed that Lawrence and Helen made a handsome pair. "I suppose," mused Boot, "that they'll marry and live happily ever after."

"Probably," admitted Trixie.

"And Lexie will marry that sodding sheep farmer."

"God forbid, but I expect so."

"Then there's little me. What would you think if I married a lovely fellow and settled down?

"I'd be delighted. Have you found the lucky man?"

Boot shook his head. "Sadly that was a hypothetical question Good answer, though."

"You will need, dear heart, to earn an honest crust if you're to support this as yet undiscovered lovely fellow."

"Or vice versa," replied Boot, happily.

"A kept man? If we're still being hypothetical, let's go for both of you being highly successful and sharing expenses?"

"In that case, I shall have to carry on writing." Boot kissed his mother and went to bed, leaving her to think of acceptable variations in lifestyle: Boot alone, living with her forever; Boot moving to live with someone rich; Boot moving to live with someone poor; Boot inviting someone to live forever at Lavender House.

She rather favoured the last option, and owned that it was unusual not to have recruited a gay person to work in the highly scented environment of Lavender House.

She had momentarily wondered about Handsome Jack Kent, reportedly divorced, but evidence was beginning to suggest he was an heterosexual gold digger/ philanderer.

Wearily, she wondered whether she was too old for his consideration. She could, she thought, keep him in relative comfort, approaching the manner to which she suspected he would like to become accustomed. He was certainly decorative. She thought she might, within the bounds of decorum, try her luck.

CHAPTER SEVEN

There was a large space on the wall by the Reception desk that had so far escaped Trixie's fondness for flower prints. One of Boot's better ideas, stemming from one of his latest best friends, Ben French, being an aspiring, and consequently cheap, photographer was to have pictures of all the therapists hung there. They all agreed both to that suggestion and to their being in black and white, the stylish option. They also adopted Beverly's notion that the pictures should be mounted in a circle, with Trixie as centrepiece to show, she said pointedly, that they were all equally important with Trixie as the hub of the wheel. While grudgingly admitting their period of training might have been longer and their qualifications somewhat higher, she and Juliet were slightly resentful of what they regarded as an unspoken hierarchy that placed the chiropractor, the acupuncturist and now the homeopath above the rest. A circle would give them equal billing.

"Except," Juliet pointed out, "there'll still be somebody at the top of the circle and I bet it won't be me or you or Jason or Lois."

"Oh, well," sighed Beverly resignedly, "as long as it's Lois at the bottom," and they both giggled.

Boot kindly offered to make his apartment available for the photoshoot. The entrance to his and his mother's flats were at the rear of the building via a double door leading to a staircase that opened on to a broad landing with another flight of steep stairs. Boot had joked about the imminent need for a Stannah stairlift, but they convinced themselves that the climb was equivalent to having a personal trainer. Trixie's third floor apartment was to the left and Boot's to the right. They had their own keys to respect each other's privacy, important to their relationship, so Trixie said.

In practice, she hardly ever entered Boot's rooms while he drifted in and out of hers which she did not mind at all. For the purpose of the photography session, she suggested that while the pictures were being taken she would offer refreshments in her flat. Beverly offered to stand by with styling brush, spray, gel and face powder. "Just like old times," she said.

The date was fixed for the following Sunday, from eleven onward.

"Bring your families," invited Trixie, cannily and correctly predicting that they might well order more photographs from Ben, a pale, sandy young man with milky blue eyes and very little drive.

Jason was doubtful whether Pippa and the boys would come as, after their regular Sunday morning Family Splash while he was working in his gym club clinic, they were usually pretty bedraggled and keen to go home for lunch. In fact they all turned up, Pippa, William, Oscar and Tom, shampooed, shiny and beautiful, sitting quietly watching proceedings. Lois arrived alone, Matthew having reluctantly promised to bring Oliver along later, also after the Family Splash and a hastily added decision to take him to the Aquarium.

The more fastidious of the visitors removed their shoes out of respect for Trixie's cream carpet, but she begged them not to fuss and seemed genuinely unworried about possible spills on it or her white sofas. The décor was more restrained than some expected. The lavender floral motif was obviously deliberately chosen for below stairs business only, and Jack Kent on this his, first visit quickly spotted two good John Piper signed lithographs on the pale grey walls.

Boot's apartment also was a surprise to those expecting high camp. The walls were white, there was a black leather sofa, a wall of black ash bookcases fully stocked and showing wide literary tastes and a few designer Swedish lamps. The large black and white photograph of a Paris street scene was signed, the vigilant noted, by Ben French.

Trixie offered to be the first sitter, a confident and well-groomed poser, free then to dispense food and drink and bonhomie. Beverly went next, not a red hair out of place and equally at home in front of a camera and wearing considerably more clothing than had been required in one of her previous jobs of which she never spoke. Juliet looked as pretty as ever but was surprisingly nervous and left immediately after her photograph was taken. Beverly stood by to arrange Lois's already artfully placed blonde hair to best advantage and then plucked up courage to offer advice to Lily who had arrived, long hair as ever in a plait down her back, her face innocent of powder and paint. After mutterings about it not being a beauty salon, Lily was persuaded to let Beverly apply a little make-up and Ben bravely urged her to release the plait. Reluctantly she let them pull the black cascade of hair, wavy after its confinement, over her left shoulder. Ben lifted and turned her head slightly to the side to offset the flatness of her features, and achieved a minor miracle. Boot popped over to tell his mother it was like a scene from an old movie where the boss's plain secretary is instructed to take off her glasses.

Jason, Lawrence and Jack pretended to resist efforts to improve on their looks, but all succumbed to a little titivating having seen the photographs in Ben's portfolio of Boot in which he looked devastatingly handsome rather than wearing the quite-nice-looking label they would normally have attached to him.

Therapists completed, Ben arranged the highly photogenic Pippa with the boys, followed by one of Pippa without the boys and then the boys alone while Jason looked on proudly. In spite of being almost forty, and a hard-working, often harassed mother of three, Pippa could have passed for a very pretty twenty.

The good looks Jason had brought to their marriage had been somewhat eroded by his rugby playing. A twice-broken nose had shifted slightly east and he had a noticeable scar over his right eye, after which injury he was persuaded to give up before Pippa burned his boots. He still had the thick, black, curly hair, soft brown eyes and engaging smile that lifted Pippa's spirits without fail. Except that just now she suspected that the young blonde woman miserably sipping Chardonnay in Trixie's kitchen was the one whom she had spotted pestering Jason outside the door of his clinic at the gym for the last two weeks. 'Pestering' had been Jason's word when she asked him about her. 'Closely conversing' was her take on the situation. He had described her as somebody from Lavender House, and had sounded untypically shifty.

She edged next to him and asked in a whisper whether that was the same woman.

"No," responded Jason quickly. "That's not her. That's Lois Palmer. That woman was one of her patients." Even as he spoke he recognised that he was being pulled absurdly into something undesirable.

"Can I ask her?"

Offended, Jason looked as hurt as he felt. "Ask her what? Of course not, Pippa. Leave it, please. It wasn't Lois. You must have seen Lois and Matthew and Oliver in the pool at Family Splash."

Pippa shook her head. "I don't remember seeing them. And what difference would that make? She gets out of the pool. All I know is that the woman you say was pestering you looks very much like the one in the kitchen."

"Keep your voice down. Yes, they look alike, but the other one's a patient. There's nothing to explain. The woman's a pest, that's all. The other woman, I mean. Not Lois."

"Shall we go now?" asked William, pleasantly full of little cream cakes and cheese puffs."

Jason nodded gratefully, thanked Boot, Trixie and Ben and hustled out his little family that had arrived and behaved so sweetly and was departing now with an inexplicable question mark over their father's happiness. He could not understand how he had allowed the nonsense to develop and felt righteously aggrieved. He and Pippa rarely rowed and never in front of the children. They hardly ever even bickered but he was aware as he drove home that his wife's silence was not signalling a happy evening ahead.

"You boys were very good," he said heartily. "I was very proud of you."

"Yes," agreed Pippa, and Jason hoped he was only imagining the slight emphasis on her next word as she went on, "They've been very good."

Matthew Palmer arrived at Lavender House with Oliver just as Lois was preparing to leave, having sensed that Ben was becoming anxious to pack up. Full of apologies, he explained that it had taken ages to find a parking place, declined firmly the offer to have his own picture taken but surrendered Oliver for sprucing up. The six-year old was chattering happily about his visit to the Aquarium while Lois, pressed by Trixie, cheered up and agreed to a mother and child portrait.

Gratefully accepting the offer of a cup of tea, Matthew politely congratulated Trixie on the progress of Lavender House. "Beautiful flat. It's nice to see you've kept the original features. A lovely project. I'm glad for Lois after all her hard work. It can't be easy carrying other people's problems like she does." He laughed. "I have enough trouble with my own."

"You don't appear to be weighed down with burdens," observed Trixie.

"Lois shields me from worries, I'm happy to say. I'm content to be an ignorant bystander."

"A sensible arrangement," said Trixie smoothly.

Soon all had gone except Ben, who seemed pleased with the day's work.

Trixie peered out of the strawberry window that overlooked the street in time to see Jack leaving, walking with his hand resting gently in the small of Lily's back until Charlie Ho drove up in his big, black Mercedes. Trixie had overheard the request from Lily's mobile and had nurtured a hope that Jack might have stayed behind for another drink and a little chat.

She wondered about Jack's chances and about Lily's surprising choice to play hard to get.

Boot found her mysteriously muttering about gathering rosebuds. He tidied up, loaded the dishwasher and considerately asked whether she would like to join him and Ben for dinner at The Green Man. She thought not, was grateful to have been invited but would be well pleased, so she said, to put up her feet and watch Songs of Praise while sipping a vodka martini.

CHAPTER EIGHT

Trixie's original intention had been to employ the therapists at The Callender Clinic, as she planned to call it. Several talks with her financial adviser had deterred her once he outlined the responsibilities: differential salary scales and demands, tax returns, insurance, pension rights, maternity leave, sick leave, not to mention the onus on her to maintain a full appointments book, and so on ad infinitum. More complicated, he explained, than running a hair salon. Easier by far to offer an attractive, well-maintained, high quality establishment at high, inclusive rents. The tenants would need to take charge of their own destinies while all she needed to do was to arrange an armed escort to accompany her as she took sacks of money to the bank, ha-ha.

She insisted that she wished to be the gatekeeper, just to keep an eye on things, but would not get involved with patients beyond bidding them good-day, booking appointments and pointing them in the right direction. He had known Trixie for years and did not see her as a passive receptionist, but let it pass.

Apart from the unfortunate matter of mad Angela Smith it seemed to be going well. Most clinics were operating at capacity, although some of Juliet's patients made only one visit. "Cured!" according to Juliet.

Clients had spoken highly of Lois's methods which might have come as a surprise to Trixie had she not thought they were based largely on her own ideology of letting people ramble on until they sorted themselves out.

Beverly seemed to be both multi-skilled and entrepreneurial; swiftly offering hot stone therapy if Reiki was unsuccessful or Indian Head Massage if that did not do the trick. Trixie admired the fact that she was able to see two patients at a time by skilful use of two couches and a plentiful supply of hot towels.

Lily, Jason and Lawrence all seemed to receive substantial amounts in fees for inflicting pain which seemed fair enough if that was what rattled their patients' cages, and Jack's homeopathy was incomprehensibly attracting women from York. Three more had 'phoned today. Trixie was determined from the start that she would not undertake any of the treatments on offer for fear it might place her in a vulnerable position and, frankly, she did not much like the sound of any of them. It had always been her motto to be friendly with all, but not so friendly that she could not take legal action if necessary. She had wondered, though, whether as a simple act of hospitality she might invite Jack to dinner one evening. When she mentioned it casually to Boot he promptly declared it a rotten idea.

"He's made loads of friends already at WOADS. He goes for drinks with that patient of Lois's, and Lily's dotty about him as you must have noticed. He hardly looks sad and neglected and anyway it's a bad policy. Invite all or none. You can't have favourites." He gave her a sly grin. "Even dishy Jack-the-lad."

It seemed to his mother that considering Boot wafted like a butterfly through the business end of Lavender House as though it had nothing whatsoever to do with him, his antennae were twitching very effectively.

By the time of Angela's next appointment with Lois, she had had her first consultation with Jack.

Firmly wedged into the high chair, Lois asked kindly, "And how did your homeopathy session go?"

Angela smiled, equally sweetly. "It was an absolute eye-opener, Lois," she said. "He's so well qualified!" She rummaged in her handbag for a piece of paper that she passed over for Lois's scrutiny. "Can you remember I was impressed by all those letters after your name in Yellow Pages? Well, get an eyeful of those. It takes years to qualify, you know. Very stringent exams. I was amazed."

"Evidently," replied Lois, experiencing a slight pang of jealousy in spite of remembering that this was part of her own game plan to offload the confounded woman. "Shall you see him again?"

"Oh, of course. But I still want to see you, Lois. Still lots for you to confide in me. I shan't desert you now, don't worry. We'll see this through together. Actually, I've become very interested in post-modern narrative therapy,—I'm sure you're familiar with it. In fact, I wondered whether this is what we're doing? You've never mentioned the type of therapy I'm paying for.

I've a lot of respect for Michel Foucault and Jacques Derrida : that's more or less what we're doing here, isn't it? More or less? I like the premise that 'the person is not the problem: the problem is the problem.' That's comforting, isn't it? Less personal involvement. Now who said that? Michael White, was it?"

Lois, who did not know Michael White from Barry White recognised the obvious bear trap. She had no idea what Angela was talking about and Angela knew it but Lois was not going to admit that just yet. She smiled a tight smile that she hoped looked encouraging.

"You've been reading round the subject, Angela. That's very good." Inspired, she went on, "These days they call it the elephant in the room. In our case that's Lucas, isn't it. The unspoken problem". She dredged up a phrase from somewhere. "'Absent but implicit'. That sums it up, I believe. He's our problem. Not you. Nor me. Lucas."

Deflated, Angela stared at her.

"I can't say I'm too happy with this elephant analogy although I grant he was a little overweight. We can hardly claim he hasn't been an important presence in our discussions. Right at the forefront, I'd say. Always on the tip of the tongue, as he was to so many lovely ladies."

Lois chose to ignore that, and pressed on. "I wish I knew how to carry out exorcisms. Have you any experience in that field? We could have quite a ceremony: light candles, chant incantations, draw a pentagram on the floor; get the shivery shakes until he floated out of the window and left us in peace."

Angela looked shocked. "Hardly Freudian, is it?" But then she gave one of her wide and frightening smiles. "But you're on to something there. Perhaps we could train as white witches, Lois. It's not greatly different from what goes on under this roof. Pin-sticking, applying weird oily mixtures, bone-cracking, hot rocks and candles. Where's the difference? Let's go it alone, Lois, you and me. Two nice, white gowns and my spare room and we're in business. Low overheads, high profits, what could possibly go wrong?"

Lois had to laugh. "It's tempting, Angela, but I'm afraid I'll have to give it a miss. I'm committed here, but there's nothing to stop you from doing what ever you like, provided it's legal," then could not resist adding, "or not even that, as you've proved."

"Miaow," said Angela. "Lois, we're making real progress here. I look forward to next week. Did I mention that Mr. Kent took me for a drink last week after rehearsals? I hope that doesn't affect his professional doctor/patient contract?"

"I imagine not," said Lois shortly. "You did mention it last time. Ask him. Best not to risk his being struck off whatever it is he's on."

Angela rose. "Perhaps I should check with Mrs. Callender. We don't want to get the place a bad name for unprofessional conduct."

"Sitting in a pub alongside a load of other thespians hardly constitutes undue intimacy, Angela, but ask him. I think you're worrying unduly, but do what you think best. I expect Mr. Kent will be surprised, but there. Keep on with your studies, Angela. You're doing very well."

"Oh, thank you! That means such a lot! Goodbye for now!"

For the first time Lois was smiling when Angela left.

Sure enough, she stopped at the desk, checked her appointments with Trixie and asked her question in, she explained, a hypothetical way.

"If," answered Trixie, who was relieved that there had been no shouting or crying or dramatic exits this week, but was having no truck with hypotheses, "if you mean are you compromising Mr. Kent by having a post-rehearsal drink in a public place, then no, Mrs. Smith, that's perfectly proper. If he were to invite you to spend a weekend in Brighton with him, I'm afraid you should no longer be his patient, even if he is only offering harmless, if beneficial potions."

Angela nodded, seriously.

"I'll bear that in mind," she said. "Thank you so much. Lois asked me to check."

CHAPTER NINE

Oscar, William and Tom Rugg were sleeping soundly before Pippa started off again. What did that woman want, she demanded to know. Not sports massage, she hoped. It was Lois, wasn't it? What did she want?

Jason had never known Pippa like this. There was an occasion many years ago when she had accused him with some cause of looking at a certain girl in a certain way, but this was new. After twelve years of trusting marriage this was all the more infuriating because his very innocence was making him appear guilty. Had he in truth been up to something he would have had a story prepared, a good well-rehearsed lie, but he had no idea what was going on. The woman, he told Pippa, whom he now knew to be Angela Smith, had quizzed him about Lois's family and their swimming habits and naturally he had honestly pleaded ignorance. She had asked him whether he worked anywhere else except the gym club and Lavender House and if he knew whether Lily was a member, which he did not. The woman was NOT Lois Palmer although she did look a bit like her. Her name was Angela Smith, she was one of Lois's patients and he had absolutely no idea why she was talking to him. He tried a lame attempt at humour. "I expect it's because I'm so irresistibly handsome," he said. That did not help, but Pippa did grumpily concede she might have the wrong woman although that did not answer the question of why that woman, whoever she was, should be chasing him.

"Chasing? Chasing is a bit strong. She's asked me a few questions and I haven't known the answers. That's not a chase, that's pestering, as I said from the start. I can't be rude to her, she's a club member and a colleague's patient. Now give me a break, Pippa."

They made up in the traditional fashion, but Pippa was plainly piqued.

Ben French lost no time in preparing proofs for examination at Reception where they were received with universal pleasure. There was rather rude general astonishment at the flattering portrait of Lily who appeared unrealistically lovely. Orders poured in and delivery was promised for the following weekend but with Boot's assistance in mounting the pictures, they were there in a couple of days.

As predicted, Lily was placed at the top of the circle but there were no grumbles about the overall effect. When the large clip-frame was hung, Trixie was amused to see how often they each checked their pictures as though they might magically have been converted to something different. She was herself proud of her appearance in the centre of the frame, smiling benevolently, beautifully coiffed and not, she considered, looking her age.

A few of the patients commented favourably, but Angela, of course, studied them for a worryingly long time before returning to the desk to tell Trixie,

"Very nice indeed. It must have taken ages to get you all at your best angles. Especially Lily. I wouldn't mind having mine done by him. I'll take a card. I guess he's a friend of Boot's?" She took a card from the pile in a dish on the desk. "Personally, I like black and white. It doesn't do justice to Beverly, though, not with all that gorgeous red hair. That's her natural colour, you know. I've known her for a long time."

Carefully, Trixie asked, "Were you at school together?"

"No, we don't go back that far. I can't say she's an old friend, more of an acquaintance, really. My late, unlamented husband set up computers in her partner's office. I expect she's mentioned it? I went to an office party there with Lucas once. Once was enough, but that's a story for another time. All I'll say now is that there were colour photographs taken that she wouldn't want her mother to see. Or Daniel. Or anybody else for that matter."

She went in to see her homeopath, leaving Trixie wondering about Angela's store of scandalous secrets. That Beverly, in her salon days, had been what was euphemistically described as 'popular and fun loving' was no secret among other hairdressers, and Trixie doubted whether Daniel would be greatly shocked, although it would be wiser not to test it out. As far as she knew, Beverly and Daniel were a happy pair enjoying life without upsetting anyone else. Wider circulation of old, embarrassing photographs could be potentially upsetting personally and professionally. Trixie swore under her breath, but had no more time to fret too much as Jack's fan club, the party of four from York arrived, fifteen minutes early.

They had previously arranged to make full use of Lavender House facilities during their visits, carefully rotating sessions of aromatherapy, head massage, and Reiki as well as their time with Jack. As one of them explained, if they were economical with petrol by travelling together, they could splash out on other treatments, adding with a laugh that they needed all the help they could get.

This was not borne out by Trixie's observation of the group, all dressed in designer track suits, carrying expensive handbags, immaculately made-up and already smelling fragrant. They were not as old as she had expected, only in their early forties, she guessed.

"That's an excellent idea," she said, "but if I may say so, you all look pretty good already."

They thanked her, but Maggie, who acted as group leader confided, "We share a complaint." Trixie was agog. "We are all migraineurs. That's why we all love Jack."

"Really? All of you? How interesting. Jack will be pleased to see you again, I know."

"He is so missed. We've all been helped so much," said Nancy, the youngest and prettiest of the group. "Not just the headaches, either. He's a lovely singer, did you know? He's left a real gap in our Operatics Society."

"It's a relief to find we can get here relatively easily," said Cecily. "It sounded like the back of beyond. No offence."

"None taken," replied Trixie. "We know we're a bit of a backwater. It's part of our charm."

In between checking other patients in and out and guiding the York ladies to their various treatments, Trixie learned as if from a Greek chorus that Jack had been in practice with his first wife, Elizabeth, also a homeopath who bought him out after their divorce.

"A mad woman!" declared Cecily. "Had an affair with a much older man. She's married him now. Pots of money but fancy letting Jack go. Some women don't know they're born. And Jack adored her, she was really beautiful, and he never looked at another woman. He's never been short of women wanting to cheer him up but I think if Elizabeth clicked her fingers he'd be back."

"Then let's hope she doesn't," said Trixie with feeling. "Perhaps we shall have to extend to accommodate all his supporters. Now, tell me. My son gets migraine occasionally. Do you honestly think homeopathy might help him?"

"Do you mean to say he hasn't tried it already? That's surprising as it's to hand." Nancy had finished her treatments and looked, in Trixie's view, paler and less relaxed than when she arrived. "If I were here I'd spend all day on couches and reclining chairs being pampered and having my psyche sorted."

"I assure you you wouldn't if you were on Reception. It's quite hectic sometimes. With eight therapists working flat out, that's well over fifty people in and out daily. I survive on camomile tea."

"But you must persuade your son to try homeopathy for his migraine. Does he live near?"

Trixie explained what plainly sounded to Nancy like an odd arrangement and agreed to broach the subject. "He'll be interested to learn he'll be called a migraineur and I suspect he'll enjoy that."

At the end of that day, Lily remarked only that some rather loud, flat-voweled voices had penetrated her clinic and that she might have to invest in sound-proofing if they were to become regulars.

Jack looked tired, but claimed it had been a delight to see old faces and that the women intended trying those services missed on this visit, which cheered Juliet and Lois, but was greeted by Lily, who already had a waiting list, with a frown.

After a shower and a solitary meal, Trixie was trying to decide whether it was an appropriate time to confide in Boot about the skeletons rattling around the place. Always happy to swap scandal, Boot might not be totally reliable in keeping things under his hat. Her own past had not been incident—free, but was in the public domain so long ago that it was of little or no interest now. A few dead affairs that she never denied seemed of little consequence and had not bothered Boot, as far as she could tell. His private life was, she hoped, not concealing anything not already guessed at. His sexual preferences were hardly unknown and no longer shocked a largely tolerant, small community. There had been occasional name-calling, usually related to his creative ways of arranging his scarves, but no physical threats. Even while thinking that through she was aware of the variables that might at any time blight his young life. Fervently she prayed that he was not as promiscuous as she had been. As his mother she recognised that she would probably be the last to know, if there was indeed anything *to* know, in spite of their perceived closeness.

Now that Boot was with WOADS, she toyed with the idea that she might ask him to keep an eye on Angela Smith. And Jack, naturally. And Jack's relationships. Boot offered amusing anecdotes regarding the producer, the terrible chorus and the petty fighting that went on amongst the members, but seemed unaware of issues that would be of real interest to his mother. Trying to enlist him as a spy suddenly struck her as such a ludicrous notion that she laughed the whole idea away as she poured herself a vodka and tonic. Bugger the camomile tea, she thought.

A particularly happy outcome of the day had been the resounding endorsement of Handsome Jack's upstanding character. At one stage she had a silly, fleeting suspicion that he must have hired the women from Central Casting, so insistent were they that he was beyond reproach. It seemed now unarguable that he was the innocent party in his divorce, a respected and successful practitioner loved and admired throughout the Yorkshire Dales. Lurking suspicions that that there might have been black clouds and dark deeds accounting for his flight from York were swept away, trailed as he was by a loving posse of migraineurs with money to burn.

Boot tapped on her door and asked whether he and Ben might have a word. Momentarily and idiotically wondering if she was going to hear news concerning their relationship, she indicated the sofa and fetched glasses.

"How do you like the idea of some better brochures?" asked Boot. "Nothing too expensive, but those leaflets are a bit boring, you must admit. No photographs, short on detail. You need something a bit more up-market now that the place is really up and running. Ben could do some super shots, you know the sort of thing, lots of glamorous therapists kneading anonymous flesh and back of the head pictures for Lois's nutcases."

"What a lovely image you conjure! I certainly agree in principle, but everyone'll need to approve the idea and you must remember they've all had heavy expenses setting themselves up and it's very early days. Still, trade is pretty good."

"Shared between eight of them it won't be much of an expense," urged Boot.

"Cost it and let me have a sample to show them. Your photographs certainly went down well, Ben."

Ben coloured as he sat quietly, pale blue eyes moving anxiously between mother and son.

"It would be nice," he said softly. "if Boot wrote the blurb. He's so good with words."

Trixie regarded him benignly. "Well, let's see what he comes up with. Nothing too abstract, dear, and no poems. I know people buy into dreams, but in my experience they do like to know exactly what they're getting and what it's going to cost. While you're here, Boot, how's your head been lately?"

Both young men looked at her blankly.

"Migraines, Boot. Any migraines?"

"I haven't had one for a while. Why?"

"There was a troupe of lady migraineurs in today from York to see Jack. They all swear by homeopathy."

Boot laughed. "I see. And for how many years has the lovely Jack been treating them, if you get my point?"

Trixie laughed as well. "I hadn't thought of that."

"How many were there? Because if they're going to be regarded in terms of regular income, you're unlikely ever to get a full complement, are you? There's always going to be someone crying off with a bad headache. Is there a collective name for them? A club for them to join? The Yorkshire Ladies Migraine Association?"

"Alright, alright! But don't come wailing to me the next time you're suicidal with pain and throwing up."

"I promise I won't. We'll be off now. Ta, Ma."

"Thanks, Mrs. Callender," whispered Ben. ""You're very kind."

"Yes," thought Trixie, "I damn well am."

CHAPTER TEN

The next few weeks passed busily and without major incident. Angela and Lois continued to exchange both barbed comments and possession of the high chair without coming to blows, and even achieved an occasional rapport. Lois was introduced by Angela to previously unexplored branches of therapy, the irony of which escaped neither. A seam of black humour started to underlie their sessions. They regarded each other as frauds and performed delicate pirouettes around the real issues that they should have been addressing.

Lois discovered that she had a stronger backbone than suspected, allowing Matthew to stop worrying about her.

Angela dug assiduously at the less attractive aspects of the Lavender House therapists and occasionally struck blackmailer's oil. Beverly was a prime target, but Angela needed to think long and hard about the best way to take advantage of the poor woman's past indiscretions. Lois remained the main victim, but had been handed a prize in the form of admission to at best murder, at least neglect. Angela wanted time for reflection. Jack was proving elusive. Courteous and attentive as he was, he remained frustratingly aloof, making no effort to push a relationship further than drinks after rehearsals, offering no hope of a successful seduction by the out of practice Angela, who was inclined to overrate her own powers of attraction. Having revealed to Lois her very practical assessment of Lily's financial allure, she regarded herself as an undeniably prettier, sexier and serious contender for the attentions of the desirable Jack. Were Lily's riches, she asked herself, to be the final arbiter? Regretfully, she concluded that they were an obstacle. But Angela rarely gave in.

In her mind she ran through her cast of characters. She knew of Trixie's past peccadilloes, but so did everybody else. Lawrence was clean, even if slightly compromised by Trixie's sponsorship. Jason was a principled, frightened fool and Juliet was an idiot without history. Angela wanted time to think. She had heard of the influx of York women with crippling headaches and had, rather cruelly, laughed.

Vulnerability was epitomized by Boot, gay, gated and doubtfully gifted. He was almost too easy a target. His current boyfriend was a shadow, an insubstantial half-presence without character or form, clever with a camera but of no interest to Angela in her search for somebody big to be shot down. She had investigated Carl, Boot's agent and found him to be the charlatan she suspected, but anyone with half a brain could see that. She was stuck with small fry.

At no time did she analyse her own motives, but a growing number of other people were trying to solve that mystery.

Lily, who had seemed to have very little interest in Lavender House beyond her own clinic, had been alerted by Jack that he had taken Angela on as a patient. Quietly, she had extracted from others the information that Lois had been harangued by this rather odd woman who had joined the WOADS of which Jack was now a member. She learned of her attendance at the gym and in the pool and of her persistent questioning.

Upright Jack would not, nor would she ask him to, reveal the secrets of his consultation room, but she began to watch Angela's movements. Lily, happy in the leisurely advancement of her relationship with Jack, believed there were many impediments to its achieving a permanent status, but she had no intention of letting Angela Smith spoil her chances. Those expecting Lily, after her photographic make-over, to be transformed into a different looking person were disappointed. The hair was back in its plait, her face owed everything to nature and nothing to art, and her belief that beauty is illusory was reinforced. What she did gain was confidence in the knowledge that she could be beautiful if she chose.

Although Lexie was on the other side of the world, pursuing what Boot described as her very peculiar inclination to interfere with dumb animals, emails were exchanged regularly. He and his mother, though often saying how much they missed Lexie, had in fact quite grown used to her absence and now that Lawrence had found himself a mate and Lexie was entangled with a sheep farmer, it was accepted that in the future they would have to endure long journeys to keep in touch. Soon Lexie would be returning to finish her degree but then she planned to have a family-only register office marriage to Jake and a life in New Zealand dealing with isolation and scrapie.

Lexie had a lofty disregard for alternative therapies which opinion her mother hoped she would keep to herself during her rare weekends at Lavender House.

A clever and studious girl, she was admired by Boot who had never felt in competition with her and spoke of her with pride. Equally proud even if disappointed by her choices, Trixie had never felt as close to Lexie as she felt towards Boot, for reasons she explained to herself as being due to the girl's self-sufficiency. Her mother's chosen path was not hers. She had known from infancy that she would prefer to spend her life with animals and no, she told Boot, she did not want to run a poodle parlour. With the return to university looming, Trixie set about tidying the third bedroom. The wholesale downsizing when they sold Pitt house, their former, spacious house, had incurred necessary ruthlessness but still there were boxes of what she could only describe as stuff. She could not resist leafing through old photograph albums, with feelings a mixture of love, pride, sadness and nostalgia. Looking at Andrew, young and handsome, posed with the children when small when she had had no idea that their marriage would crumble into bitterness and tragedy, she felt near to tears. Much later, she had learned of at least two relationships, one with his secretary in Saudi and was upset more by finding she did not really care than by the discovery itself. Boot and Lexie had seen so little of their father that they did not appear terribly upset when he died. Trixie's overriding feeling was of relief, but she tried to give an impression of grief. A photograph of Andrew she had placed in a silver frame and put on a side table was repeatedly turned face down by Boot until she removed it and gave up all pretence.

Deciding she could not make any impression on the boxes by herself, she repacked them and stacked them neatly, exactly as they were before.

Lexie's room was ready for the untidy assault she would make on it.

*   *   *

Several people were studying Lily to try to discover what lay behind her serene countenance and little button eyes, used to give an unblinking, unsettling stare when she feared she was being subjected to too much scrutiny. She was never at pains to please people, yet her clients were faithful and keen to recommend her to their friends. Clearly Jack seemed rather fond, but in an old fashioned, courtly way. Lily was observed to be close to her mother, greeting her with a kiss and chatting as she was driven away by Marilyn when Charlie was too busy to collect her.

Jack did not mention to anyone that he had received an invitation to Sunday lunch with the Hos. His acceptance was nervous because of the unfamiliar protocol. In his parents' young days, the invitation to Sunday tea, with salmon sandwiches and sponge cake was as good as an expectation that an engagement ring would soon be produced. His own generation were more likely to bring home a partner they had been living with for months. Chinese practices in these matters were a closed book to him. Not wishing to upset or disappoint anybody he was balancing a tightrope between definite interest in a long term relationship with Lily and all that that might bring, and a fear that it might come too soon.

Contrary to the views of his York fan club, he was not yearning for Elizabeth. Hurt beyond forgiveness, he was shocked not only by her faithlessness, but by the revelation that she was money-grubbing and self-centred. The first wife of her lover, Hunter Mackinlay, had sensibly armed herself with a pre-nup and pursued him successfully for vast sums to maintain the luxurious lifestyle she and their obnoxious teenaged daughters were accustomed to. Elizabeth watched with a tight smile as the fifty-nine year old Hunter's assets were reduced, but she was still elevated to a life in California and New York that had been unimaginable when she married Jack, who declared during the unpleasant divorce process that he at least had the satisfaction of knowing that she'd fallen in love with money and not another man.

Still owning the York Clinic, she made monthly visits to check the accounts laden, it was said, with jewels of vulgar dimensions.

Since the divorce Jack had warily dated a few women but was wise enough not to stray far out of a sensible age range, which limited the field, rather. There were plenty of divorcees and career women, all pleasant enough, but none with whom he wished to share his life. Lily's elusive charm and undoubted intelligence might prove enough to make her the one, but he, and, if he read it right, she, needed more time.

Wishing to avoid a faux pas, he asked what Lily's father would be wearing for Sunday lunch. Straightfaced, she told him that it might be his ankle length red brocade coat with the gold embroidered dragons and waited just long enough to see a flicker of alarm cross his face before assuring him that they were a tee-shirt and jeans family on Sundays and to wear whatever he felt comfortable in. She also suggested he might like to bring trunks as they had a swimming pool and the forecast was good. Jack began to look forward to his weekend.

He knew the location of the house, but had not been there. On their few dinner dates Lily had been insistent that she should collect Jack in her car and drive him home at the end of the evening, her reason being that she did not touch alcohol, (a minor disappointment to Jack) but wanted him to be free to have a glass or two. She dismissed his offer of using taxis, which was all very kind but removed hope of the traditional invitation to coffee. It was probably an academic point since she still lived with her parents whom he suspected of probably waiting up for her with Chinese cocoa and a questionnaire.

Came the day, after deciding against tee-shirt and jeans in favour of a white shirt with cuffs turned back, and fawn chinos, and remembering trunks and a towel, flowers for Mrs.Ho and a bottle of wine, he kissed Lily after winding himself into her tiny, environmentally friendly car. He was interested to see that she had let down her hair, allowing it to frame her face, and that she had applied lipstick and eye make-up. She wore a long, flowered print skirt and a blue, loose top that enabled him to say honestly that she looked really pretty. Lily acknowledged the compliment without apparent surprise but Jack observed a slight pink flush to her cheeks and was himself surprised to experience a similar reaction.

The Ho mansion was at the fashionable edge of town, hidden behind large but unimpressive wooden gates left open in anticipation of their arrival. The gravel drive seemed never ending, bordered with banks of blue hydrangeas until the house came into view. Huge lawns, immaculately striped, were edged with colourful herbaceous borders; roses and wisteria clung to the grey stone walls of the Edwardian building. Jack could see a conservatory at one end of the house and various ivy covered outbuildings unobtrusively placed in the less formal areas of the grounds.

As he climbed out of the car, the sweet, hot scents of the garden assailed him, while Lily said, "You'll have to brace yourself for a long walk with Mother round the back garden. It's her pride and joy. You'll be impressed by the vegetable and herb garden, I expect. Come on."

Charlie and Marilyn were on the steps to greet them, shaking Jack's hand and accepting the flowers and wine with warm thanks as they ushered him inside. He had not known what to expect in the way of décor, half-imagining restaurant-style black and red flock wallpaper, but it was all English traditional country house style, a long hall with side table with pots of lilies, a galleried drawing room with sink-in, cream linen—covered sofas with hand worked tapestry cushions; the dining room was a blur of mahogany, silver and cut glass, flowers everywhere, a library-cum study, a music room with baby grand piano, a cello on a stand and a violin on a table. Pictures were plentiful and eclectic. Old water colours, oils and prints nudged modern, abstract acrylics, signed, Jack noted, by M HO.

He accepted a dry sherry from Marilyn who suggested that they go through to the kitchen so that she could, as she put it, take a peek and a poke at the casserole before taking Jack to see the gardens. Lily surprisingly winked. Leading to the kitchen, which Jack estimated was roughly the same size as the entire ground floor of the house where he was raised, the hall wall was dedicated to Lily, with photographs of her from birth to the present day.

"I can see why you named her Lily," said Jack. "She's a little flower, cream with pink petal edges." The baby was propped up on a cream satin pillow, her straight black hair abundant, her eyes almost lost in pink, chubby cheeks.

So the pictures progressed: Lily toddling, Lily paddling, Lily on a trike, on a bike, on a horse, up a tree, on the beach. Lily in Brownie, Guide, and school uniforms; holding prizes, cups, certificates, diplomas, medals. Lily graduating, first Bachelor then Master. The most recent was Ben French's portrait of Lily as an attractive woman.

"You've been well monitored, Lily," said Jack wryly.

Charlie Ho grinned at him. "That's only the start. We have extensive collections of video films and recordings of her playing the cello accompanied by Marilyn on the piano."

Real fear suddenly overcame Jack, who understood immediately that if anyone were to hurt Lily in any way there would be unspeakable repercussions.

Satisfied that all was well upon and within the Aga, Marilyn slipped her arm into Jack's and led him through the French doors into what Charlie called the backyard. It stretched for miles, ending in a small wood. The swimming pool was just visible to the left of the garden, but Marilyn guided him to the vegetable plots.

"Everything for the restaurants is grown here," she said. "Herbs, as you see, and there's an orchard round the corner."

There was no need to feign admiration or interest, and Marilyn beamed at him as he revealed his own knowledge and enthusiasm.

"I've recently moved into a flat," he told her. "There's a small plot to call my own and I can't wait to get started again. I left behind a big garden. Nothing like this, of course. This is a park!"

"Lily shall keep you supplied with cuttings until you're established. She's also very knowledgeable about herbs and their medicinal uses, you know. Well, you'd expect that." She stopped and turned to face him. "We're aware that she made you unwelcome at first because you are a homeopath and you must find that mysterious, given her own qualification, not to mention being half Chinese."

"Yes," answered Jack, warming to this straightforward approach.

"Charlie and I didn't agree with her attitude. It was rude, for one thing, although you seem to have forgiven her. It was a personal thing, a tragedy. While she was training, her best friend was suffering from severe headaches and somebody recommended homeopathy. She had treatment for months, then quite suddenly she deteriorated: double vision, blackouts, the lot, and of course her parents insisted that she saw a consultant. All too late, she was diagnosed with a brain tumour and she died within a month. A beautiful girl, same age as Lily. You can understand her reaction. There've been other cases, too, Jack, which I'm sure you're familiar with: homeopathic remedies in place of traditional malaria prevention. They all went badly with Lily. Obviously you've persuaded her to re-think." Marilyn gave him a sidelong glance, as though suspecting he exercised greater powers than he actually possessed.

"I'm not sure that I have. There's been some bad practice," Jack admitted. "Shameful. But rare, fortunately. All disciplines have their bad apples, I'm afraid. I dare say there have been a few evil acupuncturists. I wouldn't dare suggest that to Lily, though."

"Neither would I!" laughed Marilyn, and they moved to rejoin the others. "She used to work with her Uncle Liu at his practice in Maybury and was happy there, but she needed to spread her wings a bit." There was another sidelong glance. "I suppose you think she hasn't spread them very far, but Lavender House fits the bill at present."

When they returned there was a fair-haired woman helping in the kitchen, introduced as Monika, their housekeeper. Her Polish husband worked in the garden and did general maintenance, Charlie explained.

Throughout the day other employees were introduced or mentioned until Jack lost count. There was a spread of nationalities. Billy, a Malaysian, was the pool boy when he was not attending one of Charlie's language schools, where Marilyn taught.

Prepared for close interrogation during the lunch of salmon mousse, boeuf bourgignon and fruit salad—no Chinese cuisine here—Jack was disarmed by the general tone of the conversation that ranged from musical tastes, global warming, whether alternative remedies should be provided by the NHS, to the time-consuming paper work and checking up involved in employing the non-Brits, whom Marilyn said were treated as family by Charlie. Unsure whether avoidance of his personal and professional history was a good sign in that he was trusted, or a bad sign because they did not see him as becoming involved with Lily, Jack volunteered more information than he would have done normally. He assumed Lily had told them he was divorced and added to their knowledge by revealing that Elizabeth lived in America with her new husband, but regularly visited their old clinic in which he now had no financial interest.

"We hear you have a literal following of former patients," remarked Marilyn.

Uneasily Jack admitted that he had, wondering, in view of the brain tumour story whether he should mention that he seemed to have had some success in treating migraine. He decided to do so, adding that he always advised patients also to consult their own doctors, and that several patients had been referred to him by their GPs.

"Did you know," asked Lily, "that Dr. Crippen was a homeopath?"

"Aren't you confusing homeopath with psychopath?" said Marilyn.

"Lily, please!" rebuked her father.

Jack laughed. "No, I didn't. Whatever are you suggesting?"

"Absolutely nothing. I thought it was interesting, that's all."

That was pursued no further, lunch was completed amiably and they all moved to a shady arbour in the garden, protected from the blazing July sun.

Monika was left to clear away.

"It'll be wise to wait a little while before we take to the pool," advised Marilyn. "Perhaps, Lily, you'd like to show Jack the rest of the garden while we older people rest". Jack had a momentary sensation of appearing in a production of Pride and Prejudice, but shelved it quickly as he surrendered to the sheer delight of a hot summer day with bees buzzing, birds singing and the scent of lavender and verbena in the air.

"Your parents are very kind," he said. "This idyllic lifestyle is not what I've been used to. Suburban boy, lower middle class, you know the sort."

"I've read about them," said Lily and laughed. "You know perfectly well you're a sophisticated, handsome man. But tell me about your lower middle class parents. You've probably noticed we're in trade and mixed race to boot."

"Both dead, unfortunately. Dad died of cancer when I was in the sixth form and mother died five years ago. I think you'd have liked them They were sweet people, ambitious for me and my sister. She's a paediatric nurse, married to a doctor. Two children. Lives in Inverness. Shares your low opinion of homeopathy."

"I know Mother told you why." Lily turned and faced him, very close. "I don't have a low opinion of this particular homeopath."

Jack would have liked to kiss her, or at least to hold her hand, but was fearful of one of the gainfully employed, well-treated, one-of-the-family immigrants popping up suddenly, so refrained.

"Is it too soon to swim?" he asked. They walked back, arms gently brushing. It felt to Jack that this was good, old-fashioned courting, and he liked the feeling.

Changed and sitting on the edge of the pool, Jack was able to conduct an inventory of Lily's previously well-hidden attributes. Undeniably she was heavily built, full-breasted and reminding Jack, in spite of her slanting, button eyes of a Betjeman-esque great big beautiful British sports girl, with her long, strong legs. Her skin was the colour of brown silk and he longed to touch it, but they were joined by Charlie, in bright red shorts, who slithered into the water and swam like an eel for several lengths before encouraging them in. He climbed out, wrapped himself in a striped gown and lay on one of the poolside loungers.

Lily was a powerful swimmer, reminding Jack of the photographs in the hall featuring the child Lily in a swimsuit, holding up a silver cup. He was no match and soon joined Charlie, poolside. Marilyn preferred to read in the shade and Lily emerged announcing her intention to make iced coffee.

"We shall have been married, Marilyn and I, for forty years at the beginning of August," declared Charlie.

"Congratulations," murmured Jack, mildly anxious as to where this might be going.

"I'm planning a party," Charlie went on, little, lined pixie face alight with pleasure.

"It's ruby, you know. I'm having a special piece of jewellery specially made. An ibis, with ruby eyes. They mate for life. I want a party for all our friends and relations, the people who work for us, everybody. Here, of course. We'll have a marquee," he waved his arms towards the lawns.

"and have lights everywhere, lanterns round the pool, in the trees . . . . She knows I love her, of course. I'd like the world to know."

Jack was deeply touched and envied the man's good fortune and certainties.

"That sounds wonderful."

"You'll come, I hope. We're both in our sixties now, Jack. I feel like having a damn good party before we're past enjoying them."

"I can't see that happening. I guess you'll enjoy your golden wedding. Only ten years away."

"No. Jack, unfortunately not. Don't tell Lily, please. I'm strictly time limited.

Keep her happy, please."

Deeply shocked, Jack sat up straight. Platitudes were not going to do, as he looked at Charlie's still animated face and felt the burden of this information.

"I'll try my hardest," he promised, wondering what on earth he was promising to this delightful little man. Was Charlie simply asking him to keep Lily in blissful ignorance of his state of health, whatever that was, or did he want Jack to marry her without delay to fill an approaching father-shaped gap?

Just in time, Lily arrived with the iced coffee and tiny macaroons. Whispering delicately, Jack asked what would be the appropriate time to leave, but Marilyn anticipated the question when she crossed over to join them.

"Nobody escapes before a half-hour music recital," she said. "We're absolutely relentless, Lily and I, in forcing people to hear our party pieces on cello and piano, and then you'll want to run for it before Charlie starts to sing."

She and Lily went inside to prepare, and as Jack prepared to move, Charlie laid a hand on his arm. "Before that," he said, "while I remember, there's something I must ask you, Jack. A woman called Smith, fair hair, fortyish, has been for a meal three times in our Woolchester restaurant, on her own. She said she was a patient of yours and has been asking rather personal questions about you. I had nothing to tell her, obviously, and I tried to brush her off without being rude, but she struck me and the waiters as being a bit weird. Thought I should warn you and I haven't mentioned it to Lily."

Jack breathed hard down his nose. "Thanks. I'm sorry she's making a nuisance of herself. I've just started treating her, and she sees Lois the therapist as well. Unfortunately she's also in the amateur opera group I belong to and she tends to latch on to people."

Charlie nodded and rose. "Bloody woman!" thought Jack.

The recital was very pleasant, both women playing competently. The music was unfamiliar to Jack but he was impressed by evidence of yet another area of ability in the Ho family. He thanked them for such a delightful day, Lily drove him home and kissed him tenderly on the cheek and were it not for acquired knowledge of a terminal illness and the sensation that Angela Smith was hovering over them like a big blonde albatross, Jack would have had a lovely time.

CHAPTER ELEVEN

"Luck be a lady tonight!" sang Angela in her squeaky little voice, alarming those patients sitting quietly waiting on the cane chairs, as she burst into Jack's room, fizzing like a firework.

He rose quickly. "Are you looking forward to tonight?" she asked loudly before he managed to close the door.

"You mean the dress rehearsal? My feelings are mixed, but it'll be interesting. How about you? You seem very, er, cheerful." He indicated her chair, then seated himself, hoping for an uneventful, professional session.

"It's a shame you weren't a member in time to be auditioned for Sky. You're miles better than Denzil. With a bit of luck he'll lose his voice and they'll beg you to take over."

"Please tell me that wasn't the kind of luck you were singing about. That was very unkind and I'd be extremely nervous and under-rehearsed, as the understudies usually are. I'm perfectly happy in the chorus."

This was untrue. Jack regretted his hasty decision to join WOADS, especially having learned on Sunday that Lily was a member of the Bach choir, which, all things considered, would have been his preferred option. As his mother used to say, he would have mixed with an altogether better class of person.

Before they could begin talking about her treatment, Angela left the topic in a sudden and alarming way. "Did you know," she said, "that Dr. Crippen was a homeopath?"

Jack tipped his chair back and studied her face for several moments before replying,

"It's funny you should ask and yes, Angela, as it happens I did know, but not until very recently."

"I'll tell you another funny thing. They've done DNA tests on the body parts they found in the cellar, the ones they assumed to be Cora Crippen's and they were definitely those of a man.! And evidence points to his wife really having left him, as he always said she had, and gone to live with her sister and her lover in Brooklyn. In America!" Angela sat back, triumphantly.

Jack maintained his steady gaze, his placid expression belying his mental confusion. Had Angela been lurking in the Ho's kitchen, disguised as a well-cared for Polish immigrant? Why two Crippen references in as many days?

"Is there a point to this story? Apart from Dr. Crippen possibly having been an innocent homeopath?"

"There are some people," said Angela, inclining her head towards Lily's consulting room, "who would say 'innocent homeopath' is an oxymoron."

"Where is this taking us, Angela? If you have no faith in my treatments, you should not be here taking my time and wasting yours."

"Oh, I have faith! I have! I was referring to others," and again she jerked her head towards Lily's wall. "I feel better simply looking at all your beautiful old bottles and vials." She stood and moved to his large glass cabinet with its impressive display of ancient apothecary jars.

"Good," said Jack, briskly. "I'm glad. Now let's talk about your treatment."

He was too professional to lose his grip on the situation, but throughout the session he turned over in his mind the implication made twice in a week by different people that he had something in common with Dr. Crippen. It was bizarre and unnerving. True enough his disenchanted ex-wife had moved to the States. That Elizabeth was demonstrably alive and well seemed to be becoming irrelevant.

At the end of the session he closed the door behind Angela with a louder-than intended thud, and by the end of the day he had an uncharacteristic headache, was dreading the dress rehearsal and Angela's presence at it, and hardly acknowledged Lily's parting wish for good luck as they separately headed home.

Boot, the producer, and the musical director all appeared to be heading for nervous breakdown. Some costumes didn't fit, the stage manager had still not organized all the props and the scenery was still damp. The little orchestra were struggling against players who forgot their lines and their moves. Two members of the chorus wished it to be known that they should really be in bed as they undoubtedly had 'flu. Jack wished they were.

"It's always the same," said one of the seasoned chorines, resignedly.

"PLEASE don't say it'll be alright on the night," begged the choreographer, "because it so bloody obviously won't be!"

That became even more apparent when Denzil, the maligned leading man inexplicably tripped at the top of steps leading from the dressing rooms down to the stage. He fell awkwardly and banged his head. Angela, who was close behind him, shrieked and rushed down to the wings to render first aid. It was obvious from the angle of his leg that it was a serious injury, and he was only semi-conscious. An ambulance was called while he was tended by half the cast, including his white-faced wife, the first violin. Eventually he was taken off to hospital and the producer took a couple of unspecified tablets.

Woolchester Operatic and Dramatic Society were terrible, but they were troupers.

Everyone was called on stage to be informed by the producer that the orchestra had been paid for, and the show must go on. Jack was reminded where his duty lay, as Denzil's understudy, and that he must now step into the breach.

"Let's make a drama out of this crisis!" Grant said, and, pleased by the sound of that, repeated it several times more during the evening. The players were told that hard rehearsal was vital and that it was going to be a very long night. Beer and sandwiches were sent for.

Angela's face shone in joyous expectation. Jack was shaking for several reasons. The woman's proximity to the unfortunate Denzil was most unsettling. The man was concussed and so probably ruled out as being able to give an accurate account of the fall; most people's perception was that Angela had rushed to the rescue. Had she not mentioned her hope that Denzil would lose his voice he would not have been suspicious, but she had, and Jack was.

The stage directions had been altered so often that Jack was not confident in his new role. He knew the words, music and dialogue, but there was no guarantee that many of the cast would reliably be in the right place at the right time with the right cue. Also the unfortunate Denzil was quite six inches shorter, so Boot would have a day to get Jack suitably dressed. He felt quite sick with fear.

Angela sidled up to him. "If ever there was a time for the combined healing powers of Lavender House to come into operation, this is it. I suppose now it's going to sound unfeeling to say, "Break a leg," in true theatrical tradition?"

It was well after midnight, beyond the usual milky drink bedtimes of most of the chorus, when rehearsal ended and the exhausted members went home, with the producer announcing that he was putting his faith in prayer. "Not exactly," as Boot noted, "a ringing endorsement."

The long established patterns for WOADS was for Monday, dress rehearsal, Tuesday, loose ends day, but no rehearsal, Wednesday, opening night, traditionally for half price pensioner groups, then performances on Thursday, Friday and Saturday at which the more experienced supporters attended in the belief that the company would have got the hang of it by then.

The following morning, Lily was accosted by Angela as she came through the doors of Lavender House.

"Did Jack tell you it was almost one o'clock before we got home last night?"

"I heard about the accident." said Lily shortly, and closed her door firmly.

She and Jack had made arrangements that, if Denzil were fit to receive visitors, they would go to see him that night. His leg was, indeed, badly broken and, as suspected, he was suffering from concussion. Already there was a rumour circulating, started by Pauline the prompter who was standing in the wings at the time of the fall, that it was Angela who had tripped and accidentally pushed Denzil forward. Jack was not happy to hear this.

Neither was Trixie who knew, via Boot, what was being said and was furious to learn the woman had been invited by Ben French to pose for some of the pictures to appear in the brochure. Boot had evidently noticed that Angela had perfect feet and lovely hair and recommended that she be asked to sit for Juliet's Reflexology, and for Beverly's Indian Head Massage. Ben was due at twelve. Angela had arrived before nine declaring herself content to sit quietly waiting with a magazine, being no trouble to anybody.

It was unfortunate that Mrs. Delia Parkin, who had received a Lavender House gift token (one of Boot's bright ideas), from her daughter and was enjoying Reflexology with Juliet, found the toe-stroking interrupted twice when Juliet had quickly to excuse herself and was heard throwing up in the cloakroom. While sympathetic with the girl's nausea, it was not the experience she had reckoned on, swiftly coming to the accurate diagnosis that she was party to a bout of morning sickness. Mrs. Parkin was in the middle of re—arranging the visit with the embarrassed and apologetic Juliet, when there was a wail from the reception area. They quickly stepped outside to find Angela, Boot, Jack and Lily clearly distressed, with Trixie trying to keep things calm, having taken and relayed the message that Denzil had suffered a massive stroke and died, with his wife Audrey at his side. It transpired that Lily and Marilyn both knew Audrey from playing occasionally with her and another violinist, usually at wedding receptions, so reinforcing Jack's belief that everybody in Woolchester knew or was related to everybody else which was not necessarily a good thing.

Grant, the producer, went immediately to see Audrey at home to offer condolences, sweating and silently hoping that the company were fully insured against such contingencies, and to ask, as delicately as he could, what

Audrey thought Denzil would have wanted regarding the forthcoming performances.

Audrey was a forthright woman. Glaring at him from tear-swollen eyes, she said,

"Clearly, Grant, I have no way of knowing what Denzil would have wished. Oddly enough it was not a possibility we had discussed, and frankly, Grant, I don't give a flying fart one way or the other."

Squirming, Grant frowned, nodded three times and said, "We'll go ahead then, shall we, and dedicate the show to poor Denzil?"

After being assured that there was nothing at all he could possibly do to help, Grant left to spread the bad news regarding Denzil, and the slightly better news that the show would go on.

It was difficult to judge the sincerity of Angela's distress. Certainly she had paled and let out a loud cry, but in no time at all she had pulled herself together, cancelled her photoshoot with Ben and the still vomiting Juliet, and, by 'phone, offered to help Grant in tying up loose ends, by acting as his personal assistant and 'keeping the show on the road' as she put it.

Boot was trying, between the pesky clients, to catch Jack for fifteen minutes to try on some suits and hats. The aim was always to keep down to a minimum the number of hired costumes, and he had worked wonders in securing suitable, borrowed attire. He had become really friendly with the nice people at the Citadel who had been most willing to lend Salvation Army uniforms and to put up a poster.

It was a revelation to Ben that Boot had no qualms about cajoling, begging or borrowing from people who seemed immediately to become his best friends.

There is nothing like death for enhancing a reputation and Jack's own feeling that he was not physically suited to his new role was, unwittingly, confirmed by the many who acknowledged that Denzil's voice was not the greatest but that he was a nifty mover and engaging performer. Jack felt neither nifty nor engaging, and Lily tried to instil a more positive attitude.

"By Saturday you'll be fine," she said. "It's a sell-out for the last two days. We're all coming, you know, including your York migraineurs who've made a block booking. They've hired a minibus."

"Oh, dear God," said Jack.

Boot gave Mrs. Parkin, with her vertical zones only partly rebalanced, complementary tickets for the show. She thanked him and told him to advise Juliet to take arrowroot, and winked. He had no idea what she was talking about, but was reconciled to finding much at Lavender House beyond his comprehension.

Later Mrs. Parkin told her daughter that they were all very nice people but seemed rather stressed out for some reason and that she'd probably enjoy 'Guys and Dolls' better as a means of relaxation.

Two of Jack's York women arrived for their appointments. Celia, first to go in, told him with a gleam in her eye, "Elizabeth's coming, you know."

"Coming where?"

"To your show. Nancy bumped into her and mentioned we were coming on Saturday and Elizabeth was dead keen. We managed to get her a ticket but she's driving herself down in her new Lexus. Her husband's in Miami at another conference. We knew you wouldn't mind. She hasn't been best pleased with us for transferring to you, but we still go the nail clinic, and they do Botox now as well—watch my lips! So it's not exactly being disloyal to you or taking the bread out of her mouth either is it? We had a word between ourselves and thought it would serve her damn well right to see this lovely place and realize you've got a happy life without her."

Nails! Botox! Jack was stunned.

"I appreciate the thought but I'm happy chiefly because of the clean break. It's a bit embarrassing because I'm taking over a part at short notice that I'm not well prepared for. The man died yesterday."

"Honestly? They take a pragmatic approach down here, don't they? You'll be fine, Jack. We're all looking forward to it."

CHAPTER TWELVE

Kindness suggests a veil be drawn over the Wednesday opening night. It was not the worst that WOADS had experienced. 'Kismet' took the honours for that to date, but it was up there with the highest for lost words, late entrances, malfunctioning props and general awfulness. Jack was word perfect and acquitted himself well, all things considered. A replacement was found for Audrey, the newly widowed first violinist, although Grant clearly felt that she might have pulled herself together and made the effort to play. He had prepared a carefully worded eulogy, read before the curtain rose, confidently expecting that the audience would be sympathetic because of the tragic circumstances, and forgive any errors. There was much to forgive, but the mostly elderly audience were familiar with the songs and cheerily joined in with rather more gusto than the players, whom they forgave, declaring they'd had a really good time.

Grant announced after the curtain fell that he believed it had gone very well, all in all. The audience applauded Jack heartily for his heroic, last—minute efforts, as did most of the cast.

Lily received with a strained smile the news that the former Mrs. Kent was going to the show, but really did not know what to think or say, so made no reply to Jack. A slightly more worrying aspect of this prospect came when Trixie took a 'phone call from Mrs. Hunter Mackinlay, whose name she did not recall, asking her to join her for Sunday lunch at The Holly Bough Inn, where she said she was staying on Saturday night. Aware that the name had not registered, the former Mrs. Kent explained her status and that she was accompanying the migraineurs to see 'Guys and Dolls', but was also most keen to discuss a business proposition. While quite seeing that Elizabeth might be miffed at the exodus of some of her clients, Trixie thought it a damned sauce even to approach her, lunch or no lunch.

"Well," she began, but Elizabeth interrupted,

"Please come. I've heard so much from the girls about your lovely place that I'm dying to meet you. There's no ill-feeling between Jack and me, you know. Water under the bridge and all that, but don't mention this to him, please. Our secret. I'm back to the States on Wednesday and I'm cramming things in as best I can. Do say yes."

Trixie said yes.

By Thursday the show was significantly improved, Denzil's death seemingly having had a positive impact. All tickets were sold for Friday and Saturday and Grant's last minute instruction to give it 100% and enjoy! appeared to do the trick. Pauline the prompter was virtually unemployed, the musical director managed to keep up with the chorus who gave their all and the leading players were on form, especially Nicely(Brummie) Nicely who received encores at all performances. Bouquets were presented to the leading ladies and there was a bottle of champagne for Jack as a reward for his courage. (Cheers from the migraineurs.)

Some members of the audience hung about until the cast were changed and ready to meet them in the auditorium, but Lily, Marilyn and Charlie were not among them.

Elizabeth with her shining, platinum hair piled high, slim and elegant in blue silk had been easily spotted among the York posse and Lily felt too clumsy and plain to risk comparison. Angela also picked her out and with no such qualms went at once to make herself known.

"Jack's probably told you all about me," she said. "He's so talented, isn't he? We all love him!"

"So I see. Lucky Jack. He always was catnip to the ladies. The show must have been *such* fun for you all," and Elizabeth moved gracefully away to greet Jack as he approached.

"What a pleasant surprise," he said, unconvincingly.

"I wouldn't have missed it for the world. I'm afraid I must go, though," and she left, after bidding goodbye to the York contingent who were raising the noise level by several decibels.

Normally, after the last performance everyone was invited to take a bottle to Grant's spacious house near to the theatre, where there would be cans of lager, orange juice and bowls of crisps kindly offered by his wife. Sex, drugs and rock and roll it was not, and most members of the company were relieved to have the excuse that it seemed unseemly so soon after Denzil's death to celebrate too conspicuously, and were happy to go home. Jack had already told Lily of his intention to do that and hinted that, should she feel like joining him after she had driven her parents home, he would guarantee a warm welcome. She had not turned down the offer and he returned to his flat to make optimistic preparations.

When Trixie arrived at The Holly Bough Inn at Sunday lunchtime, Elizabeth was sitting at the bar sipping a Perrier water. Irritatingly, she was one of those women who look eye-turningly attractive even in the white shirt and jeans she was wearing, her long, platinum hair in a plait over one shoulder. Believing she might need an unclouded head for subsequent discussion, Trixie matched her with an orange juice. A secluded corner table had been booked, set only for two, to her relief as she had feared being outnumbered by the migraineurs threatening to kidnap Jack.

In response to Elizabeth's pleasant enquiry, she outlined the history of the conversion from Bagshot House Hotel to Lavender House, explaining that it was also now a comfortable home for herself and Felix.

"Is that Boot?"

"Yes, that's Boot. There's very spacious accommodation for the seven therapists. That's the maximum without building on at the back, which I don't intend to do. It's large enough to be viable but small enough for us to function as a supportive group with a family feeling. I suspect you know all this already?"

"Could you get planning permission if you wanted it?"

Eyes narrowing involuntarily, Trixie repeated, "I don't want it. That's our garden: there's a small lawn and a large patio with pots and garden chairs for any therapists who want to relax outside. In practice they don't do it yet, but they could. I shan't build on. The question won't arise."

Elizabeth nodded thoughtfully. "I've extended my clinic and managed to buy the properties on either side. We've broadened our services and introduced new cosmetic procedures and every imaginable spa treatment. It's a money-spinner, I can tell you. Trade's booming. Jack wouldn't have countenanced it, I know, but I'm in the lucky position now of having my own money to invest."

"Congratulations," said Trixie, in honeyed tones. "Of course, I've moved away from the hair and beauty salon end of the business. Ours is purely therapy."

"I think that's an imaginary line," laughed Elizabeth. "Fewer wrinkles and fuller lips have a decidedly therapeutic effect, I can assure you."

They paused to order lunch, Trixie going for the steak and ale pudding with baked potato as a matter of principle.

"It's lovely talking to you," she said, "and I understand your interest, but did you want to raise a specific matter?"

Elizabeth flicked her plait from her shoulder and nodded. "I'm willing to make an offer for the place well over the market price. Lock, stock and barrel."

"Including Jack?" laughed Trixie.

"Including everybody if they'd like to stay. You could carry on as manager. I understand your people are self-employed. I employ all mine at above the going rate, which they all seem very happy with. We could come to an amicable arrangement concerning the flats." Trixie shook her head

Internally, Trixie was open-mouthed, but she retained her usual composure, smiled and said, "You haven't even set foot inside. Talk about a pig in a poke!"

"I receive full, very detailed reports from Jack's groupies and, before you ask, I didn't encourage them or send them to spy. Actually I was less than thrilled when they started coming down here, but you've met them and know by now they're chatterboxes one and all. Naturally, I'd prefer to think they're loyal to me, but I can't compete with Jack for their homeopathic allegiance. They still practically live at the salon for one thing and another. Between us we must dominate their lives."

Gazing at her navvy sized steak and ale pie, Trixie considered how satisfying it would be to land it on the beautiful head of the greedy, jealous woman opposite daintily engaged in playing with minute amounts of crab and strips of lettuce.

"It's not for sale, Elizabeth. Not everything in this world is."

Beautiful blue eyes widened as she replied, "Most things are, I've found, if you offer the right inducements".

"Not this time. It's not for sale. Lavender House is my baby, only a few months old."

Mrs. Hunter Mackinlay shrugged. "It could grow into a beautiful adult with a serious injection of cash. Do you have room for dessert?"

Trixie shook her head. "Provided you don't subject me to pressure about selling, you're welcome to look round, Elizabeth. I shan't invite you while we're open—it might unnerve people, especially Jack, but if you'd like to come out of hours before you fly off, I'll gladly give you the guided tour."

"That's nice of you. I'd like that. I'm driving back to York later tonight. Could I come at about seven?"

That agreed, the women appeared relaxed as they chatted about developments in the sweetly scented world of pampering.

Relaying this to Boot when she reached home, Trixie was disappointed and shocked to hear his first question was to ask how much was being offered.

"Boot!" she exclaimed sharply, "there's a matter of principle, here. Can't you see it's a revenge offer to poke Jack in the eye?"

"What if Jack doesn't mind being poked in the eye if the money's right?"

"Oh, for God's sake, pour me a large vodka. I've raised an amoral Philistine."

"I was just testing, and you're right, of course. We don't want to make lots and lots of lovely money, do we? We're happy as we are, living over the shop, up three flights of stairs and loving it."

Trixie was outraged. "Actually, Boot, yes I am, very happy and proud as it happens. But if you want to continue living rent and board free over the shop, I suggest you think before you speak."

Boot obeyed, realizing that this was no joke.

"Why are you letting her look round then? What's the point? Obviously she'll be making an inventory and calculating how she can persuade you to budge."

Sighing, Trixie softened. "Honestly, I don't know, love. I'm fond of the place, that's all, and I don't want to think the others can be bought. Stay with me when she comes in case she pins me against the wall and forces me to sign something."

"Mother, don't try to come over all helpless and vulnerable. It doesn't suit you and isn't convincing. She gets the swift tour, an offer of a drink then out on her arse she goes, okay?"

There were times when Trixie felt quite proud of Boot.

Punctually at seven, Elizabeth arrived bearing a large bunch of lilies that Boot took upstairs to arrange and the tour began, Trixie using her master key to show several rooms as examples. Jack's was not included, to his ex-wife's obvious disappointment. "Has he still got those apothecary jars?" she asked. "I gave them to him for our fifth wedding anniversary. They're worth a fortune now."

Trixie nodded. "Sentimental value, you mean?"

Elizabeth had the grace to laugh. When asked about the décor of her own establishment, after being visibly unimpressed by Trixie's lilac scheme, she described how it was done throughout in black and white, with a small, red rose as the salon's insignia.

"How lovely!" said Trixie, "Just like the Labour Party."

She learned that the name had been changed from KENTS to ELIZABETH'S.

Stopping to study the photographs, Elizabeth remarked that they were a good-looking bunch, pointed at Lois and asked whether she was the girl in the chorus of Guys and Dolls who had come over and spoken to her. Trixie explained that Lois bore a strong resemblance to her but that she had obviously met Angela, a patient.

"She gave me the impression she was Jack's girlfriend."

"She probably would, but she's not."

"She's his patient?"

"Yes. She's also seeing Lois, our counsellor."

"How fascinating. She struck me as a bit off-beam."

"She's improving," said Trixie, and moved on.

When they reached the flat where Boot was waiting to offer refreshment, which she refused, Elizabeth praised the refurbishment and declared it all a most desirable enterprise.

"Your mother's to be congratulated," she told Boot, graciously.

"Indeed she is," agreed Boot, equally graciously, waiting for an offer that was not made.

Elizabeth thanked them both, mentioning that she was going to pop in to see Jack before driving to York where she had two days work before flying to the States.

On the way out she picked up one of Ben French's business cards from the desk, causing Trixie and Boot to wonder whether she intended trying to poach him, too.

Ten minutes after she left, they noticed her cream cashmere cardigan on the sofa.

"If she's going to Jack's I'll drive round with it," offered Boot. "Shan't be a minute."

Trixie thought it prudent to 'phone Jack to tell him that his wife was on the way and that Boot was close behind her with a cardigan.

This accounted for Boot recognising Lily's green car being driven away from Jack's in the direction of her own house. Elizabeth's Lexus was turning into the drive, but more mysteriously, Angela's red Honda was parked on the opposite side of the street with Angela at the wheel.

It was an ambition of Boot's to own one of these flats as soon as he could afford it. He liked the plain, white, anonymous, stuccoed fronts, the entry 'phones, the lift and secluded gardens. It was a disappointment when he pointed the place out to Ben to find his preference was for a honeysuckle-covered cottage in the country.

He caught up with Elizabeth just as she had pressed the video 'phone and was receiving instructions to go on up. She thanked him profusely but did not suggest he should accompany her. In any case, Boot thought, Jack might well be ruffled by Lily's hasty exit even though he was a free man perfectly entitled to entertain whomsoever he chose. He also felt he should have mentioned the lurking presence of Angela in the street, but did not know how to phrase it, so drove away, pretending he had not seen her noticeable blonde head or her familiar red car.

Trixie learned of this with a wry smile. "It's like a French farce. It only needs the migraineurs to turn up and poor Jack will be a nervous wreck."

They analysed Elizabeth's behaviour for a while then agreed to forget it.

Boot had helped Grant to pack away the remnants of 'Guys and Dolls' and been told that the police had interviewed all those who had witnessed or been in the vicinity of Denzil's fall. A representative of the Health and Safety Executive made worryingly copious notes regarding the condition of the steps and banisters, but found them beyond reproach. Pauline the Prompter did not repeat her observation that it was Angela who had tripped and accidentally shoved Denzil, and Angela tearfully described her inability to save him and how she would never forgive herself.

An accident, pure and simple, it seemed. This view was reinforced by Audrey who confirmed that this was not a company given to reckless behaviour.

After listening to this account, Trixie asked for Boot's assessment of what had happened.

"I think you've been shielding me from some very interesting information about Angela Smith. Ben thinks she's got beautiful feet but is mad."

"On what grounds?"

"Not many, actually, but Beverly has hinted more than once that she's a nasty piece of work who upset Lois on her first visit. And she's outrageous at rehearsals,—makes passes at Jack all the time. He puts her in her place but she's like a bouncing ball. Hell hath no fury etc. Ben's quiet, but he doesn't miss much. People are used to him being around taking photographs, but he hoovers up little snippets of conversation for my entertainment. This was a good one:

he heard Angela telling Pauline that Dr. Crippen was a homeopath, just like Jack! And she told Grant she hoped Jack would play Denzil's part if he got ill or anything. Clairvoyance or what?"

"Surely she wouldn't push somebody downstairs to secure a part for a man she fancies? Would she?"

Boot shrugged. "He's dead, however it came about. Voodoo doll most likely."

"I shall be glad when she's gone from here. It's her last session with Lois next week, and I expect Jack'll try to shake her off soon."

"I hope she's not sticking pins in Lily."

"That would be an ironic role reversal, wouldn't it?" They laughed and went on to other areas of interest.

Characteristically plain-speaking, Lily had informed her mother after taking them home after the show that she was going back to Jack's and might well stay overnight. Marilyn, equally characteristically, suggested items to be packed in her bag.

"Give us a ring if you're coming home for a meal," she said.

That Charlie would be unhappy at this development was predictable, but even his over-protective instincts accepted that Lily was well over the age of consent.

His hopes of one day becoming a grandfather were almost extinguished, acknowledging that Lily was settling into a literally single-minded way of life, which was comfortable for them all. His liking for Jack was causing a reappraisal. If a match were to be made, he would have no problems in welcoming him into their family. An engagement, followed quite soon by marriage would be a desirable outcome, but Charlie was aware that nowadays people lived together, had children and even then did not feel obliged to have a wedding. Going after Jack with a shotgun was not an option. Lily had survived one broken relationship that accounted for her long period of distrust towards the few who had made advances of any kind. That Jack was generally admired, good-looking, apparently solvent and respectful, made him an ideal suitor, but Charlie could see that people might have suspicions, as he unwillingly had himself, of gold-digging. Rationally, that did not matter. If he made Lily happy, there was no reason to exclude him from the family fortunes. Marilyn was not now, nor had she ever been, a great beauty. He could have chosen from a selection of pretty, young women, but saw in Marilyn the qualities that lasted throughout marriage. Jack's first, failed marriage to the lovely Elizabeth had perhaps served to encourage him also to look for inner beauty. All these thoughts whizzed through his mind as he watched Lily's preparations to return to Jack's on Saturday night, and kept his thoughts busy for the greater part of Sunday, which seemed an unusually long day.

When the 'phone rang at about eight on Sunday evening to say she was on her way home, it aroused no concern until Marilyn revealed that Lily was tearful because Jack's ex-wife was about to arrive for what was described as a flying visit.

Lily flew out herself in a marked manner.

Charlie fetched his black baseball cap, a bottle of water and some crisps and announced, to Marilyn's alarm, that he was going for a little drive and would keep in touch.

He passed Lily in her little green car travelling towards home, waved at her and carried on till he reached Jack's block of flats. He parked on the opposite side of the road, a few metres behind the Honda, where Angela was also evidently prepared for a long vigil.

After fifteen minutes, Elizabeth emerged and drove away. Angela waited for a minute then took the parking space close to the front door, got out, pressed the video 'phone and received a message that clearly displeased. She climbed back into her car, slammed the door, revved up noisily, drove back to park the Honda untidily in front of Charlie's Mercedes, got out and rapped on his window.

"Lily's left," she informed him. "So has his ex-wife. Boot's been and gone and I'm just about to leave. You can make your report now, Mr. Ho."

She drove off, leaving Charlie to 'phone Marilyn with the news which she relayed to Lily.

"Sounds like the Keystone Kops," said Marilyn, drily. "You should have stayed, Lily, and marked your territory; stood by your man. You were the only person actually invited. The rest are, well, God knows what, but not in a loving relationship with Jack 'Phone the man and make up. This wasn't his fault."

Reluctantly, Lily did that and eventually went to bed, slightly mollified, with memories of a blissful Saturday night and a most peculiar Sunday.

CHAPTER THIRTEEN

Standing by early on Monday morning, at Jack's request for a quick chat, Trixie had already decided that 'don't tell Jack' was not a binding command since Elizabeth could look after herself and Trixie knew where her own loyalties lay. As half expected, Jack had been told by Elizabeth about the visit to Lavender House and the offer to buy. He waited nervously to hear from Trixie whether she was entertaining the proposal. Clearly he was less than pleased that his ex-wife had been invited to tour the place and only slightly reassured by learning that at least access to his own clinic had not been included.

"It would have been churlish to refuse," insisted Trixie. "I'm certainly puzzled by her motives: there are thousands of suitable premises all over the UK. Why here? Why not expand in the States? I understand her wanting to show her financial independence, but why pick on us, unless it really is personally directed at you? The migraineurs still patronise her place, and since there's no longer a homeopath there to treat them I see why they're still loyal to you, but I'm left with an uneasy feeling. You say the split was amicable? You might like to know that she enquired after your apothecary jars!"

Jack raised his eyebrows and smiled. "She bought them for a few pounds at a collectors' fair not knowing their value. Now she does, and serve her right. She came here to tell me . . . ."

Trixie held up an imperious hand. "Your private life is none of my business, Jack"

"Trixie, last night I think I said goodbye to my private life for ever. I've never been subjected to so much surveillance, what with Angela and Charlie Ho with binoculars trained on my front door and Boot chasing Elizabeth, it was no wonder Lily legged it. Who could blame her?"

"She wasn't forced to leave *too* early, I hope," asked Trixie archly, forgetting her declaration of uninterest in his private life.

Jack smiled. "No, not too early, we'd had a lovely day, thank you for asking. Trixie, I'm going to cut down on Angela's appointments: they're quite unnecessary. And the York patients, too. Frankly, most of what I'm doing for them could be done by 'phone. I'm developing into more of an agony uncle than a homeopath, and I do have a waiting list now. If they want to come here for their Reiki and aromatherapy, fine, although I'm beginning to wonder whether they're not all double agents."

"They've been a welcome boost for one or two of the girls, Jack, but I understand how you feel. Incidentally, this'll make you laugh, did you ever hear that Dr. Crippen was a homeopath? Pauline the prompter told Beverly, and Beverly told me."

"I believe that's the fourth time in a week. I've never felt even slightly homicidal until lately, but so help me I'll kill the next person who mentions it."

"I'll go then, before you offer me one of your evil little potions."

Laughing, Jack put his arm gently round her shoulders.

"I'm sorry. I'm afraid that one way and another I've upset the applecart. The worst's over, I think."

"Unfortunately not. The worst, the search and destroy missile, is arriving in a minute to have her allegedly beautiful feet photographed by Ben. Just hang on in there, Jack."

Angela duly arrived at the desk with a mock-tragic expression on her face.

"Do you know, Trixie, on Wednesday it'll be my last appointment with Lois. I feel we've grown really close."

"If you don't mind my saying so, you're a different person from when you first came," said Trixie, wanting to add, 'but not in a good way.'

"I do feel different. More confident. I'm setting achievable goals for myself, and you've probably noticed how much Lois has benefited, too. And the times with Jack have been . . . just lovely."

"Ben should be here in a minute," said Trixie quickly. "Perhaps you'd like to go along to Juliet's room."

"She's not going to actually touch me," said Angela. "We're only posing."

"Fine," replied Trixie. "Like good men, pretty feet are hard to find."

"Then, after the mock Reflexology, Ben's photographing the back of my head, facing Lois."

"Lovely," said Trixie.

"Incidentally," Angela went on, "if you're ever hard-pressed on Reception,—and I've seen that Boot isn't always available,—I'll gladly hold the fort. I'm computer literate and know all the therapists very well now, so don't hesitate to ask. My technical writing work has pretty much dried up, so I'm usually free."

"That's very kind," replied Trixie. "I'll bear it in mind."

The 'photo session was reported by Boot to be a success. Most therapists offered each other unidentifiable sections of their bodies for Ben to display to best advantage. Pretty Nancy of the migraineurs offered to be shown in full, receiving a tiny bottle from a serious—looking Jack, even though she and the others had been warned already that he wished to reduce contact time. They expressed regret but not distress, and diverted their appointments and their money to other therapists willing to listen while they worked.

Jack declared himself too busy for more posing, but only Jason found difficulty recruiting a volunteer, Ben insisting that a hunky, hairy portion of male anatomy was essential, which ruled out Boot who would have been happy to oblige.

Eventually, a reciprocal arrangement with Lawrence was set up, in spite of his overhearing a disparaging remark from Jason to the effect that chiropractic was neither his cup of tea nor an altogether respectable process. Lawrence thought he heard him say 'chiroquacktic', but was not sure enough to do anything but ignore it, but he brooded about it, causing Boot to report to Trixie later that he had never before seen Lawrence so quiet and moody.

It took Helen over an hour that evening to winkle out of Lawrence that he had been offended by Jason's comments. To date, no-one had cast doubt on the validity of his profession; certainly his patients expressed no qualms, and personal recommendations were the basis for his success. Helen advised him not to worry.

"If you're happy with what you do, that's all that matters," she said, and was taken off-guard when Lawrence replied sharply,

"But it's not, obviously. That's like telling a car thief that it doesn't matter as long as he's happy."

"Now you're just being silly," she said. "You can't get upset by criticism from a sports masseur with twelve months training. Think of all those years you were at college."

Lawrence nodded. "True. I could have trained to be an orthodox doctor in the same time."

"That's just what my Dad said," agreed Helen, misguidedly. "He wondered why you chose chiropractic."

"Why didn't he ask me when he had the chance then? As I remember your Dad thought at first I was a chiropodist."

Helen did not like the tone of Lawrence's voice, and told him so as she went to pick up her jacket and bag.

"Since you've raised the matter, there are a lot of unanswered questions about chiropractic. You haven't been asked because nobody's wanted to upset you."

"Well, that doesn't seem to be worrying you now," said Lawrence, pink-faced and puzzled as to how their relationship, ready for trips to IKEA, should suddenly have nose-dived so disastrously.

The sound of the door of his newly-mortgaged flat being slammed was like a shot to his heart. He sat down, blaming Boot and Ben and the stupid photoshoot and wondering whether he should be the first to apologize and, much, much more worryingly, what was the matter with chiropractic all of a sudden.

That morning, Lily and Jack had hugged each other in reconciliation. By evening, with the exception of Lawrence, there was a feeling of restoration to an even keel.

Tuesday passed without drama, and there was an air of quiet, scented purpose.

On Wednesday, Angela arrived with a large box of chocolates for Lois and trotted up the stairs to her room.

"Well, here we are," Lois greeted her cheerfully. "For me? That's really kind. How has your week been?"

As Lois stood to accept the gift, Angela slipped niftily into the higher chair.

"Very busy. I was telling Trixie that my contract work has virtually dried up, but it's just as well, actually, because I've been here, there and everywhere on various missions. I've decided against training as a psychotherapist. I recognise in myself an urge to tell people to pull themselves together. Keeping busy, that's the key, I find. All this talk about 'issues' is not my scene. You did right to tell me to get out and about and stop obsessing about my own little problems like having an adulterous husband who died prematurely. I'm moving away from homeopathy, as well. I've been researching it and well, really, it's for the suggestible. Don't tell me, please, that the Queen uses it. Her life is so abnormal she can't be held up as a medical adviser!" Angela rummaged in her handbag.

"I printed this out for you to study. Read it later," and she handed Lois an envelope.

"So! I'm confident and happy. How about you? I felt your pain, as they say, and I acknowledge I may have added to your worries, but I trust you'll deal with your own problems. Take charge of your own destiny, etc."

Lois listened without moving a muscle.

"I'm sure you'll be fine," she said, "and so shall I. All I want to suggest to you is that you resist becoming too involved in other people's affairs, especially as you've decided against pursuing a career in therapy. The matter between us, the one that brought you here, stays with me in complete confidence. Of course, if you were to make any accusations against me, I would deny them. There were no witnesses; I would claim you were in a disturbed state and I would feel obliged to mention your murder confession. So, it's all over, happily settled for us both. A classic, steep learning curve. I shall miss seeing you round the place."

"Well, as a matter of fact, the possibility is that I shall still be about. Trixie and I have had a chat about my doing some part-time work in Reception."

Lois stared, thrown off track "Boot does that," she said.

"I think we all know that he does not regard that as his chosen occupation." Angela gave a little laugh. "He needs time to concentrate on his writing, and Trixie pushes herself too hard."

"Well, anyway, Angela," said Lois, struggling not to appear fazed at this final stage, "I wish you good luck and happiness, and thanks again for the chocolates." She rose, and shook hands with Angela who seemed reluctant to vacate the high, green chair.

"Goodbye," she said eventually, stood up, kissed a surprised Lois on both cheeks, and walked out very slowly.

Allowing five minutes for her to be gone, Lois scuttled downstairs. Her next patient who invariably looked as if she'd been crying, was sitting on one of the cane chairs.

"I shan't keep you a moment, Fenella. Please go on up."

Trixie recognised the look on Lois's face and braced herself.

"Tell me it's not true! You haven't engaged Angela Smith to work in Reception?"

"I can tell you it's not true. But she certainly offered. She'd love it, wouldn't she?"

"Jesus! She made it sound like a fait accompli, just as we'd exchanged tender words and undying love, the lying little bitch."

Trixie nodded in the direction of the stairs. "You'd better attend to Fenella Phipps. Her dog's dead."

The women rolled their eyes in cold-hearted synchronicity.

CHAPTER FOURTEEN

In spite of the diagnosis of leukaemia and its worrying prognosis, Charlie was thinking for the umpteenth time of the charmed life he continued to enjoy. He climbed from the pool and lay on the lounger alongside a dozing Marilyn. The early evening sun was still hot enough to dry him with a minimum amount of patting, and as he looked up at the sky, the sunset looked as though drawn by an enthusiastic child with a box of pastel crayons. He inhaled the scents of lavender and honeysuckle from the hedge behind and again counted his blessings.

Partly in view of his undisclosed health problems, he had told his managers and Marilyn, who was delighted, that he was embarking on partial retirement. His language schools had competent managers as did the restaurants, and he had begun limiting himself to irregular appearances in them. Mildly worried about the peculiar Smith woman, he intended going to the Rising Sun this evening, but felt disinclined and closed his eyes, happy in the knowledge that the profits would come rolling in regardless.

When his mobile rang he expected to hear from Lily who was having dinner with Jack, but it was a barely intelligible

Chinese voice eventually recognisable as Ken, his restaurant manager, reporting, he finally interpreted, a police raid.

Charlie sprang up, wide awake now. Marilyn watched in wonder as he shouted to her to fetch his clothes and bring the car round.

The police, it later transpired, had received an anonymous tip-off that he was employing immigrants without the necessary paper-work. Most of the officers were familiar customers of the Rising Sun, fully aware of the multi-national workforce and respectful of Charlie and his impeccable credentials, known as a solid, law-abiding citizen, Rotary Club member and generous donor to local charities. They asked in a slightly embarrassed way about his personal house staff and were clearly relieved when he called his secretary to produce the essential pieces of paper, all up-to-date, with every last leaf-picker legitimate and documented in scrupulous detail.

They were not allowed, they said, to reveal who had started this hare running.

"Female?" asked Charlie.

One officer silently inclined his head slightly.

"Blonde? Fortyish?"

Again, the merest inclination of the officer's head.

"That explains it. At least it explains who I suspect it is. She's a bit deranged. A trouble-maker. My apologies, gentlemen."

The gentlemen left, speculating in the two cars that had brought eight policemen, whether this was the work of an aggrieved lover, which they considered unlikely, a disgruntled competitor, which was possible, a racist protest against a perceived loss of jobs for locals or a disappointed customer, unhappy with her chow mien.

Whatever the cause they felt secure in the knowledge that when they took their wives or girlfriends out for the evening, there would always be a good table at the Rising Sun.

Marilyn drove Charlie home, concerned by the greyness of his complexion and in agreement that responsibility for all the nonsense probably rested with the strange Mrs. Smith, who had her eyes on Jack.

Lily was home, surprised by the scribbled note to the effect that they were off to the Rising Sun, and even more surprised when she heard the reason. Her parents did not mention their suspicions, but Lily jumped immediately to the same conclusion.

"Ignore her," she advised, tight-lipped. "I don't want to mention this to Jack. She'll soon get tired and leave us all alone."

Charlie dictated a letter for distribution to the Rising Sun staff, expressing regret and concern for the police intrusion. He mentioned that the men were only doing their duty and that, as they well knew, they had nothing to fear and had been shown to be legally employed. He added that in small recompense there would be a small bonus in their pay packets at the end of that week. Jennifer, his P/A Secretary, assured him that no offence had been taken and that extra cash was not necessary but would be gratefully received.

"After two kitchen inspections in a month they're getting used to being checked out," she said.

"What did you say?" asked Charlie, worried now. When she repeated it, he revealed he knew nothing of such inspections and that Ken had not mentioned them.

"Well, there was nothing to report. Nary a cockroach. Everything shipshape, as it always is. Ken wouldn't want to bother you."

Charlie put his hand to his forehead, wearily. "Jennifer, it's late and I'm tired, but tomorrow I shall want to see those papers and I shall want you to find out from the Food Standards people who authorized and conducted the visits. I smell stinking fish, which is perhaps not an appropriate phrase under the circumstances, but you get my drift."

Jennifer, sixty-ish, small, slight, fair going to grey, with the capacity to terrify very large men, had been with Charlie for twenty years. Clever, loyal, hard-working and very highly paid, she determined immediately that if there were any funny business going on she would root it out. Charlie was an exemplary employer and she did not intend to see him or his workers harassed.

The minutae of Charlie's domestic life were familiar to her. She was aware of Lily's affection for Jack, who was being welcomed into the Ho household; she knew, as Marilyn as yet did not, of Charlie's leukaemia; she had been put in charge of the secret arrangements for the Ruby Anniversary party; she knew, too, of Angela Smith.

When Charlie and Jennifer examined the hygiene certificates the following day, and checked them against earlier ones, the smell of rat grew stronger. When the office concerned denied all knowledge of recent visits, Charlie and Jennifer believed they knew where the trail might lead. The 'why' was not hard to diagnose, but the 'how' was trickier.

The 'inspector' was described as having dark, curly hair most of which was tucked into the regulation white, peaked hat. She wore a white coat, black-framed, slightly tinted glasses, disposable gloves, had a strong Irish accent and a clip board.

A wig, an assumed accent, computer proficiency, a clip board and a brass neck all added up, they agreed, to Angela Smith. She was known, though, to restaurant staff. Would she dare? Could she have pulled it off, knowing that eventually the deceit would be revealed? Who else could it be?

Charlie deterred Jennifer from calling the police, declaring that one police encounter a week was enough.

"I'll sort it," he said. "Let it go, Jennifer. You'll be busy with the party. In fact, I'd rather talk about that now. I'll 'phone their office and say we think it was just a silly prank. I don't want them meddling in it."

Most reluctantly she agreed, but inwardly had no intention of letting the matter drop. She turned her attention to the party, mildly worried by the ever lengthening guest list that was going to entail bigger and bigger marquees.

In addition to relatives from both sides of the family, there were friends, business colleagues, employees, Lily's friends and colleagues from Lavender House and, it seemed, anyone who crossed Charlie's mind.

Jennifer examined with a critical eye and a feeling of near hysteria, Charlie's draft for the invitations.

PLEASE COME TO CELEBRATE
08.08.08 (A propitious year in CHINA)
AND JOIN MARILYN AND CHARLIE AT HOME
ON THEIR FORTIETH WEDDING ANNIVERSARY.
(Map enclosed, with parking provision marked)

Please, no presents, but if you wish to mark this joyous occasion, (which is also the start of the Beijing Olympics) with a donation to the local hospice, that would be greatly appreciated.

BRING SWIMWEAR (Heated Pool)

The Party will be from 12 noon to 12midnight. We suggest that from 6p.m. it shall be for adults only.

R.S.V.P.

Jennifer complained that it was more of a short story than an invitation and that there were rather too many brackets.

"You're the secretary. Sort it out, but keep the relevant information."

She thought it would be a miracle if Marilyn were surprised. Charlie was hopeless at keeping secrets and, in any case she planned to drop a heavy hint so that Marilyn would be prepared with a new dress and hair and nails in order, rather than the very real possibility of being caught in tee shirt and gardening trousers.

Most of the town would be involved in printing, marquee hire and assembly, in catering for twelve hours, in staffing the event including parking and pool supervision. Some secret.

Adequately pre-warned, Lily was taking two days off with instructions to take her mother shopping on Thursday, to stay overnight in an hotel and bring her back in time to be astonished on Friday morning by finding the garden transformed into a scene of wonder, with bands playing, two marquees erected, a bouncy castle, lanterns to be lit when the sun went down, enough food and drink for the entire town and a steady parade of friends, relatives and other well-wishers. Naturally, even without Jennifer's hints, Marilyn had caught on that the date would not go unremarked and happily jumped at the prospect of time with Lily that included a trip to the theatre. She was prepared to feign astonishment.

She and Jennifer were such old friends that Marilyn sometimes referred to her as 'the other Mrs.Ho', although that was not a coveted position. Jennifer had once declared that she would walk on hot coals for Charlie, but had no ambitions to wash his socks. She was devoted to them both and, to a lesser degree to Lily, whom she found awkward and unforthcoming. The knowledge of Charlie's illness was like a stone in her heart; fruitlessly she urged him to share this with Marilyn and Lily, but always he replied, "Soon. Not just yet."

In fact, he wanted to get the party over without the cloud of mortality hanging over the proceedings. Lily was treating them to a weekend in Paris, where he planned to break the news to Marilyn. At the moment he was refining the menu.

"Fortune cookies?" asked Jennifer.

"They're the most important item," agreed Charlie.

CHAPTER FIFTEEN

When Trixie opened the front door on Thursday morning at eight o'clock, it was to find Carl, Boot's agent, sitting on the doorstep.

"I'm the bearer of good tidings," he announced, creakingly rising to his feet and bowing in a manner that did nothing to endear him to Trixie, who merely raised one eyebrow, always a useful accomplishment.

"The books, Mrs. Calloway dear, the books! I'm en route to distribute them to half a dozen outlets, and I've a box for Boot in the boot. Ha!"

"You'd better bring them in, Carl. I'll fetch Felix."

She did not wish to be the one to ask the therapists whether they had any objection to having a pile of them displayed on a table by Reception, where Boot planned to spend the day signing copies. In truth she had forgotten her promise to arrange this, but Boot eagerly accosted people as they arrived for work. No-one liked to object, all admired the green cover with its gilt embossing and agreed to buy a signed copy before blanching at the asking price of £25. The poems were not, Boot explained, what was termed 'accessible', but readers were assured they would be rewarded by further study of the shapes and apparently random words. Some tried at intervals for the rest of the day, but found no hidden messages.

Clients did not feel the same sense of loyalty and sales were limited to two migraineurs who liked the covers.

Angela turned up for what Jack had amiably agreed should be her last session. From his point of view she had enlisted of her own volition and he was pleased to see her leave the same way.

"I'm sorry it hasn't been quite what you expected," he said.

"Your description of homeopathy was very appealing when we were sitting over a drink, do you remember?" asked Angela. "I think your nice, blue eyes had something to do with it. I suppose when you were looking at me in what I thought was a fond fashion, as if you were attracted to me, what you were actually doing was classifying me as a nux vomica or a sulphur or a pulsatilla type. None of them sounds particularly pleasant but I'd have preferred sulphur in the hope you might have regarded me as a creative genius rather than subject to bouts of irritability, being weepy and disliking butter, which I understand are characteristics of the pulsatilla personality."

"I was an off-duty homeopath when we had a post-rehearsal drink together," Jack replied stiffly. "On duty, most certainly I would try to adopt an holistic approach and try to assess your whole being, not simply the mild depression you reported, that fortunately does not seem now to be manifesting itself."

"I've done a bit of research," Angela began, but Jack stopped her, his eyes not quite as attractively crinkly.

"Lois showed me your little extract from the web and I understand how you came to dismiss the theory from that small piece of criticism, but there are libraries of volumes of studies and hundreds of thousands of people satisfied with the practice. Forgive me, Angela, but you need more than 'a bit of research' to demolish the science and the art."

Angela listened, head on one side, unsmiling.

"Fortunately, I've plenty of time to do more than 'a bit of research', and that's my intention. After that I shall be looking into acupuncture."

"I see! Suddenly you're an investigative medical researcher. Excellent news! Remember, won't you, that you have to be impartial and carry out empirical studies."

"Actually, I don't. It's all been done and widely published on the web, in newspapers and in books. All I have to do is read and extract information. Strictly speaking I should have said 'search' not 'research'. What I then do with all the information I haven't altogether decided. But I've truly enjoyed my time with you, Jack and I hope this won't affect our relationship, especially at WOADS. They're talking about doing the 'Desert Song' next. That should be fun."

"Not for me, I'm afraid. I've retired from all that. It was too time consuming, but you should carry on. I'll definitely buy tickets."

Irritated, Angela tapped her right foot. "It would be silly to leave now. You're a shoe-in for the leads now the competition's gone."

"Poor Denzil, yes. I've already told Grant and he was very nice about it."

"Oh, he's an idiot to let you go." She sighed, dramatically. "But there, Jack, you're your own man, as they say."

"Yes, they do say that, don't they. I've really no idea what it means. Tell me, are you feeling content now, in mind and body, as it will say in the new brochure?"

She nodded. "My feet and my hair will feature in it to remind you of me. Yes, I'm fine. I'll see you around. I may even be manning Reception."

Angela was almost out of the door when she turned and said,

"Sometime, when you're not too busy, perhaps you might take me through Avogrado's number, and the 30X dilution that I think means I'd have to drink 7,874 gallons of water to get one molecule of medicine. Easily swallowed by the gullible, I imagine, but pretty hard to swallow intellectually."

"No," said Jack, on his feet now, and aware that his neck was reddening embarrassingly. "I shan't have time to do that, Angela. You seem very well, and I'm happy about that. Good luck with your studies."

The last few words were squeezed out through gritted teeth as she finally closed the door.

He was, in truth, highly put out by the paper Lois had passed to him. Reading it as expressed by a non-believing analyst was like being a committed Catholic being told your lifelong faith was so much fluff and piffle. That a certain amount, perhaps even a significant amount, of suspension of disbelief was needed by patients he did not deny. Had he been of a more analytical bent when he first became interested, he might have been talked out of dedicating himself to the work, but he had gone along with the theories and reached a point of no return, encouraged by people who claimed to be healed, or at least improved, by the teensy weensy drops of nothing.

Lily's woeful tale of her friend's fatal experience had been untypical, and he could relate plenty of gaffes made by orthodox medics, but it had rankled, and he had to admit that the York migraineurs regarded their appointments more as pleasant social encounters, meaning neither more nor less than half an hour with Juliet, that ridiculous Reflexologist, or a lunchtime Botox. Most of them no longer suffered migraine or headache of any kind, which they regarded as proof positive of the efficacy of homeopathy. Secretly he nursed suspicions that the word 'migraine' had often been misapplied, in many cases a self-diagnosis in the first place.

He had once come across Boot in the throes of a migraine in all its disorientating, light zig-zagging, speech-disabling, nauseating, head-drilling, death-wishing glory and doubted whether Nancy, Celia and the rest had ever experienced anything comparable.

Jack wished, how he wished, he had some teensy weensy, non-attributable drops that would prove fatal when dropped in Angela's coffee. He, himself, was developing a throbbing headache, so took a couple of Paracetamol.

At lunchtime, Lawrence popped his head round Jack's door.

"You look as cheerful as I am. Do you fancy coming round tonight for a couple of pints? I'd like to get as genuinely pissed as I feel right now, and I'd rather fall down indoors."

Jack grinned at him, surprised. "I can't imagine why you're down: a handsome, young feller with a devoted following, a burgeoning career and the love of your beautiful bride-to-be."

"Bride-not-to-be, I strongly suspect. We're not in communication at the moment, largely due to the apparently dodgy nature of my calling."

"You too? Well, I think I'm okay with Lily at present, but she'll be at choir practice tonight and otherwise discontent and paranoia have settled on my shoulder. I'd love a drink or three, so a taxi it is. What time?"

As they sat in Lawrence's previously pristine flat later that night, surrounded by empty take-away cartons and beer bottles, listening to Leonard Cohen's collected works and growing steadily more maudlin, they tried to assess how their lives had begun to career off course. Jack decided he'd like Lawrence for his new mate, describing how he'd arrived in Woolchester divorced and friendless.

"Orphaned?" suggested Lawrence helpfully.

"Orphaned," Jack confirmed. "Lily and her family have entered my life in a meaningful way, but she believes homeopathy is the devil's work. Also that batty Smith woman is collecting all the negative data she can find and half-threatening exposure to all and sundry. Why she's picking on me I can't imagine."

"She fancies you."

"Understandable, but a bloody silly way of trying to seduce me. Now, what's happened to you?"

Jack topped up Lawrence's glass while he listened to the description of Helen's sudden attack on chiropractic.

"She didn't dismiss it as such, and she's never had a go before, but now she's plainly critical. And bloody Jason Rugg said something snide as well when they were doing those shots for the brochure. I could be wrong there, but it sounded damned rude at the time."

"Jason did? Are you sure? Jason never says anything. Keeps his head down, takes the money and goes home. We're not threatening his livelihood, are we? Other thing, Lawrence, other thing, and keep this under your hat: my wife wants to buy Lavender House."

Lawrence laughed. "Your ex-wife, you mean, the glamour-puss. Saw her at 'Guys and Dolls' in the audience. Rich now, so Boot said. Why'd she want to buy Lavender House?"

"She's given up practising homeopathy herself, and doesn't employ any others—lost her faith, she said. I suspect she doesn't want to pay the going rate when she can fill the place with seventeen year old girls doing nail extensions and hot rock stuff. She's making squillions out of beauty treatments. She told Trixie, and not a word, Lawrence, she told Trixie she'd keep everybody on, but if she intends turning us into a beauty parlour, I'm out of there. And unless you change into a Botox technician you'll be forced to join me. Same for the acupuncturist."

"Trixie wouldn't do that, Jack. She's been like a mother to me."

"Are you an orphan as well?"

"No, and my parents are proud of me. Helen's aren't, though; think I should have studied medicine. More respectable. They're right, of course, but it's a bit late now."

They drank silently for a couple of minutes.

Jack perked up.

"I don't know why we're worrying our pretty little heads about all this. We could easily open a Jack and Larry Clinic. Plenty more pebbles on the beach for you Larry, old son, if Helen's gone cold. And the lovely Lily had better watch her step."

"What about the naysayers? Angela Smith and company?"

"Sod 'em."

They moved on to cheerier music and more beer until it became obvious that Lawrence's sofa was to be Jack's bed for the night.

The following morning, Trixie enquired after their health and mentioned to Lily that they both looked very unwell and she hoped it wasn't a bug going round, especially as Juliet had confided that she was definitely pregnant.

Simon had evidently expressed delight, insisting that she should give up work at six months.

"Just how demanding can sitting down, stroking people's feet be?" Trixie asked Lily.

Personally, she had carried on working until labour pains interfered with the perm she was doing, and it was her opinion that there was far too much fuss about the whole procedure these days.

"She won't be able to bring the baby to work, though, will she?" Lily hoped.

"Keep it under your hat, dear, but fortuitously I've been approached by a kinesiologist who'll be looking for a room as soon as he gets his certificate in a few months time. I doubt Juliet'll want to come back. I may suggest to Simon that she could work from home. Nice, profitable little sideline. No overheads. Simon would appreciate that."

Lily realized that Trixie's business acumen was not too deeply buried under her kindly exterior.

She went to offer to soothe Jack's clammy brow.

As hoped, Ben's photographs for the brochure were well received. The anonymous, silky-brown legs, Angela's well-publicised perfect feet and hair, the wrinkle-free, peachy-skinned face, the spine about to be subluxated, the hairy calf receiving the attention of Jason's strong hands, all were shown to advantage.

Each of the therapists had written his own blurb to be edited into enticing prose by Boot. Each complained mildly that they deserved more space until Trixie pointed out that they would still have separate leaflets for each speciality, for which they were individually responsible and which could contain as much detail as they saw fit. Having read some of the more extravagant claims for some of the treatments, she preferred to distance herself from liability.

Asked to design the cover, Boot had kept it simple and, he claimed, tasteful.

EVERY BODY DESERVES LAVENDER HOUSE it stated in bold black type on pink, the words encircled by shadowy sprays of lavender. Underneath that was

MENS SANA IN CORPORE SANO in slightly smaller type, which Beverly kindly translated for Juliet after she was heard pointing out that they didn't have a men's sauna.

"Honestly," Beverly said to Jason, "If that girl had one more brain cell she'd qualify as a turnip," which Jason thought was funny but harsh and quietly suggested to Juliet that he had a little Latin and if she wanted an upstaging tag for her own leaflet she might consider 'a capite ad calcem' helpfully translating it as 'from head to toe'.

She smiled, happily. "That'll show 'em," she said, and shared with Jason her good news, which was by now anyway an ill-kept secret.

Later, at home, she told Simon that Jason was the pick of the bunch, a gentleman and a scholar.

The therapists graciously approved the go-ahead for printing.

Boot was very busy sitting by the window inside the local newsagent's, hoping to sign and sell copies of his book, piled high on a table on a sale or return basis. The indications were for return, but there he sat, his hair an artfully lightened whiter shade of pale, elegant in cream cashmere and black scarf, smiling until his face ached at people buying 'The Sun.'

Tomorrow he would have sessions at Woolchester's only two bookshops where he hoped to meet a more intellectually aware set of people, ready for a challenging, kinaesthetic experience. Sadly, he would find the eye-catching space near the doors was stocked with the memoirs of a Big Brother participant, and he could only wonder and shake his head in sorrow at the sorry state of culture today.

His mother had swiftly enlisted Bunty, an old friend, to assist when needed on Reception, in return for a few nights out. Although she intended being there for the duration of Boot's absences, Trixie wanted to pre-empt any opportunistic offers from Angela, who still showed up regularly on some pretext or other.

Lawrence confided in Trixie that his engagement was on a knife edge, causing her a brief flicker of hope that Lexie might walk through the door and, in a late but welcome turnaround, Lawrence would forget the beautiful Helen, and Lexie would disregard her hearty sheep farmer once she again clapped eyes on Lawrence.

Trixie's low expectation of any of this happening was proved correct.

When Lexie, without prior warning, arrived home that night, tanned to the look and consistency of old leather, with her fiancé, Jake, tall, built like a plaid-clad barn, brimming with health and bonhomie, Trixie conceded defeat and clasped them both to her welcoming bosom.

Boot yelled, as they always used to do, "It's Big Sis!"

He received the time-honoured response, "Big Sis yourself!" and they hugged, affectionately, Boot adding as he introduced Ben, "Don't shake her hand. We all know where it's been."

Ben was rendered even quieter than usual by these noisy exchanges and Jake looked on in slight apprehension.

Liking to get things straight from the start, Trixie enquired whether Jake would prefer to have the second twin bed in Lexie's room or to use Boot's spare room, and was assured by her daughter that as they'd been sleeping together for a year, they'd like to continue as they meant to go on. They appeared to be travelling light.

The plan, Lexie explained, was to introduce Jake to her friends and family, to travel in their hired campervan (on display in the car park if anyone wished to examine it,) to look up his Welsh relations before she returned to university for her final year, for Jake to return then to New Zealand and for them to be reunited there for a register office wedding and life on the farm which was owned by his father who was semi-retired, and there was a farmhouse for them and, asked Lexie, breathless, wasn't she the luckiest person in the world?

Trixie had to acknowledge that it sounded idyllic for anyone fond of sheep.

They all spruced themselves up and went out for a celebratory dinner at The Red Sun, much to the delight of Charlie Ho who welcomed them warmly and insisted on providing champagne. He also added Lexie and Jake's names to his elastic guest list, but they had to offer regrets that by 08.08.08. they would be in Wales.

While courteous in his admiration of Lavender House and its therapeutic intent, it was soon obvious that Jake found the place overheated, over-scented and claustrophobic and unable to conceal his relief when, two days later, they set off for the Brecon Beacons to stay with his uncle on another sheep farm for a week or two.

The new brochures were admired, displayed and distributed, but a greater stir was caused by Lily's distribution of invitations to the ruby wedding anniversary, which came as a pleasant surprise. Apart from the occasion, most were curious about Lily's house, known to be on a grand scale, and a local talking point. It seemed unlikely there would be refusals.

Jennifer had skilfully edited Charlie's draft, pointing out for one thing the inadvisability of offering swimming for the adults. The women, she said, will not want to change out of party dresses or get their hair mussed up, apart from the added problem of providing changing areas and the necessary supervision for hordes of people in a pool, not to mention the inevitable drunken guest, probably Uncle Ho, who would fall in and drown. It was agreed to limit it to the few children who would be there and only until six p.m.

Lily explained to them the significance to her father of having the party on the actual day, and the parents among the therapists made child-minding arrangements to enable their own attendance at the evening party. Both Jason's and Lois's ever-obliging mothers-in-law were called on, their conversations in front of Juliet making it clear for the first time that the logistics of having a social life as well as children were trickier than she imagined. Silently she planned to start now on a plan to endear herself more to her mother-in-law who lived nearby.

The shopping trip for Lily and her mother was successful on all counts. Lily chose her mother's dress, Marilyn chose Lily's. Neither professed any particular expertise but knew what Charlie would admire. They enjoyed the theatre, the relaxation of staying in an hotel overnight and arrived home, as promised, promptly at ten a.m.

There was no need for Marilyn to feign amazement. When she first glimpsed the hedgerows leading to their gates, decked out in balloons, ribbons and garlands of flowers she cried out in delight.

CHAPTER SEVENTEEN

While the arrangements for the party, under Jennifer's skilful guidance, had been progressing swimmingly, as the day grew nearer there were rumours of some discontent in the little town. Woolchester's two small factories had been forced to make skilled people redundant. Three long-established cafes had closed already and there were closing down sales notices in the windows of the handbag boutique and the organic food shop. The Wig and Pen 'let go' one of the barmen and reduced the hours of their cleaner.

Whereas in previous years Charlie's business acumen had been hailed as entirely praiseworthy, his community spirit recognised publicly by the local Chamber of Commerce, now there were murmurings that his restaurants were still flourishing and his fully-booked language schools still profitable because of their large intake of foreign students and his employment of mostly immigrant labour, paid, it was said, the minimum wage, if that. News of the raid, even though Charlie was not guilty of any offence, had been widely reported. Increasingly, as people's job security wavered, there were many beginning their sentences with, "I'm not a racist, but . . ."

As yet Charlie was unaware of this unpleasant undercurrent although he was realistic about the broad economic problems affecting Woolchester. He understood that, as ever, his middle class clientele, like those of Lavender House, were mostly cushioned against the harsher effects of the credit crunch.

With antennae more sensitively attuned than her employer's, Jennifer suggested that offering a day's work at the Ho mansion might be a small but good PR move, preferable to Charlie's intention to offer jobs to his language students. She ignored Marilyn's jibe that it was a good idea in spite of the students in the main having a better command of English than the majority of Woolchester townsfolk.

An advertisement was placed with the local Employment Agency for kitchen help, waiters and waitresses, pool supervisors, cleaners, car park attendants and litter collectors. The entertainment had been booked well in advance, with a classical trio, a small jazz band and a disco, a Chinese dance troupe and a pyrotechnician,—Chinese of course: "Who do you think invented fireworks?" asked Charlie.

Naturally there was also a huge TV screen to relay the opening of the Beijing Olympics. "Nice of them to mark our big day," said Charlie.

Acting realistically on his orders to spare no expense, Jennifer had enjoyed managing the huge budget except that periodically she had experienced waves of puritanical dismay at the thought of so much money going on one event, but she shrugged off the feeling while realising that others would be bound to comment. The only real economy she achieved was in providing the temporary employees with the silk-look, red polyester, mandarin-collared jackets worn in Charlie's restaurants. They had an infinite supply of these and she saw no point in hiring anything else.

And so it came to pass that Angela Smith applied for, and was given, a job as a one day kitchen assistant at Charlie's party.

Fortuitously she had 'just popped in' to Lavender House to collect a brochure or two to send to her mother, she said, at the moment that the invitations were being distributed and pleasurably received.

Beverly, when asked, showed it to Angela who said she guessed it would be a lovely occasion and that any people who managed to stay married for forty years definitely deserved a celebration to remember, and she hoped they all had a wonderful time.

"She looked," Beverly reported later, "like a kicked kitten."

"She'll probably gatecrash somehow," forecast Trixie.

Never short of a cunning plan, Angela was currently plotting to compile an 'An Alternative Alternative Brochure,' as she described it to herself. In it she would list people actually harmed by the same therapies as those on offer at Lavender House and named on a website. Angela considered it her duty to publicize their suffering to a wider audience. That this might be construed as an act of revenge for something quite unconnected, did not enter her mind. Lois had been a trigger for the release of a scatter-gun approach to getting her own back on society in general for having dealt her what she considered to be a very poor hand. When she had tried to do someone a good turn by giving a relatively gentle nudge, the fool had died instead of fulfilling her intention of inflicting a mild enough incapacity to enable Jack to step into his shoes. It was disappointing that Jack did not have the ambition to take full advantage of the situation. In fact he had been a disappointment in many ways and she regretted wasting time on him. His infiltration of the Ho family was asking for trouble and altogether self-induced. Lily was a pampered, plain woman who deserved a lesson in humility. There was clearly something wrong with anybody who enjoyed sticking needles in people. Angela could see a long period of righting wrongs. Opportunities were opening up every day, many of them landing in her lap with hardly any effort, which surely indicated, she thought, that she was being given a mission in life that she was going to exploit to the full with huge enjoyment. She knew she was blessed with higher than average intelligence. It should not be wasted.

She had taken to frequenting the Wig and Pen, favourite of a few WOADS members, of Boot and Ben and occasionally Lawrence and his teacher fiancée. The old-fashioned, high-sided booths were ideal listening posts. She heard Boot reveal one day to Ben, who plainly didn't care, that Lawrence and Helen were not speaking, a piece of information she shelved for future use.

When Lawrence received his party invitation for the pair of them, he broke his angry silence by asking Helen to have lunch with him, hoping she would wish to accept, would make up and accompany him to the jolly event.

Angela was in pole position when Helen arrived to join Lawrence. She heard their stilted greetings, their discussion of the menu, heard him tell her she was looking very pretty and noted there was no acknowledgement of the compliment. They ate in near silence until Lawrence produced the invitation and asked whether Helen would like to go with him.

"I suppose," said Helen, icily, "we'd be in the Lavender House group? All the healers lumped together?"

Lawrence said nothing, but sipped his Perrier water.

"I'm not sure I could keep quiet about my views on acupuncture and Reiki and that cranio-sacral whatnot."

"And chiropractic?" asked Lawrence, heavily. There was a very long pause.

"I'm sorry, Lawrence. I don't think I can be a support to you. I still love you, but I don't like what you do. I've read a lot more about all these alternative and complementary therapies and I've come to the conclusion that it's faith healing, it's exploiting the vulnerable, there's no scientific basis for most of it and I'd be an embarrassment to you and, frankly, you'd be an embarrassment to me."

Lawrence stood, white and shaken, and put on his jacket.

"I've paid the bill," he said, and left the pub.

Thrilled by this exchange, with two bright red spots of excitement burning her cheeks, Angela considered her next move.

It was swift, and took Helen by surprise.

"Do you mind awfully if I sit here? I've ordered an omelette. I'm sorry, but I couldn't help overhearing your conversation. I'm Angela Smith."

"Should I know you?" asked Helen, coldly, recognising the name but not the context.

"I've some connections with Lavender House. I went for bereavement counselling and I've grown to know them all very well, including Lawrence, of course."

Helen thought that one through for several seconds.

"It was a private conversation. I'm about to leave."

"Please, I wish you'd stay. I feel terrible about eavesdropping and I'm so sorry about the two of you, but I wanted you to know that I've also been researching, and I agree with you absolutely. I'm working on an expose. It's all a big con, in my opinion."

Helen searched Angela's face, but could find no sign of obvious disturbance, just a very direct, blue gaze.

"Look, you seem to know a lot about us, somehow, but I'm feeling upset at the moment and I'm not in the mood for a long chat. Or even a short chat, for that matter. I'm not setting out to hurt Lawrence. He's a good, sincere man."

"Could we meet another time?" Angela persisted. "Would you like to have lunch with me tomorrow when the dust's settled? Not here, perhaps. It's not very private."

Helen gave a short laugh at that, and feeling in her bones that she was about to do something stupid or dangerous and possibly both, she suggested that they meet at the Willow Café on the High Street at noon the next day.

Restraining herself from punching the air, Angela said truthfully, "I'll look forward to it."

Helen prepared to leave as the omelette arrived, planning already to cancel, pleading a headache, to which end she asked for and was given Angela's 'phone number.

Never in her life had Angela co-operated with anybody over anything, but she felt that she and Helen had so much in common. She admired the unwillingness to compromise for the sake of love. She recognized the possibility of developing a working alliance based on sheer ruthlessness. Helen might, she allowed, prefer to believe she was acting according to her conscience, but no matter, one way or another they would achieve a common aim. She truly believed that by the end of 08.08.08. the pair of them would be firmly in the ascendant.

CHAPTER EIGHTEEN

Marilyn wept, on and off, throughout the day as one delight followed another. The visual impact of two, huge striped marquees, the banks of flowers and balloons and banners she saw as they drove through the gates showed it was not going to be a quiet family affair with a few favoured friends.

"Oh, God, Lily," she cried. "What has the silly man done?"

She and Lily changed into their new dresses for Charlie's approval and, alone at last with Marilyn, he gave her the specially commissioned brooch of the entwined ibis with big ruby eyes. She pinned it proudly to her dress, then presented him with a pair of ruby cufflinks, for which he had to change his shirt, weeping as much as his beloved wife.

Jennifer made her final scuttle round the house and estate, was satisfied that all was well, caterers in control, performers accounted for, hired help decked out in their red jackets and in receipt of clear instructions from herself and Monika, the housekeeper, which amounted to doing anything they were asked to do, the host and hostess were looking good and the sun was shining. She poured herself a glass of well-deserved wine.

Although Angela was known to Jennifer, in the kitchen she became just another red-jacketed helper and there was no flicker of recognition. The chances of her being spotted by any number of people was high, for which probability Angela had prepared a little speech to the effect that she was so fond of the family that she wanted to do her bit towards a wonderful celebration, and it was a privilege to be there in any capacity.

At twelve the jazz musicians made their first appearance on the specially erected decking, and people began arriving. In spite of the protestations against gifts, most brought offerings and Monika asked Angela if she would take charge of displaying them on the huge dining table, taking care to keep the donors' names attached. This was a far pleasanter occupation than anticipated and had the double benefit of giving Angela entry to the main house, denied to all but the closest members of family and staff.

Ben was there to photograph all and sundry, from Charlie's many business associates and their spouses, his and Marilyn's family and friends and about two dozen children, including the three little Ruggs and Oliver, who lost no time to start splashing around noisily in the pool.

Lawrence arrived at twelve-thirty, with the intention of making a polite appearance followed by an early departure. He apologized for Helen's absence and explained why to Lily after giving Marilyn their highly suitable gift of a Victorian cranberry jug, which she loved. Angela hovered near to take it inside in her new, important role of gift organizer. Had she not said, "Hello, Lawrence," he would not have noticed who she was, but she went on to tell him in sorrowful, confidential tones that she had bumped into

Helen and heard of the break-up. She did not tell him of the rebuff she subsequently received.

Lawrence wondered how she had 'bumped into' Helen, but merely said, "I'm afraid I can't stay. I've a client at two and I've some preparation to get on with tonight."

After many years away at university, Helen was out of the habit of asking her mother for advice about anything, but she found she needed her sensible head and comforting shoulder as she had done when lovelorn, aged sixteen. After listening closely and without interruption, her mother revealed that, nice as Lawrence was, neither she nor Helen's father rated his occupation highly. They wouldn't have minded at all if he'd been something very ordinary like a postman or a plumber, they weren't being snobbish, she told Helen, but his was such a cranky kind of profession. It was obvious to them that Helen hadn't come to terms with it and the best thing she could do was to hand back the ring, have a little holiday and relax. Regarding the Smith woman, it was hard to say. Helen must consider whether she wanted to become associated with such a controversial issue. The woman sounded perfectly capable of doing her own work, and her mother's advice was to 'phone to break the appointment. No need to lie, just say she'd thought it over and decided not to get involved but to wish her luck.

Helen followed her mother's advice on both counts and when told by Angela in a very cross voice that she'd regret the decision, it had the reverse effect and she was immediately relieved to be rid of two complications in her life. She turned to the internet to book a holiday on Lake Garda.

When, in the early hours of the morning of 08.08.08, a brick came hurtling through their bay window, they immediately ruled out Lawrence as a likely suspect and found it hard to believe that someone like Angela Smith was capable of such a thing.

The police said there was a lot of it about.

Unaware of the above, Lawrence went into the marquee to console himself with some of the delectable food on offer, intending to then return to Lavender House, although his story of a two o'clock appointment was fiction. He enjoyed the meal so much and found the jazz greatly to his liking so could see no reason for not attending again in the evening as a free man needing solace. He would otherwise spend a solitary, brooding night while his colleagues were enjoying lovely, free food and drink and entertainment. He could, if he wished, get drunk, or flirt or do anything he chose with people who did not consider him to be a purveyor of snake-oil or a charlatan bone-cracker. By the time he reached Lavender House he was in a sufficiently cheerful frame of mind to tell Trixie that the party was off to a splendid start and he intended to return without his newly ex-fiancee.

"I see. Oh, dear," said Trixie. "Well, I'm sorry of course. She's a lovely, clever girl but she wouldn't have been right for you, Lawrence dear. Plenty more fish in the sea, as they say. Boot and I shall be going by taxi. We'll pick you up and bring you back, if you like. Have you told your parents yet?"

Lawrence nodded and gave a wry smile. "They're not too upset. Apparently they thought she was a stuck-up little cow. All that aside, you might like to know that Angela Smith's in command of the Ho's dining room, arranging the gifts."

Trixie laughed. "You have to give the woman credit for sheer determination. I hope they've counted the spoons. Why on earth would she want to do that job? And what possessed the Hos to let her in?"

"Search me. I suspect she's simply trying to get accepted as an efficient, dependable person. We've been a bit hard on her, I think. She's looking for affection."

"For Pete's sake, Lawrence. Don't give her any inkling that you're available again. You'll be a marked man. We'll see you later."

Marilyn and Jennifer, sharing a small table with Trixie, found her engaging company that compared favourably with most of Charlie's stuffy business wives with their talk of new conservatories, dull children and autumn cruises. Trixie's rather brash style, this evening in her favourite purple sequinned outfit with her hair piled high, only added to her larger than life charm as she told slightly risqué stories and gossiped about the other guests.

Suddenly, Marilyn said, "Just remind me, Jennifer, why are we so suspicious of that Smith girl who suddenly seems to be in charge of our latest possessions? I know Lily's not fond of her and we know the reason for that, but what else has she actually done?"

Trixie quickly chipped in.

"Actually, nothing proven. She upset one of our therapists on her first visit,—I'm afraid I can't tell you the details. As you know there's been a fair bit of stalking and pestering. She was inches away from that singer who fell at rehearsal, the one who died. There was a suspicion that she was responsible for the police raid. Oh, and the food hygiene queries I believe you were subjected to. She's a knack of always being where things are about to go wrong: there's a whiff of sulphur wherever she goes. She wants to be our receptionist but I'm fearful the place would burst into flames."

"This is the woman you put in charge of our valuables, Jennifer?"

"I didn't recognise her in uniform. That's the point of uniforms, isn't it? Sorry. In fact she's been very good, efficient, pleasant without being intrusive, everything organised perfectly. Don't worry, she'll be fine. Come on, Marilyn, time to mingle."

As they walked off, out of the corner of her eye Trixie saw Lawrence deep in conversation with Beverly, whose husband Daniel was on business in Germany. She knew that recently there had been a few arguments in that household. Absurdly, it seemed that Daniel was jealous not of other men, as he might reasonably have been, but of her job. She worked long hours, offered several different kinds of treatment for which she held certificates and juggled her patients to manage the maximum number.

Trixie calculated that she was now earning more than the 'specialty' therapists, including Jack. Daniel felt threatened by her success, fearful, so Beverly said that she would become so independent that she wouldn't need him. Agony Aunt Trixie advised her to make a special fuss of him and put on the 'helpless little me' act to reassure him, thinking privately that he needed a damn' good kicking. Knowing all this, and aware of Lawrence's recently shattered love life she felt nervous at seeing them walk together round the garden, Lawrence's hand placed gently on the small of Beverly's back. She had good cause to worry.

Lawrence noticed apparently for the first time that Beverly's thick and curly, long hair was a particularly fetching pre-Raphaelite Titian, that hers were the silky brown legs featured for good reason on the brochure and that she had merry eyes and a quick wit, none of which would have mattered had he not told her so, emboldened after a few glasses of red wine. When they seemed to be heading for one of the three summerhouses bordering the copse, Trixie closed her eyes and sighed.

In the first hour after arrival she had enjoyed three separate, quiet moments of reminiscences with middle-aged, respected burghers of Woolchester, out of earshot of their comfortable wives. Still, even though she was in no position to sit in judgement or even offer advice, she hoped Lawrence might settle for something less dangerous than an affair with a married woman.

She was pleased to see Pippa and Jason Rugg, minus the children, walking happily hand in hand or chatting with friends, Jason had been able to point out yet again that Lois, there with husband Matthew, was not Angela who had surprisingly and briefly appeared, red-coated and busy organizing the gifts like one of Santa's little helpers. When Pippa asked what she was doing there, Jason shook his head in wonderment. "She's like that character Zelig who appears uninvited in photographs of the rich and famous. She's omnipresent. And a bloody nuisance."

Their gift to their hosts was an illustrated book of Chinese Love Poetry, which genuinely moved Charlie and Marilyn who considered it a most sweet and thoughtful present. The number of identical ruby wedding plates received was becoming a minor embarrassment as were the bouquets of flowers filling as many containers as Angela could find during her extensive searches. Many people handed over envelopes with donations for the hospice to put in the box file provided by Jennifer, who remarked on the generosity of Charlie's friends.

Simon was kept busy finding seats with cushioned backs for the slightly pregnant Juliet who conspicuously drank only orange juice, and was fed dainty tit-bits by her husband who, according to Pippa, was an idiot who would soon tire of that nonsense.

Charlie's older brother, Lui, known by everyone as Uncle Ho, was the self-appointed master of ceremonies, an even twinklier version of Charlie, light on his feet and insistent that everyone should dance, whether to the disco or the Mozart trio. The exquisite Chinese dancers, who earlier in the day had taught a sparkler wielding dance to the little ones, now delighted everybody with their ribbons, twirled as they glided as if on wheels. One of Marilyn's language students gave a virtuoso drum solo before people were yet again directed to the marquees where even more fresh food had been laid out.

"I want everybody back here for eight o'clock sharp! On the dot!" ordered Uncle Ho through the microphone.

It was observed that Jack, though looking extremely elegant in a light grey, linen suit and pink shirt, was keeping a rather low profile, shadowing Lily, making sure people had chairs when and where needed and that they were eating their way through the delicacies on offer. When the crowd followed instructions and trickled out of the marquees and away from the gardens for the eight o'clock deadline, Uncle Ho struck the huge brass gong wheeled out for the purpose, and everyone turned toward the small stage where Charlie and Marilyn stood at the front, flanked by their families and, interestingly, Jack.

Uncle Ho stepped forward.

"On behalf of the Ho family, I welcome you to this celebration of the wedding forty years ago, of young Charlie here and his beautiful, beloved Marilyn. Without any doubt theirs is one of the happiest marriages on record and here and now I invite you to re-congregate in ten years time to celebrate their fiftieth anniversary.

The time is eight p.m. on the eighth day of the eighth month of the eighth year. A day and night of wonder! Please raise your glasses to toast Marilyn and Charlie!"

The gong was struck eight times as cries of, "To Marilyn and Charlie!" echoed round the garden. Even comparative strangers were moved to tears.

Lanterns were lit and launched into the darkening sky, and the two poor fellows who had undertaken the job of lighting the forty floating, water lily tea lights on the swimming pool climbed out to join in the cheers.

Charlie thanked everyone in the traditional manner, paid tribute to Marilyn, his soulmate, and revealed another happy cause for celebration. He took the hands of Lily and Jack to announce that they had become engaged on this happiest of days.

More champagne, another toast, more cheers as they kissed, modestly.

All the helpers had been invited to come out front to join in this part of the night's enjoyment and to raise a glass. One of them, unnoticed by all but Lois, slipped off her uniform red jacket, worn over a little black dress, and joined the invited guests. After much clinking, people dispersed to eat more, carry on drinking, chat, dance or watch the Beijing Olympics showing on the massive screen.

The Lavender House crowd moved to congratulate Jack. Lawrence appeared, slightly rumpled, accompanied by a pink-faced Beverly, but only Trixie seemed to notice.

Lily, smiling happily, held Jack's hand tightly and kept murmuring, 'Thank you, thank you.'

Inevitably, Angela popped up in the centre of the small crowd of well-wishers.

"I hope you'll be very happy," she said, quite loudly and with the emphasis on the word 'hope.'

Then she turned to Jason and said sweetly, but obliquely, "So many happy days to remember." And walked away.

"What did she mean?" asked Pippa, sharply. It was useless for Jason to repeat wearily again and again that he really had no idea.

At ten there was to be a firework display, fenced off on the far side of the pool. Gradually, as it grew nearer to nine thirty, the party-goers moved nearer to get a good vantage point. Angela murmured to one of the helpers that her feet were killing her and, undoubtedly, they were poor, swollen versions of those so admired on the brochure. She moved to ask Jennifer,

"I know you don't want people in the pool, but would you mind if we two sat on the edge and dabbled our feet? I'm not used to all this standing."

Jennifer glanced down and nodded sympathetically. "That's fine, Angela. Obviously we didn't want visitors actually in the water, things can get out of hand so easily, but I can't imagine anyone plunging in at this stage."

As she watched Angela and her new friend walk away across the grass she thought to herself that at least they would know where she was. Jennifer had secured the dining room and locked away the cheques because, as she confided in Monika, she didn't know half the folk there, and suspected neither did Charlie.

Jennifer also had something else on her mind. Even though she knew of Charlie's illness, she was shocked to hear from Uncle Ho, who had drawn her aside, that a few months ago Charlie had consulted him in his capacity as Dr. Ho, practitioner of Traditional Chinese Medicine. As far as she was aware, the family did not use Uncle Ho's practice even though Lily had at one time worked in his acupuncture clinic.

Charlie had asked his brother for help in what was vaguely described as 'heart trouble.' Uncle Ho obliged, but felt bound to reveal to Jennifer that Charlie was not a well man. She was able to tell him of Charlie's promise to tell Marilyn of his illness during their forthcoming weekend in Paris. Uncle Ho admitted that he had advised Charlie to again seek orthodox help.

"I've done what I could," he said, shaking his head.

Jennifer's response was under her breath.

The line of people sitting cooling their toes in the pool now stretched its entire length.

"They're like sheep, aren't they?" observed Monika. "One in, all in."

It made a magical setting: on the hottest night of the year, in the foreground the tea-lights were twinkling with dwindling flames on the pool. The first of the fireworks lit the sky, followed by bangs, screeching rockets and sparkling showers of rainbow colours, reflected in the water.

The viewers oo-ed and ah-ed appropriately until the set piece, a ruby coloured 40 was the grand finale at which there was a general cheer, followed by scrabbling about to put on shoes and wraps before a gentle tide of people moved back to the house.

Although the invitation had said 'till 12', most of the crowd began to make preparations to leave. Charlie and Marilyn stood on the decking as they were thanked and people made their way to their cars and taxis.

Tessa, the kitchen helper sitting by Angela, prepared to go inside to collect her things.

"The caterers are packing up now," she said. "There are paper bags in the kitchen for us to help ourselves to the leftovers. Crumbs from the rich man's table but I don't mind. I'm not proud. I've got two teenage boys and they eat like horses: costs a fortune. I do these events for our holiday fund. My husband's very good, he keeps an eye on them and it's a change for me. In term time I work in the school kitchen."

Angela listened with growing distaste to this vignette of working class life.

"I think I'll stay here a bit longer, and I'll pass on the party bags. I live on my own and I don't eat much. I'll see you later."

"Yes, see you."

A tap on the shoulder momentarily scared Angela, especially as she turned to find Lois and Matthew looming over her.

"Aha!" said Matthew, rather too cheerily. "It's true. You two are lookie-likies. When I saw you on the stage I thought it could have been Lois except she can't dance."

"Other people have remarked on it," agreed Angela, amiably. "I suppose we should find a way to capitalize on it, but evidently a stage career's ruled out."

"Alibis in a life of crime," Matthew suggested, unusually garrulous, or drunk as Lois chose to call it. "That could work. Loads of scope there for two beautiful, unscrupulous women. I can be your agent."

"Shut up, Matthew," hissed Lois as she took his elbow and steered him away from the poolside. As she took his arm and calculated the extent of his unusually fuddled state, Lois, also slightly tiddly, made a risky decision.

"She tried to blackmail me, you know. Angela, my lookie-likie, as you call her. She threatened to tell you I'd had a fling with her husband."

Matthew stopped, thought, and tried to bring his wife's face into focus.

"And had you?"

"As if! He was an obnoxious little toad and he's been dead for two years."

Matthew blew out his cheeks and laughed. "That pretty well rules it out then, doesn't it, sweetheart?" and he leaned heavily on her arm. "Silly cow." He did not specify which of the lookie-likies he was referring to.

Lois smiled, thinking she'd save the story of the murder confession for another occasion.

Half an hour later she could not dissuade Matthew from taking another glass of wine with him as they went to say their thanks and goodbyes to Marilyn and Charlie, who rolled their eyes as the pair walked unsteadily away.

Matthew then insisted on returning to the pool.

"We didn't say goodbye to Angela," he said. "I'd like to say goodbye to Mrs. Lookie Likie," and he walked with the careful steps of a man who thinks he'll just about make it. By the time they reached her, a solitary figure still sitting with her feet in the water, nearly all guests had gone.

"You okay? Your feet must be cold," said Lois. "We've come to say goodbye."

To her further embarrassment, Matthew sat down and took off his shoes and socks and clumsily sat down, ignoring her reproaches. Off came his jacket. Lois looked round, but no-one was paying attention. Jack, with Lily the only ones remaining of the Lavender House group, was still on the decking, chatting and laughing with the Hos. Lois headed at a fast pace towards them to seek help to persuade Matthew to be bundled into a taxi. She stopped in her tracks when she heard two soft splashes and, appalled, saw Angela being pulled feet first into the pool by Matthew.

Lois shouted for help, turned back and ran to the pool. Angela and Matthew were a wildly thrashing tangle of arms and legs as he pulled her to the centre of the pool and seemed to be holding her head under water.

Sober, Matthew was a good man and a strong swimmer; drunk, he was out of his mind, out of his depth in four feet of water and floundering. Lois kicked off her shoes and slid into the water as Jack and a few others heard the noise and ran, stripping off their clothes as they went. Billy, the pool boy, threw in the lifebelt kept by the pool and soon Matthew, no longer struggling, was pulled out by Jack, both gasping for breath. A member of the jazz group and Lois managed to grab Angela and propel her to the side of the pool where Charlie and Uncle Ho lifted her out, unconscious.

While Jack and Uncle Ho tried to resuscitate her, Marilyn 'phoned for an ambulance as, horrified, she watched their desperate attempts and realized that Matthew too was giving up the struggle.

Lois, dripping, breathless and weeping but still quick-witted said, "She just slithered in. Matthew went in to try to save her, but she was fighting him off." She burst into tears as Jennifer came running with blankets, already waiting for confirmation that Angela, certainly, and Matthew probably, were dead.

That this day of days, the propitious eighth of the eighth of the eighth should end in a double tragedy was almost unbearable. She hoped someone was looking after Charlie.

Angela's mauve, still face held out no hope; Matthew had been turned on to his front while Uncle Ho and Paul the jazzman continued to work on him.

Billy, who had been about to collect in a bin bag the spent tea lights from the pool, had arrived in time to hear the splashing. He went to make sure the road was clear for the ambulance that arrived in ten minutes.

The unaware guests lingering in the parking areas, chatting, saying farewells and offering invitations that they would later regret, were taken aback by Billy's request.

"There's been a mishap," he reported, which one of the guests said later was the understatement of the year. "Police and Ambulance will be here soon."

"Not Charlie?" asked one guest, anxiously.

"A lady guest and her husband," replied Billy, mistakenly, which was how the rumour spread rapidly that it was Lois, married to Matthew Palmer, who had drowned.

Lily, sitting on the grass with the exhausted Jack, was upset and furious that typically, Angela Smith had created havoc, albeit for the last time.

Drained of feeling, Marilyn mustered her inner resources to insist that she should accompany Lois to the hospital, realising that if, or rather when, Angela were officially confirmed as dead by drowning, and whether or not Matthew survived, there were traumatic times ahead. There would be questions regarding pool safety, enquiries about Angela's next of kin, about how she came to slip into the water from that position. She heard one of the paramedics at the scene mention what Uncle Ho had also noticed—a large bruise at the back of her head that would easily match the metal hand rail that she had somehow failed to clutch. Someone, at some stage, would question her state of mind, as she was seen sitting alone by the pool. Already Tessa was volunteering the information that Angela had mentioned she was living alone and didn't eat much. Billy, who didn't drink, volunteered to drive. He was clearly upset by the fact that had he been a few minutes earlier clearing the pool of spent tea lights, and drawing the pool cover, the accident would not have happened.

"Five minutes," he kept repeating, "Just five minutes and people's lives are ruined."

Marilyn did her best to comfort him. "There's no point going along the 'if only' route,

Billy. If only Charlie hadn't wanted to throw a lovely party, this wouldn't have happened, but something else might have done. It's not Charlie's fault and it's certainly not yours."

She could not help recalling that Lily's immediate reaction to the accident was not to express sorrow at Angela's tragic death, but to declare that she could not even die in normal circumstances that didn't impinge on others to the extent of ruining both her parents' wedding anniversary and her own engagement. Jack had protested mildly that he didn't think Angela had done it on purpose. Lily was not convinced, and Marilyn was beginning to wonder.

Lily and Jack were the only Lavender House people left, the others having departed before the accident. Juliet and the walnut sized foetus needed to be in bed by ten, so Simon insisted. Beverly shared a taxi with Pippa and Jason, leaving Lawrence to go home with Trixie and Boot, who was developing a migraine.

Ben stayed on, having taken full advantage of the hundreds of photographic opportunities, from the sparkler wielding children in the afternoon, the spectacular entertainments and the more intimate pictures of hosts, family and guests, later on.

The pre-firework picture of the line of women with pretty party dresses hoisted to their knees as they cooled their toes in the water while holding their expensive, high-heeled, strappy shoes carefully in their hands, he thought was a winner.

There was another good, post-fireworks shot, reminiscent, he thought, of the carefully posed Princess Diana sitting on the bench at the Taj Mahal. There was the unpopular Angela, in a little black dress, all alone, looking up at the dark blue sky.

Then there was one of a man he did not recognise, sitting beside her, removing his shoes and socks. This was followed by the man wriggling out of his coat and being remonstrated with by Lois, who was now standing behind him. As Lois walked quickly away the man went into the pool, larking about, Ben thought, grabbing Angela by the ankles and tugging her into the water. Ben watched as it all started to go wrong, seemingly in slow motion. Disliking the water, he carried on filming until suddenly conscious of increasing distress, decorum dictated that it was time to stop. As soon as the police and ambulance arrived, Ben put on his jacket, made his way to the car park and was offered a lift home by Paul, the musician, who was so stunned by the way the feeling of general happiness had plummeted that he could hardly speak, for which Ben was grateful. Instead of going home he went to Lavender House, where Trixie was ministering to Boot.

In the migraine twilight between consciousness and hammering pain, Boot heard Ben's voice and his mother's startled cry of, "Oh, God, no! Jesus,no!"

Boot blinked anxiously. "It's not Lexie, is it?"

Trixie and Ben shook their heads, and Ben explained in a quiet monotone that Angela had drowned in the pool, Matthew Palmer was unconscious and on the way to hospital. Ben wanted to measure his words carefully.

"According to Lois, Angela more or less fell in. Slid in, she said and Matthew went in to try to save her when she started getting into difficulties, but he was in trouble himself. Lois went in then and so did Jack and Paul, the saxophone player, and between them they dragged them both out."

"It's not a very deep pool," observed Trixie. I can't visualise how it could have happened. Mind, Matthew was as drunk as a skunk by the time we left, which can't have helped."

She looked expectantly at Ben, whose eyes, she noticed, had become paler than ever, with fatigue, she supposed.

"Can I come and see you tomorrow, Trixie? Lily asked me to make a video and I've other stuff on my digital camera."

"Ben, dear, what are you saying? You can stay here tonight. What's the hurry?"

Ben put his hand to his forehead and sat down.

"Trixie, I've been filming all day and all night. I expect the police will want to see what I've got. I need to get home."

He had no need to spell it out further. Trixie took his hand while Boot tried to concentrate.

"What did you see, Ben?"

"What I saw wasn't what Lois described: the sequence was different. Angela didn't fall in, or slide in,—it's not possible with that sort of edge. She was sitting, perfectly still. Matthew went in first, deliberately, then dragged her in by her ankles . . . ."

"Christ Almighty, Ben!" Boot cried out.

" . . . .I thought he was just mucking about, he was obviously pissed as a newt, but he grabbed her and her head kept going under. When Lois saw them she yelled and she and Jack and Paul piled in and there was a horrible struggle but they managed to get them both out of the water. Dr.Ho and Jack kept on trying to bring them round until the ambulance came."

None of this was helping Boot's migraine. Dazed and amazed, he asked, slowly, "And while all this was going on you kept on filming, like a war correspondent? You didn't consider jumping in before it turned nasty?"

"I'm sorry, but I'm no good in the water so, yes, I kept filming. By the time I realized it was serious, I'd passed the critical point."

Also speaking slowly, Trixie said, "You've described a murder, Ben. And you've filmed it."

Ashen faced, Ben looked beseechingly at Trixie, "What should I do, Trixie? From what I heard, it's unlikely Matthew'll pull through. Lois put him forward straight away as a sort of hero, trying to rescue Angela. Tomorrow he's likely to be either a dead hero or a dead murderer."

At that precise moment the 'phone rang. Marilyn confirmed that Angela was certified dead on arrival and that Matthew died at 12.30a.m. Lois's parents had arrived with Oliver and were waiting to take her home. Marilyn wondered whether Trixie happened to know Angela's next of kin, which she did not, other than she thought they lived in Fuengirola." They exchanged sympathetic comments, with Trixie pledging whatever help was needed.

Trixie relayed the message to the two men then said, "I suggest, and it's up to you Ben to decide, that we stay with the dead hero scenario. That will make things easier for Lois, as she was quick to realise. Frighteningly quick, from your account, Ben, but there's the poor Ho family to think about as well. What a mess!"

"Then I've got some editing to do. Actually, if I erase everything after the fireworks display it won't look as though it's been tampered with, and fireworks are a natural climax."

He rose wearily. "With a bit of luck no-one will mention me, but by tomorrow the police are going to be swarming all over the place. I'd like the Hos to have a pleasant record of their day, poor devils. I'll walk home. I could do with a breath of fresh air."

Eyes now reduced to painful slits, Boot went to bed, but not before disturbing his mother with his parting shot.

"This is my first experience of involvement in covering up a murder, and may I be the first to say good riddance to Angela Smith. I shall not subscribe to the wreath."

Wondering whether she should 'phone the Lavender House people still ignorant of the catastrophic end to the party, Trixie noticed the time and decided against it. The town would soon enough be buzzing with the story which was guaranteed a long life, what with post-mortem results, inquests, witness statements, speculations about people's private lives and the added excitement of it all being based in the gardens of a rich Chinese businessman. She wondered whether the inevitable connections with Lavender House would be good or bad for trade. Time would tell. Poor Lois, poor Lily, poor Jack, poor delicate, pale-eyed Ben, who had no qualms about witnessing a murder without intervening and none whatsoever about destroying evidence.

CHAPTER NINETEEN

Contrary to expectations, both Trixie and Boot slept soundly, which was just as well as the 'phone calls started at seven a.m.

First was Simon, checking that in spite of the tragedy, Lavender House would be open for business. Juliet was keen to come in, he said, and he believed it would help to take her mind off things, and she didn't want to let down her clients. Trixie mentally amended this to the more accurate 'client' while promising Simon that of course she would send for him at once if Juliet showed any signs of distress.

It transpired that Jack had 'phoned his new best friend Lawrence, who 'phoned Beverly who 'phoned Juliet who 'phoned Jason, all of whom decided to come in early. Lily had no Saturday clients anyway, so was staying home with her parents and Jack.

Bunty, engaged for emergency cover, was thrilled to be put unexpectedly in charge of Reception, her first task being to cancel Lois's appointments for the following week, sorrowfully passing on news of her bereavement. The tragedy was widely known by eight-thirty, thanks to the local radio. Showing surprising initiative, Bunty successfully suggested to Lois's bereaved dog-owning client that a transfer to Juliet for reflexology might be equally helpful.

The therapists congregated in Jason's surgery and agreed over coffee to send condolences and flowers to Lois's home where she was said to be under sedation while her parents cared for Oliver.

They listened as Trixie related the carefully edited account of what had happened, but she could tell from the raised eyebrows and furtive exchange of glances that the narrative was unconvincing. All were aware of Matthew's excessive wine consumption the previous night, Jason commenting that it was out of character for a 'normally one pint man'. Angela's mode of entry into the water was discussed at length. Nobody understood how she could have slithered into the pool. Juliet's theory was that Angela had decided on a little swim, but could not explain her doing it in a nice black dress. Jason suggested she might have fainted and toppled in: it had been an exceptionally oppressively hot day, and she had been standing for most of it. If Lois had only glimpsed her going into the water, she could easily have been mistaken at the manner of it. This was accepted as being the likeliest explanation, plus the fact that since Matthew could hardly walk by the time most of them were heading for home, he was hardly fit to engage in successful lifesaving. The other facts that the depth of the water was only four feet at most, and that they were both swimmers which should have enabled them both at the very least to wade to the side, they explained away by the probability of panic setting in. Similar theories were also chewed over by all their clients who, without exception, found it all quite fascinating.

Periodically that day in different parts of the town, there were bouts of mea culpa from those who had experienced

Angela's peculiar machinations, and understandably taken against her. Pippa Rugg was spoken to quite sharply by Jason earlier that morning when she burst into tears on hearing the news and accepted all blame for thinking ill of Angela and Jason, which had obviously driven the woman to suicide.

The suicide theory was posited elsewhere several times. Audrey, widow of Denzil, who had heard disquieting rumours that Angela might have been responsible for his tumble down the stairs, asked whether it might have been a guilt-induced suicide.

Angela's alleged attempts to cast slurs on Charlie's restaurants and on his employment practices received an airing from Jennifer who considered Angela to be disturbed and unpredictable. She was bound to admit, though, that mounting a suicide bid in order to throw Charlie's supervision of the pool under suspicion would have been somewhat extreme.

So far, and fortunately in private, Boot was the only one to declare a disinclination to mourn the loss of Angela, although everywhere general sympathy was muted. Undeniably, and unsurprisingly, her death was receiving a great deal more speculation than Matthew's.

The police arrived early at the Hos. Jennifer handed them the guest list and Angela's handbag, left in a staff locker and fortunately containing her parents' address. It also contained, very oddly, the pretty, cranberry glass jug which seemed inexplicable, especially as she had been placed in charge of the anniversary gifts.

The woman police officer and Inspector Bird took statements from Jack, Jennifer and the Ho family. Dr. (Uncle) Ho said he'd assumed from the bump on her head that it was an accidental fall, possibly a faint. He had not noticed the redness round both ankles, he replied, perfectly truthfully, when asked, but he had not examined her with much care because of the concentrated efforts to resuscitate the poor young woman. It was agreed by all that she had not been drinking, which no doubt the post-mortem would confirm. Tessa was interviewed as possibly the last person to speak to Angela.

She confirmed that Angela had drunk only pineapple juice all day, and that she seemed a lonely person, which did not count for much in the way of evidence.

Jack was asked immediately why Angela had sought homeopathic treatment, a fact divulged by Lily. When he revealed that she had transferred to his clinic after a course of therapy from Lois, but had not wished to continue after becoming dismissive of homeopathy in general, Inspector Bird showed sudden increased interest.

"Did you have a disagreement?"

"Only a professional one. More of a discussion," said Jack. "Nothing personal."

"I saw you in 'Guys and Dolls'", said the Inspector, apparently off target. "Very good, very good. She was in it wasn't she? I remember her name in the programme. Younger than your average chorus member."

"Yes, she was. I think she enjoyed it. Actually it was Lois who suggested she might join to meet some new people."

"What's next?"

Momentarily puzzled, Jack realized they were still speaking of WOADS.

"The 'Desert Song', I believe, but I've dropped out,—it was too time consuming."

"No arguments?"

"None at all."

"No other reason?"

"Certainly not."

"Tell me again what you saw last night. Mrs. Palmer said you were right behind her and jumped in to do what you could."

Jack nodded. "None of us had noticed anything. The jazz trio were still playing, but then we heard Lois screaming and we all ran to the pool, but we were too late to do anything. Matthew was still flailing his arms about, but they were both in a bad way."

"No help from homeopathy, then?" asked the Inspector, unsmiling.

Jack gave him a black look, but the Inspector almost smiled. "My sister goes to your place to have her toes tickled by Juliet. Reflexology, I believe. She says it helps her backache and she enjoys it, so . . . ." He shrugged while Jack weighed up the advantages of dissociating himself from that area of activity, but the Inspector nodded and moved to Billy, who had worked himself up to a state of great anxiety and a belief in his own guilt.

"I only went for the bag. I was only a few minutes. I'm so sorry. It's my fault. Just a few minutes and that happened."

The Inspector took pity on him and told him that all he wanted to know was what he had actually seen and heard and that nobody was blaming him.

Billy said that before he went to get the bag from the kitchen, he heard Mr. Palmer laughing and calling Mrs. Smith a 'lookey-likey'. This had to be explained to the Inspector who thought it might be an Indonesian expression, but it set him off on a whole new train of thought when its meaning sank in. There was confirmation that the two women did look alike, but it took the events no further because even if Palmer had mistaken the one for the other, he was evidently drunk and, so it was said, trying to carry out a rescue. Billy was advised to go and make himself a cup of tea.

The Inspector felt deeply sorry for Charlie Ho. The man looked grey with worry, clearly fearful that he had not made sufficient provision for pool safety.

"We were so careful when the children were in the pool in the afternoon, and there was no trouble at all. It was my decision and it seems my mistake, to leave the cover off, but there were garden lights all round it, and the tea lights—forty of them, floating on the pool. I wanted the fireworks to be reflected on the water, and they were, and it looked so beautiful, Inspector. Billy worked so hard to keep it safe.

He watched carefully when some of the ladies decided to sit along the edge and dabble their feet in the water. High heels, hot day, you can understand. At the deepest it's only four feet. I'm told a lady named Tessa, one of the agency workers, was the last to get up, leaving Angela Smith sitting there alone. She was an intelligent woman, Inspector, and sober. She'd been very helpful all day

"Bit of a thorn in the flesh, though?"

Useless to deny it, thought Charlie.

"You could say that. Your colleagues at the station will know we suspected she was the one who wanted me investigated about my employees' legal status and hygiene standards. I honestly don't know why. I didn't know the woman and I can't think of anything I might have done inadvertently to upset her. The only thing was that she's said to have had a crush on Jack, my daughter's fiancé and there might have been a sort of misplaced jealousy, but I'm no psychologist and I just don't know. Monika and Jennifer didn't recognise her when the agency sent her, which accounts for her being in my house for most of the day, but she did a good job, arranged the gifts, kept note of the donors, no problems."

"Except it seems she pinched one of the presents."

"Did she?" Charlie had not been told and was genuinely surprised. He managed a smile. "Not one of those ruby anniversary plates by any happy chance? Why on earth . . . ?"

The Inspector shook his head. "I don't suppose we shall ever know now. I need to speak to the others. Thanks for your help, Mr. Ho."

Marilyn, Lily and Jennifer had little to add except that Jennifer admitted responsibility for admitting Angela to the house. "She may have been piqued at being left off the guest list, but there was no earthly reason to include her, and what happened in the pool makes no sense at all."

Lily was terse. "I'm very upset about what's happened, especially for Lois, losing her husband like that, but I can't pretend I liked Angela or trusted her. She was making an absolute nuisance of herself. I suspect she had a psychological disorder."

"I understand she had received therapy from Lois? Are you hinting she was a suicide risk?"

"No, no, I'm not. She didn't appear depressed, quite the reverse. I got the impression she hadn't finished plotting mischief. She's certainly caused some now."

Inspector Bird left the WPC to take the remaining statements while he drove to Lavender House, looking forward mostly to renewing an old, close relationship with Trixie.

Bunty 'phoned upstairs to let her know of his arrival and he went up to the flat.

"How's Trix?" he asked amiably, while she took note that his curly hair had receded a little and was quite grey, that he had gained a little weight but that his hazel eyes that turned down a little at the outside edges still had a magnetic twinkle. She reminded herself that this was a professional call during which she needed to keep her wits about her.

"I say," he said, looking round, "this is all very luxurious."

"*Inspector* Bird is it now? Well done, Dicky. Sit down. How's Penny?"

"She's well and happy, thank you, as far as I know. We no longer share a roof. We were divorced five years ago and she's living in Devon with a computer programmer called Hector who keeps regular hours."

"Really? Oh, I'm so sorry," said Trixie cheerfully.

"I'm trying to get a picture of last night's events, Trixie. From what I've gathered you and all your people left early, just after the fireworks, and missed the, er, incident. I've never known you leave a party before midnight, Trixie. You're slipping."

"Boot had a migraine so we came home. He's still a bit fragile but if you want to interview him I'll fetch him. He lives in the flat next door."

"Presently. Is he still . . . ?"

"Gay? Yes, Dickie. It doesn't wear off."

"I was going to say at university, but never mind. Now, there are links here, Trixie. Mrs. Smith was a client, yes?"

Trixie nodded and again explained that Angela had seen Lois for a course of ten sessions, then Jack for a couple, had offered to man Reception, and was a trifle pushy. "I'm told she'd set her cap at Jack Kent."

"What a sweet, old-fashioned expression. She'd been a widow for two years. What goes on in the therapy confessional is confidential, of course, but I do know that Lois encouraged her to get out and about more and she did.

She joined WOADS and I think she hoped Jack might fall for her, but as you know, he's engaged to Lily Ho. Boot said she was embarrassingly keen."

"So she was a bit of a pest."

"Let's just say she didn't endear herself to people, though funnily enough by the end of their sessions, she did seem to have a kind of rapport with Lois."

"It's said they looked alike?"

Trixie shrugged. "Same age, same build, blonde hair. There was a resemblance."

"One of my colleagues remembered a rumour that Angela's late husband was a bit of a Don Juan. Put himself about a bit."

"And?"

"And had a quite long relationship with Lois Palmer."

"I wouldn't know," lied Trixie, feeling a blush forming under her necklace. "Would you like a drink?"

"I'd love a coffee," smiled the Inspector. "You're very loyal, Trixie. What do you think happened?"

"It's been suggested that the heat simply made her faint. She'd been on her feet all day and that's why she and another helper were cooling their toes. You can see how that could happen."

The Inspector nodded. "It's feasible. And Lois's husband Matthew, the cuckolded one who'd been drinking, staggered to the rescue and they both drowned in spite of the best efforts of Lois herself, and the man Angela really fancied."

Trixie felt sick "You haven't mentioned Paul, the saxophonist. He went in, as well."

"So he did, so he did. May I speak to Felix now?"

Boot told how he'd been so busy talking to friends and listening to the music that he didn't go near the pool at all; that he'd managed to spoil his mother's and Lawrence's evening by getting a migraine that meant they all left early, but in fact it was a kind of blessing as they'd missed all that unpleasantness.

Inspector Bird nodded sympathetically. "You still look a bit green round the gills. I'll leave you alone. Thanks, Felix. Oh, and good luck with the book. I saw it in Horace's shop. Very original and interesting. I bought a copy for my daughter."

Inspector Bird's stock rose significantly.

When called, Jason confirmed that he'd seen nothing untoward and had left with his wife before the fireworks to relieve his mother who was babysitting. Angela was known as being a bit odd and had turned up at the gym asking personal questions about people, but he'd managed to steer clear of her otherwise.

Beverly and Lawrence separately kept their fingers crossed that their tryst in the summerhouse would not somehow feature in the drama, but they knew nothing, had seen nothing, and had also left early.

Juliet confided in the Inspector that, being pregnant, she had spent a lovely quiet evening there with her husband who took her home when the fireworks started as they didn't want to take any risks. Inspector Bird thought that over without comment.

"Of course," Juliet went on helpfully, "Angela was trouble from the word go. She had a couple of shouting matches here with Lois which was quite upsetting. I told my husband about it at the time, but their sessions quietened down, thank goodness. There are some funny therapeutic methods these days, aren't there?"

The Inspector agreed gravely that indeed there were.

Alone again with Trixie before leaving, he suggested that they might meet up one evening for dinner or the theatre, perhaps. She was, he said, as attractive as ever. No ties now. Why not?

"Why not," agreed Trixie.

When she related this to Boot he was all in favour as Inspector Dickie Bird was clearly a man of taste and discernment.

CHAPTER TWENTY

Lily checked that there were no restrictions on her parents travelling to Paris the following weekend and was assured there were not. The atmosphere in the Ho household had clouded even more when Jennifer was overheard having a heated argument with Charlie about his consultations with his brother and his use of what Jennifer rudely described as Chinese voodoo medicine for a serious condition. Their refusal to tell Marilyn what the row was about caused an unprecedented chill.

When, as he had promised, he revealed to her on their return from France the gravity of his illness, and the advice he had taken from Uncle Ho, she was temporarily shaken to her core. Quickly she resolved not to risk a family rift by upsetting the two brothers, but she rearranged appointments with consultants who were not best pleased at having been sidelined, read everything she could find about his illness and, with Jennifer's help, determined to get the best possible care for Charlie. He felt overwhelming relief and submitted, gratefully. At no point did a shaken Lily suggest anything other than orthodox treatment for her father. Uncle Ho's intervention was kept from her, for fear of war.

Jack received an e-mail from Elizabeth congratulating him on his engagement and asking him to commiserate with the Hos for the bodies in the pool incident which must, she said, have cast a cloud over their day.

When back to near-normal on Monday morning, there were warmer wishes from all at Lavender House with a large card and champagne, and flowers sent from the migraineurs who were anxiously booking appointments in order to keep abreast of the scandalous goings on in poor Lily's pool.

It was unusual for Helen's mother to take early morning tea to her daughter, but local news on their radio alarms on Saturday morning had given them both a shock.

"I feel terrible now," she told Helen. "Perhaps if you *had* met Angela Smith and got together on researching homeopathy this might not have happened. Don't look at me like that, Helen. I advised you badly and there's been a tragedy and I feel culpable and I'm sure you do, too. They're saying accident: I'm suspecting suicide. Obviously she was an attention seeker, and if she could just have found an outlet this wouldn't have happened. Well, that's my theory."

"Thank you so very much, Mother. That makes me feel much better."

"Don't get narky with me, Helen." She sat on the edge of the bed. "Your Dad and I were talking about your breaking off your engagement and we wonder now whether we weren't all a bit hasty. It's only Lawrence's profession that's the barrier, and if everything else is alright, you could still make a go of it. Confidentially, Helen, I never really wanted to be married to a chartered accountant. It wasn't my first choice, but it made no difference. I had my job and he had his. He's always provided for us very well."

She seemed unaware that Helen was slowly pulling up the duvet.

"I picked up one of the brochures from Lavender House the other day when I was passing, and your Dad and I calculate that Lawrence must be making well over £50,000 a year already. That's not to be sniffed at. With your salary as well you'd be very comfortable. Think about it."

Head now completely covered, Helen muttered, "Go away. Please, go away."

Her mother stood up, lips pursed, picked up the cup and saucer and went to report to her husband.

"I think I've persuaded her to think it over," she said.

When she eventually rose, Helen told her parents that she was going to 'phone Lawrence, not to arrange a re-union, but to express sympathy for the unfortunate deaths and to let him know that she intended carrying on with researching into alternative medicine. She promised to keep an open mind, but already she had found much to cause concern.

Her parents told her she was being unfair and advised her to do nothing until she returned from her holiday in Italy, which counsel she ignored, naturally. She was slightly put out, though, by Lawrence's receiving the news with fortitude, without pleading for her return or a change of heart.

In fact Lawrence had just had an interesting conversation with Beverly, who had come into Lavender House looking somewhat disconcerted. Her husband Daniel, expected home in a few days, had 'phoned with the news of an offer of a new job in Hamburg, which he had accepted. ("Without consulting me!") Higher salary, an apartment, generous benefits, a five year contract. It seemed he would not be home for four weeks, then away until Christmas, then probably a longer spell.

Initially, this had not gone down well with Beverly who resented his cavalier behaviour, but gradually she admitted to Lawrence that she could not overcome a feeling of release, and a hope that his visits home would be few. He had organized their finances quite generously, but that wasn't the point. What did Lawrence think, she asked.

Lawrence thought that Christmas had arrived early.

Sipping the tea brought by Paul's pretty wife Ella, Inspector Bird glanced round their immaculately tidy drawing room. An off-white carpet, two pale pink, linen covered sofas, a wall of neatly ordered books and a surprisingly small collection of CDs did not reflect his expectations of the home of a jazz musician, usually associated with chaos and the smell of certain substances. His wife was a pretty, dark-eyed woman, plump, friendly and relaxed as she described Paul's arrival home on the night of the pool disaster. She told him how he came in, left his saxophone in the hall, as usual, and held up a pair of soaking wet boxer shorts at which point she noticed that his hair was damp and he looked near to tears.

He told her the tale now familiar to the Inspector, of the screams from Lois, the dash to the pool to find Matthew and Angela struggling, distressed and too far gone to save. Paul had, she said, given a lift home to Ben who was crossing the car park and who lived round the corner.

At this point Paul entered, his excuses having already been given by Ella who explained he'd popped to the postbox. He re-iterated their panic as they'd stripped off and jumped in the water. He had heard Lois's cries that Angela had fallen in and that Matthew had followed to try to bring her out but, no, he hadn't actually seen that as he was still playing when the shouting started and there were still a few people standing or dancing in front of the small stage, obscuring the view. Everybody turned and ran to the pool. It was horrible, he said, a sickening nightmare. When he realized they were both probably dead he just wanted to get home out of the way, so he pulled on his clothes, fetched his sax and left.

"Who is Ben?" asked the Inspector.

"I don't remember his surname. We're on nodding terms usually. He's a photographer. He was upset and about to walk, but I was glad of the company. He's friendly with Boot Callender and he told me he'd recently taken photographs at Lavender House of Lois and Oliver, and he'd met Angela Smith, so he felt it personally. He was shaking like a leaf, poor chap."

"Did he go in the water?"

"No, he was dry. I don't expect he was very near, but it rattled him. Well, naturally, it upset everybody."

"Could you give me his address?"

"It's literally round the corner: a ground floor flat in the small white block. There's a big pot of geraniums by his front door. I didn't notice the number."

After thanking them, Inspector Bird walked round to have a word with this photographer, so far not mentioned by anybody else. The geraniums were located and Ben was home, pale-faced but resigned and prepared for a grilling. The thought flashed through the Inspector's mind that Paul might have nipped out not to post a letter, but to warn him of an impending visit. Inspectors are trained to think like that.

Ben volunteered the information that Lily had asked him to make a video because she was pleased with those he'd taken at Lavender House. He'd been filming most of the day right up to the fireworks at the end.

"Wasn't quite the end, though, was it?" Ben feared Inspector Bird would hear his heart beating. "The band was still playing and a few people were still dancing and drinking."

"Yes, but I'd got my film. There was a shape to it and the fireworks were the climax"

"You must have wandered round a fair bit. Did you see anything to concern you? Any drunkenness, for instance?"

"Some people were a bit merry, but it wasn't a riotous party. It was good natured and pleasant. Are you asking about Matthew Palmer? He'd certainly had too much. I saw Lois trying to control him once or twice, but he was only loud, not aggressive or anything."

"When you became aware of the trouble in the pool you didn't jump in?"

"I was too far away. I'm not happy in water, and there were loads of people piling in to help."

"You didn't consider starting to film again? The newspapers would have snapped those pictures up."

"I don't do photo-journalism and that would have been morbid. At first I didn't realise how serious it was, then it was just so horrendous I wanted to get away. I know how pathetically weak-kneed that sounds, but I was too upset to think straight."

"Did you take any shots of people in the pool earlier?"

"Adults didn't go in the pool earlier. The only one was of the row of women sitting along the edge, which was very pretty and in other circumstances I'd have submitted it for competitions, but it would be too tactless, now. I didn't take photographs of the children in the pool. You understand how it is, Inspector, I'm a gay loner with a camera. I don't go looking for trouble. There is a nice shot of the Chinese dancers teaching the children a sparkler dance in the afternoon, but that's it. My speciality is actually portraits, not parties. You're welcome to view what I've got. Would you like to take it now? Then I'll pass it to Lily when you're done."

"We may want to see it, just in case there's something we've missed."

"Have you spoken to Boot, yet? He wasn't well on Friday night and left early."

The Inspector nodded. "He's still looking a bit fragile, but he was up. I see you have his book. Are you a special friend?"

Ben gave a rare grin. "You'd have to be a special friend to buy it."

The Inspector warmed to the young man. "Thank you," he said.

After the Inspector's departure, Ben sat and wondered at the ease with which lies and half-truths had slipped from his lips like oil, without previous practice. The experience had been exhausting, though, and he did not wish to repeat it.

Dr. Bertram Hallam and his wife, Dr. Veronica Hallam left a note for the Inspector advising him that they were staying at their late daughter Angela's house until further notice, and would be pleased to see him. He took WPC Shirley Pickering with him to provide support and tissues in case of scenes of intense emotion, which he found hard to handle. She had already visited the spacious, detached bungalow nestling with others of its kind in a leafy cul-de-sac, and spoken to keyholding neighbours who expressed shock at Angela's unfortunate death. As is usually the way they described her as pleasant, quiet, a keeping—herself-to-herself kind of person. She paid for a gardener after her husband's death, but they didn't have children or pets or known relatives or any visitors as far as they were aware.

The two doctors,—PhDs, not medical, they were quick to point out, were like two wisps of grey smoke, thought by the Inspector to be the thinnest, palest, British expats to have lived in Fuengirola, notably a place filled with sun-baked, gold-chained, plump and sociable escapers from a damp climate.

After telling them that Bertram was making coffee, Veronica seated them in the large lounge, fetched a plate of sorry-looking assorted biscuits and paper napkins and declared they'd start asking questions when her husband joined her. It was clear that she was determined the interrogation should be directed at the police and not conducted by them.

To fill the gap, the Inspector commented on the many botanical watercolours on the walls.

"Mine," said Veronica. "I'm surprised she kept them. She didn't appear to like them when I gave them to her. I am a botanist and Bertram is an entomologist. We've been working in Spain on an illustrated guide to the flora and insects of the region where we live. It was a disappointment to us that Angela wasn't cut out for academic life, not necessarily in our field of interest: we tried to encourage a career in marine biology, but she said it was boring! She became engaged to Lucas at seventeen, very much against our wishes and, as it so often does, any ambition she did have flew out of the window. All she wanted was to work in advertising. Alien territory to us, I'm afraid."

For the first time since learning of Angela and her activities, the Inspector felt defensive on her behalf.

"People tell me she was very intelligent," he said.

"Undoubtedly," agreed Bertram, arriving with the coffee, "but without focus. However, that's really of no importance now." He and his wife looked depressed, but remained dry—eyed. "Please tell us exactly what happened, Inspector. The account we received seemed too extraordinary to be credible. We were told she was engaged by an agency to help at a party. Surely that's not so? Why would she do that? She wasn't in need of money."

Tricky question, thought Dicky Bird. "Impossible to answer what her motive was, but she knew Lily Ho and her fiancé Jack Kent and we think she may simply have wished to be present at the party. Did you know it was a ruby wedding event? Jack and Lily's engagement was also announced, but that was a surprise."

The Hallams looked whiter than ever. "So she was a paid gatecrasher, which I suspect is an oxymoron," commented Bertram. "Tell us how she came to drown at a party where there were people all around."

Yet again the Inspector related the circumstances as he knew them, eyeing them both as their papery faces registered puzzlement, disbelief, and revulsion in succession.

"What is her connection with the man who died? Angela could swim," added Veronica. "Four feet of water? We're assured she wasn't drunk, but that the man who allegedly rescued her was, and that more people joined in in what sounds like a free-for-all."

"It was most certainly not that," retorted the Inspector, robustly. "Everyone was trying to help. It was a particularly hot day, Mrs. Hallam, and Angela had asked Mr. Ho's PA for permission to sit on the edge of the pool with one of the other kitchen workers to cool their hot and swollen feet." Veronica flinched. "She stayed there alone for a while and the suspicion is that she simply fainted and fell in. Mr. Palmer saw her first and went in after her, then Lois shouted for help and went in herself, then a few more, but it was too late to save either of them. Matthew actually died in hospital, as I'm sure you know."

The more times the Inspector went over this story the less happy he felt with the details, but he tried to sound confident.

"We'd like to see where it happened," said Bertram, firmly.

WPC. Pickering, feeling her skills of empathy were not being fully employed, asked whether they would not find that too upsetting and was rewarded with a withering look from Veronica.

"Yesterday we identified our daughter's body. I can't think of any experience more upsetting than that. We're aware that the Hos are an important family in the small business world of Woolchester. I trust they'll be subjected to the same scrutiny as if they were cash-strapped academics."

"Or even policemen," replied the Inspector, coolly. "That goes without saying. I'm certain Mr. and Mrs. Ho will wish to meet you. They are still deeply distressed. Mr. Ho's brother, Dr. Liu Ho, was on the scene to help with the resuscitation attempt and I'm sure he'll make himself available."

At the word 'doctor' they nodded, impressed. The Inspector hoped he would not have to reveal Uncle Ho's Chinese Traditional Medicine qualification that he feared might impress them less.

Bertram asked Veronica whether they ought to make contact with Lois, but were told she was still too distressed to meet anybody, which was untrue, as the officers were on their way to speak to her.

Again murmuring condolences and thanks for their help, they promised to arrange the visit to the Hos. On the way out, WPC Pickering noticed a collection of Victorian cranberry glass displayed in a large pine dresser in the dining room, but did not comment on it until in the car, when they could conclude only that Angela had been a very rum customer indeed.

Their feelings about the forthcoming interview were a mixture of sympathy, curiosity and mild distrust. When they arrived at the house with its dry lawns showing evidence of a resident child with way too many toys, the Inspector intended to be kind, but probing. He preferred his young widows to be too distraught at a death scene to be immediately claiming heroic status for their late husbands, but he forced his mind to remain open. Both he and Shirley Pickering agreed that Angela seemed to be damned from all quarters with very faint praise: even her parents appeared not to have liked her, stressing what a disappointment she had been. Both officers could see that this lack of esteem could easily have blighted her life. They hoped this was an accidental death, and not the suicide being hinted at by some.

It was a surprise to find Lois's double-fronted house stuffed with people. Oliver was understandably clinging to his mother. The Inspector and Shirley were introduced to Lois's stepmother who appeared to be trying to force food and drink on all comers, then in rapid succession to Mathew's parents sitting red-eyed, silent, hand-in-hand, clutching mugs at the kitchen table, to Lois's sister, Fay, and her sullen teenage daughters who looked ready to pick a fight if anyone put a word out of place, to Matthew's grandmother who kept trying to prise Oliver away from the disturbing scene and to a couple of mug-nursing women neighbours taking a bright-eyed interest.

There were several bouquets on the dining table and a pile of sympathy cards. Oliver clung on even tighter when the Inspector asked to see Lois alone, but his grandmother persuaded the wary child with a promise of chocolate from the corner shop.

Elegant in grey silk shirt and trousers, Lois was carefully made-up and slightly scented, with a determinedly chin-up air that Shirley admired and Dicky viewed with suspicion. The three went upstairs to Matthew's study which served as a sporting shrine, hung about with caps, scarves, jerseys and trophies. Lois indicated the two chairs and perched on the edge of the bed.

"It's a madhouse," she said apologetically. "I can't wait to get back to normal so that Ollie and I can pick up the pieces and grieve in peace. Everybody means well, but they're all so cut up themselves, it's unbearable. The Press have been on to me, trying to make a 'tragic hero' story out of it, but Fay sent them packing. I happen to think that's exactly what Matthew was, but it's our private tragedy. It hasn't sunk in yet. Ollie and I both think Matthew's going to come walking through the door any time soon."

The Inspector nodded, and spoke sympathetically. "The word 'sorry' doesn't begin to cover it, Lois. We'll try to be brief, but this has to be done. Now, I understand that you were trying to get help to steer Matthew away from the pool,—we know he'd had a few drinks. You say Angela fell in while you were doing that. Is there any possibility, any doubt in your mind that he might actually have been the first one to fall in? That it was Angela who went in then to rescue him and not vice-versa?"

There was an audible intake of breath and Lois's lips tightened.

"No doubt at all. I heard the first splash and turned before Matthew went in. It would have been instinctive. He was a swimmer, Inspector, but Angela was pulling him down when he tried to save her—not deliberately, of course. I imagine she panicked and just wouldn't let go. I'll find it hard to forgive her for that, but I accept it was an accident."

"Do you believe Angela slipped, or fell or fainted?"

"It looked to me as though she just slipped in, and fainting's the obvious conclusion, I should think." She looked inquiringly at him. "No-one's suggesting suicide, are they? She was an odd person,—attention-seeking—but I didn't regard her as suicidal."

Ignoring that, the Inspector went on, "Lois, I know you're a therapist yourself, but if you'd like to talk to Shirley here, she's a qualified bereavement counsellor, and there's a family liaison officer if you think Ollie might be helped. She'd spend as much time as it takes. Just say the word."

Lois gave a bright, brave, little smile. "I don't think it's time limited. I know all the theories, Inspector. That's very kind, but my family's supportive and I want to try to get back to work straight after the funeral. I shall be fine." She stood up. "Would you like tea or coffee? There's a non-stop buffet down there and you'd be welcome."

They declined, said their goodbyes and left.

"Poor thing," said Shirley. "It must have been so traumatic. She's bearing up incredibly well."

"Incredibly well," agreed the Inspector, literally. "We used to have a Plod's Law in Liverpool that any party involving fifty or more people and a swimming pool invariably ended badly. For a party it seems strange that she was the only witness to how it started, but it was the fag end of the affair with middle-aged folks gone already and nobody paying attention. It seemed a remarkably sober do, apart from the late Matthew who was pie-eyed by all accounts. Lois's version is impressionistic, to put it kindly, and I don't really buy it, but I think it's all we're going to get. The video ended at the fireworks, so nothing there, unless there's been doctoring done, but I don't think so. I can hand that over to Lily now. As both the poor devils are dead, and nobody else is being blamed, it's academic. Talking of which, or whom, we must prepare the Hos for the Hallams."

CHAPTER TWENTY-ONE

Having established that Trixie was still a carnivore without allergies, Dicky prepared moules marinieres with coriander bread, and a chicken and mushroom risotto. She had taken no persuading at all that it might not be wise to be seen eating out together until the dust from the drownings had settled.

She remarked favourably on his minimalist décor, forced on him, he said, by slicing up the more lavishly furnished matrimonial home, and having recourse to IKEA. He had salvaged, though, two large, abstract paintings that had not been favourites of the first Mrs. Bird. His kitchen/diner was decked out with an impressive display of state of the art stainless steel appliances and implements of which he claimed a working knowledge.

There was an implicit agreement not to talk of the deaths, which was easily managed. Dicky had a few DVDs in reserve in case boredom threatened, but it did not.

Relaxed by the wine, chosen with care, they skipped back a decade or two to slip into the fondly bantering relationship previously enjoyed. Trixie felt that she was being gently courted, with no pressure, the door left open wide for further pleasant and possibly closer evenings,—or not.

When Boot came to collect her at the decorous ten-thirty previously arranged, she was able to answer his question honestly.

"Very nice, thank you, dear. I've had a lovely evening."

Dr. Bertram Hallam, Dr. Veronica Hallam and Dr. Liu Ho sat with Charlie, Marilyn and Lily on the decking facing the pool, stiff with mutual distrust.

However the description of events was related, Angela's parents would not be persuaded of the concept of accident. They suggested, and were as near as they would ever be to the truth, that it was horse-play that dragged her unwillingly in, or that she was pushed in by a drunken reveller, or that she was so exhausted by unaccustomed physical work that she dozed off and slid in. They tried to blame lack of supervision, poor lighting, too much food and drink. Finally, Uncle Ho declared firmly that the coroner's inquest would collate all the evidence and reach an impartial conclusion and that the deaths of two young people were undeniably tragic, but that no amount of finger-pointing would bring them back.

By the time of this meeting the Hallams were aware of Angela's unpopularity, and more evidence was contributed by Lily who would not be dissuaded by the frowns and eye signals from her family from disclosing the small scandals associated with their daughter. Gradually and mostly unwittingly they let slip that she had been a 'non-conforming' girl who was expelled from her first boarding school, and that after her marriage to Lucas their contact was limited to birthdays and Christmas.

The atmosphere lightened when Marilyn walked them round the garden, with both Hallams keen to share their encyclopaedic knowledge of insects and plants. In spite of themselves they were impressed by the house with its feeling of understated wealth, and were drawn a little closer by the shared interest in gardening.

As a precaution, Marilyn had asked Monika to prepare lunch for six without expecting that they would actually wish to stay, but stay they did, ate heartily and accepted a glass of wine. Visibly relaxing they let slip a few more little nuggets of information regarding Angela's unlovely traits as a child: the purse stolen from an aunt, the scribbling over one of her mother's pictures, the running away from home on two occasions and her refusal to consider higher education, choosing instead to work as a junior in the office where she met Lucas, whom they disliked from the start.

The Hos listened attentively as the picture formed of an emotionally neglected, attention and love-seeking girl attached to an uncaring husband. Even Lily began to feel a certain sympathy for Angela, though not for her cold, self-obsessed parents.

When the conversation turned eventually to the nature of Lavender House, rather than the dismissive comments expected, they became very interested in all that it had to offer, wanting explanations of some of the more esoteric treatments. Bertram knew of a study with animals that had lent credibility to the use of acupuncture and there followed a discussion on whether that disproved the theory that it was mostly faith that effected cures, since animals had none. This encouraged Veronica to decide to make an appointment with an unwilling Lily to try acupuncture for a painful knee. She tried to pass her over to Uncle Ho, but the Hallams were eager to visit Lavender House so that was that.

This was achieved two days later, with Veronica vouching for a feeling of relief. ('Not the only one,' said Lily.)

While there, the Hallams studied the photographs in the foyer and were startled by the picture of Lois which led to Bertram becoming convinced that his daughter had been killed, either deliberately or accidentally, as a case of mistaken identity, a theory he promptly relayed to Inspector Bird. Equally promptly he rejected it on the grounds that, even though Palmer was the worse for drink, he would still have recognised his own wife, apart from which there was simply no motive, and no evidence that they were anything other than a happily married couple and good parents.

Reluctantly, Bertram accepted the logic of that.

During the following days, the public's interest waned as news trickled round the town that everything pointed to accidental deaths, awful tragedies, but without any fascinating, scandalous exposures of drugs, sex or even rock'n'roll, the celebration revealed as more of a tea-party for the early-to bed middle-aged than a riot of fun and frolic. True, Matthew Palmer, known to many as a sportsman, had evidently had a few too many, but he had still tried to save the life of an unfortunate young woman who got into difficulties.

A surprising development was the Hallam's revelation to Dicky Bird that Angela's house would be put up for sale very soon and that she had made them aware after Lucas's death that her will stated that proceeds from the house, in addition to her not inconsiderable stocks, bonds and shares, were to go to Peachblossom House, a children's hospice. There were a few small bequests, but it was all cut and dried, signed and sealed and made with their full approval. Their own needs were met with an apartment in Fuengirola and a house in Bath. Who could argue that the hospice was a marvellous choice. Cheers all round. Good old Angela.

The nerve-twanging wait for the inquest was eventually resolved without angst, the verdicts being accidental death in both cases. The Hos were absolved from any blame; Matthew Palmer was posthumously commended for his brave efforts, and Angela's death was ascribed to a fainting fit. Condolences were offered to both families for these untimely deaths. There was a concerted sigh of relief.

Funeral arrangements were discussed by the Inspector and Shirley Pickering, (who was allowed to address him as Dicky in private) as they sat in the police car, reminiscing over others they had attended in the line of duty. Dicky's ten years in Liverpool, then a stint in London, sometimes ended in arrests, but were almost invariably noisy, emotional, tear-stained, flower bedecked events. His particular fondness was for those with horse-drawn carriages. Shirley's equally battle-scarred service in Birmingham caused a nostalgic moment. She observed that she found it odd now that neighbours and even strangers did not, as they commonly did in her previous experience, lay bunches of flowers at the garden gates or at the scenes of a crime with sympathy expressed in text-message English.

Dates had been decided, Matthew's first. This was to be a traditional church service followed by cremation, Lois requesting that black should not be worn, family flowers only but donations to Peachblossom Hospice would be gratefully received. Friends were welcome to meet afterwards in The Wig and Pen for drinks and a buffet. Oliver was to attend the service before being taken home by Pippa, who still felt personally responsible for the whole bang shoot.

There were eulogies a-plenty. Sporting and business colleagues lined up to confirm that he was an all-round good egg, and that they were devastated, but not surprised by his fatal act of heroism, typical of the man.

Trixie, Boot and Ben sat at the back, looking straight ahead and joining in the hymns and prayers. They hugged Lois but asked to be excused from the cremation and the refreshments. On the way home, Ben said he had been so carried away by the ceremony that he now believed his eyes must have deceived him.

"Let's all believe that," said Trixie fervently. "Life will be much easier."

"Did you keep a copy of the original video?" asked Boot.

"Well, naturally," replied Ben. "Do you take me for a fool?"

Shirley and the kindly funeral director worked hard to steer the Hallams through the painful process of arranging a service. She and Dicky feared there would be a poor showing of mourners wherever or whatever they chose. The Hallams were Methodists, Angela a non-believer and to their credit they tried not to let their own beliefs get in the way of Angela's stated request in her will for a secular service. The director remarked that it was unusual to receive such explicit instructions from one so young. "She must have been a very thoughtful person," he said.

A Humanist was produced to advise on a suitable form of words. The Unitarian Hall was booked for the service to be held prior to a woodland burial in a wicker casket. There would be tea and cake back at Angela's house.

The hall soon filled. Representatives from Lavender House, the Ho family, Lucas's former colleagues and his parents, and almost the entire membership of WOADS, including Audrey, Denzil's widow who loudly announced her intention 'to check the little cow's really dead.'

Lois sent a wreath with the cryptic message on the card, **WILL ALWAYS BE REMEMBERED BY MATTHEW'S FAMILY.**

There was a wreath of pink roses from **THE GUYS AND DOLLS** which puzzled the Hallams, unaware of Angela's thespian links.

The lady Humanist, enlarging on what she read in the local paper and the Hallams' half-hearted inventory of Angela's good points, made a moving little speech based on 'a promising life cut short,' making much of her willed gift to Peachblossom House, which Juliet tactlessly commented was doing rather well out of their tragedies.

A slight chill was felt at the back of the hall when Helen, attending in the hope of speaking to Lawrence, discovered him sitting unnecessarily close to Beverly. She sat behind him, alongside Boot, Ben and Trixie who was embarrassed by the situation, but smiled benignly. Helen slipped away immediately the service ended, Trixie guessing that her tear-filled eyes had little to do with grief over Angela's death.

The woodland burial, set in grounds with memorial saplings planted for the unnamed dead in among shrubs and bordering a copse where the trees were rustling slightly in the summer breeze, was unfamiliar to most, but appealing to many as a pleasant, green means of dispatch.

The lady Humanist recited 'Farewell', by Walter de la Mare,-Bertram's choice, which also received general approval, and a large body of people headed for Angela's house and the promised tea and buns. Hospitality on any scale was not Veronica's forte, and it was left to Trixie, Beverly, Boot and Ben to do what was necessary, encouraging the crowd to move into the garden. The Hos made polite apologies and left quietly. The Hallams explained several times that Angela's instructions were for them to dispose of her possessions as they saw fit, a task they would begin the next day.

The Inspector and Shirley had wondered about broaching the delicate subject of the stolen jug. Charlie had begged them not to, but when Angela's handbag was given to Shirley to pass on to the Hallams she did point out to Veronica that the little jug inside was a ruby wedding gift, as the label showed.

"It must have slipped in accidentally," said Veronica without a blush, and handed it over, but Bertram whispered, "We've had to do a lot of that over the years, and may have to do a bit more."

Out of earshot, Shirley murmured to Dickie, "Kleptomania to add to the list."

Gradually the mourners, to give them an undeserved title, made kind little speeches of insincere offers of help of the 'if you ever feel the need to talk, or need running anywhere just say the word' sort, as people do on such occasions. The Hallams were surprised, but politely assured them of their ability to cope.

The following week Bertram, attempting to pull down the loft ladder slightly and rightly fearful of finding a cache of stolen goods, wrenched his shoulder. Pleased by her acupuncture experience that made her feel, so she said, like Saint Sebastian, a claim that prompted Bertram to comment that that was a worryingly RC kind of thing to say considering her Methodist credentials. Still, he took her advice and made an appointment to see a chiropractor at Lavender House. Bunty, still on emergency Reception duties, took the call and passed it on to Lawrence as an emergency, for which he agreed to stay till six to attend to the suffering Bertram, although he was not feeling at his best.

Remarkably, the two funerals were the first he had ever attended and they had left him with depressing intimations of mortality. He had other concerns, too. It was no surprise that Beverly compared unfavourably with Helen as an intellectual companion. Beverly's knowledge of music was limited to rock and pop, her literary tastes were chick-lit, her interest in current affairs was non-existent. The conversational void was so far filled excitingly by the dramatic upsurge in his sex life. His initiation into the novel and acrobatic experiences enjoyed with Beverly were of a far more frequent, intense and exhausting nature than he was accustomed to, and he found himself hoping for an occasional night off.

Jack was too busy with the Hos to be free for a quiet drink, so he hoped he might find an excuse for a relaxing evening at home on his own, watching TV, after he had dealt with Dr. Hallam, for whom he felt increasing sympathy.

After the usual introductory questions about general health, said to be good, Bertram described the site and intensity of his pain, and the manner of his acquiring it.

He was placed in a comfortable position, his jacket and shirt were removed and Lawrence explained carefully, as he always did, that he would give neck manipulation for what he diagnosed as Vertebral Subluxation Complex needing neck extension and rotations of the head. Bertram relaxed, was unworried by the clicking noises and Lawrence performed the moves until it became horribly plain that his patient was suffering convulsions.

Appalled, Lawrence assessed the situation and 'phoned for an ambulance, dashed into the foyer, empty of everyone except the evening cleaner who ran upstairs to fetch Trixie who rushed down in double quick time with Boot.

By the time the ambulance arrived, Bertram had fallen into a coma despite Lawrence's best efforts. Trixie edged him out of the way to tell the paramedics that Dr. Hallam had just sat down to explain where his pain was, when he apparently suffered a massive stroke and the ambulance was called straight away. One of the savvy paramedics asked whether treatment had begun. By this time, taking his cue from Trixie, Lawrence indicated his notes and said he was just starting to interview the patient and explain the form the treatment would take when the convulsions began.

"The poor man has been under great pressure. His daughter died tragically, you know. He was clearing out her house. I guess this is stress-induced. I'll go and collect his wife and take her to the hospital," said Trixie. It was agreed that Lawrence should go along in the ambulance.

Boot marvelled again at his mother's skills of improvisation.

An hour later, by which time Veronica had almost recovered from the shock, she, Trixie and Lawrence waited in a side room, each in a state of high anxiety, for differing reasons.

"He's always looked fragile," said Veronica, "but I didn't expect this. Do you think he damaged himself trying to get into the loft? He's not used to that kind of physical exercise and he moved awkwardly. I didn't realise it could be serious enough to bring on a stroke. If only he'd gone for chiropractic treatment immediately this wouldn't have happened, I'm sure. It must have been such a shock for Lawrence, too."

Sitting between them, Trixie squeezed Veronica's right hand and Lawrence's clammy left one, closed her eyes and prayed for Bertram's full recovery and her own personal redemption, neither of them seeming probable.

After another thirty minutes a tired-looking radiologist appeared to report to Veronica that there was damage to the blood vessel wall,—a blood clot, consistent with a wrenching of the neck.

Veronica confirmed that he had indeed injured his neck at home while stretching awkwardly at the top of a ladder.

Since Bertram remained comatose, and Veronica expressed no wish to sit and hold his hand, Trixie suggested that she should go home with her to Lavender House to be nearer to the hospital so that she could get some rest but be there in ten minutes as soon as he came round. Lawrence was sent home, with Veronica's thanks for his swift action when Bertram collapsed.

At six a.m. they received a 'phone message to inform them that, sadly, Dr. Hallam had passed away without regaining consciousness. Persuaded that Bertram would have preferred to die rather than face the great possibility of being left brain-damaged, Veronica was stoical, telling Trixie that she regarded herself as fortunate in having spent her life with such a clever companion and that she would devote what was left of her own to completing their book. Trixie was impressed by the woman's dignity, but slightly worried that she showed no sign of shedding any tears. She wondered whether this emotional frigidity was a genetic flaw or whether Angela's strange behaviour was environmental, and whether there was any point in asking the so-called therapist working at Lavender House. On balance she thought probably not.

Quietly, she called Lawrence, urging him to come into work as usual and not to deviate from the non-contact story which was, insisted Trixie, as true as dammit. Lawrence said he did not feel able to come in. Trixie told him to get his arse over to Lavender House or she'd personally drag him out.

Lawrence contemplated suicide. He had spent the night assembling the names, addresses and 'phone numbers of his professional association, his insurance company and likely sounding lawyers, and arrived at Lavender House at eight a.m. white with fright, but showered, shaved and in a clean white shirt as per Trixie's instructions.

He had let his parents know that a man who suffered a stroke while in his consulting room had subsequently died, and they sympathised and suggested he should go to their home for a nice meal, an offer he declined.

By the very worst of coincidences Helen, unaware and about to leave for Lake Garda, had left an envelope for him at Reception. The contents detailed deaths and injuries incurred worldwide by patients receiving chiropractic. Helen thought Lawrence should read it, and she helpfully also gave two website addresses that she was sure he'd find informative. Amongst other advice she referred him to the sixty-two Edmonton chiropractors who warned of the risk of stroke resulting from neck manipulation, and to Professor Ernst who listed milder adverse results and to others who reported incidences of epidural haemotoma, intracranial aneurysm and peripheral nerve palsy. Helen further suggested that he should have a word with his new, close friend Beverly, regarding the craniosacral therapy she offered in amongst her other more beneficial and no doubt enjoyable massages.

Lawrence contemplated murder, then suicide again, but instead showed the letter to Trixie, who went, "Whoooo!" and could not help admiring the girl's turn of phrase if not her timing. Clearly Lawrence was not in the right mental or physical state to see patients who might well, given the circumstances, be deterred by his clammy, trembling hands.

"I'll 'phone them," she offered, and took his list that included two migraineurs who had been handed on from Jack and were agreeable to being handed on again as there was gossip in the air. Juliet was delighted to receive four clients for Reflexology to add to the only one already booked. Beverly gave two spaces for whatever they cared to choose from her extensive list.

Lawrence was told to keep Helen's letter to himself for the time being, and to go upstairs where Boot would make him coffee and something to eat. Feeling like a six-year old sent to his room, Lawrence obeyed, and gratefully ate up all his scrambled egg with parsley decoration and the toast tastefully arranged into dainty triangles. He considered the advantages of spending the rest of his life as a six-year old.

To Trixie's disappointment, it was not Inspector Bird who arrived to conduct interviews, but Sergeant John Evans, ignorant of how near he was to the truth, when he had rudely suggested to Dicky that he was deliberately engineering incidents related to Lavender House in order to get his feet well and truly planted under Trixie's table.

She spent most of the day helping Veronica, who surprised the funeral director by asking him to arrange another woodland burial, which evidently had impressed Bertram. The choice of a good, old-fashioned Methodist service pleased him, and he was kindness personified to the widow who was yet to show real signs of feeling bereft. This time there was an obituary to be placed in The Telegraph and a request for help from Trixie in finding a suitable place for the funeral refreshments as Veronica believed there would be many people wishing to attend. Finding this hard to believe, especially as the only relatives mentioned were Bertram's aged sister who lived in the Orkneys, and a couple of cousins in Bournemouth, Trixie postponed a hasty booking as there was still the matter of the inquest before a date could be settled.

Juliet, looking very pretty in her sleeveless, embroidered, oversized smock, explained within minutes of her new clients' arrivals that she was expecting a baby in six and a half months time but had more or less stopped experiencing morning sickness, for which they were grateful. Though sympathetic women, they agreed afterwards that the forty minute monologues on pregnancy did not add to their enjoyment and if, (God forbid) there should be a next time, they would decline the offer. Juliet's reticence regarding Dr. Hallam's demise was due not to professionalism but to lack of knowledge other than that the poor old fellow had dropped dead in Lawrence's room.

"He was very old, I think," she said helpfully. "In his sixties, I'm pretty sure. We do seem a bit jinxed at the moment."

The jinx word was raised again when the reporter from The Woolchester Bugle turned up early to question Trixie, who spoke in a dignified way at dictation speed:

"It's very sad, especially so soon after his daughter's tragic accident and our thoughts are with his wife at this difficult time. It seems he suffered an injury at home that caused his death. We're all deeply shocked, especially the chiropractor who was just preparing to treat him. No, we don't believe in jinxes. We have seven highly qualified therapists helping hundreds of people, many of them travelling long distances because of our reputation. Some things are beyond our control, I'm afraid, as life and death don't follow a pattern. Thank you."

CHAPTER TWENTY-TWO

Between sessions, all the therapists nipped up briefly to offer support and sympathy to Lawrence. Jack and Lily, outwardly the most positive, but inwardly the most shaken, suggested the three should spend the evening together. Beverly, as yet ignorant of the jibes in Helen's letter, offered a comforting evening at her place. Jason said that there but for the grace of God went all or any of them: it was like cruises where a number of people were expected to die every trip simply because of the average age of the passengers. Older clients were, by definition, wearing out and every now and then one would pop his or her clogs in their presence. Bad luck, Lawrence.

While being driven to the airport by her father, Helen received a call on her mobile from Lawrence, who berated her, furiously. When it became apparent to them both that she had not heard about Dr. Hallam's death, she burst into tears and forced her father to turn the car round, cancelled her holiday by 'phone and made for Lavender House, instructing her fuming father not to wait.

Bunty, whose initiation into working on the Reception desk was more exacting than she had imagined, nervously 'phoned upstairs and was asked to show Helen into

Lawrence's consulting room. He kept her waiting for ten minutes then went down, and, immediately melted by her woebegone face, longed to hold her, but did not.

"I don't know why you're crying," he said. "Here's another statistic to add to your list. Except that it's not. I wasn't treating him when he collapsed. It was co-incidence, but nobody will believe that if you're going round spreading slanderous, libellous statements extracted from some Canadian's theories."

Lawrence added himself to the growing list of fluent liars, believing in their own lies.

Helen pulled herself together sufficiently to mount a robust response.

"I am personally sorry for what happened here. Of course I am, but I can't retract what I wrote simply because its timing was bad. I'm here because I love you in spite of your being a chiropractor. Those aren't theories, either, they're case histories that you'd do well to read."

"Thanks a million," replied Lawrence, curtly. "I thought you were going to Italy?"

"I was. I cancelled."

"That was stupid. You can't do anything here. All I can do is wait for the inquest. Veronica—Dr. Hallam, doesn't blame me at all, but the death will always be associated with me. I'm just hanging on. See if you can get the next flight."

Helen shook her head. "I wouldn't enjoy it now," she said, and stood up. "If you want me I shall be at home."

Lawrence escorted her to the front door, turned ready to go back to the safety of Trixie's flat when Beverly appeared, nodded towards his room and shooed him in.

"What happened, really?" she asked. "Did you accidentally press on the carotid artery? It's easily done.

We're taught that when we do our cranio-sacral procedures we must keep to the lightest of touches, if any. It's used with babies, so you have to be careful."

Having now fully persuaded himself that it was Veronica's theory of the awkward ladder stretch that had killed Bertram, Lawrence was deeply affronted.

"So you're assuming I killed him? Be careful what you say. You can't compare chiropractic—four years intensive training,—with that non-scientific rubbish you're peddling."

"I assure you," said Beverly in tones of pure ice, "I can do and say whatever I please. My patients all walk out alive and well!"

"And believing in twenty-first century quackery. Good luck to you, but don't confuse your mysterious practices with serious procedures."

"Forget my invitation for this evening. Obviously you don't need a remedial massage."

Lawrence watched as her lovely Titian hair bounced as she left. The words 'cut', 'nose' and 'face' came into his mind as he stepped out to return to the security of Trixie's flat, but he was waylaid by Sergeant Evans, who wanted a word.

Exactly when did he notice the doctor was unwell? Had he touched him at all?

His shirt was off, so hadn't the manipulating, if that was the word, begun? What did the doctor say had happened with the loft ladder? He'd managed to drive alone to Lavender House, though, hadn't he, so he can't have been feeling too bad? You wouldn't have thought he'd be able to drive at all with such a severely damaged shoulder, would you?

Lawrence explained, quietly, that there were many recorded cases of people with dreadful injuries carrying on normally for surprising lengths of time due to an adrenalin surge that apparently deadened the pain. Mind over matter.

Cynically, the Sergeant commented, "That's the motto here, I suppose."

Hackles rising rapidly, Lawrence replied, "We can debate the philosophy of what we do, if you wish, but I thought you might simply want a factual statement."

"Absolutely right," agreed the Sergeant, "and I believe that's what I've got, so I'll leave you alone. Where do I find the cleaner who was here when Dr. Hallam arrived? Then I'll be seeing Felix and his mother just to tie up the loose ends. Thanks for your time."

Elizabeth e-mailed Jack regretting the misfortunes that seemed to be surrounding him.

The migraineurs were keeping her posted, she said.

Encouraged by the others to 'get back in the saddle' as soon as possible, and because his shaking had stopped and only one person had cancelled an appointment, Lawrence felt sufficiently confident to resume his normal schedule. The only difference was that having read, thanks to Helen, that the parent of an Edmonton woman who had died, just like Bertram, after Vertebral Arterial Dissection following neck manipulation, had been told by the hospital doctor, "Never let those buggers touch you above the shoulders," Lawrence moved his manipulations south, to be on the safe side.

He was aware of the practice—and theory—of 'Therapeutic Touch', which involves no contact at all, the therapist instilling 'healing energy' by keeping his hands inches away from the body as he moves them from head to toe. Undeniably, apart from the risk of overlooking real illness or damage, this was harmless, and certainly there was no shortage of people willing to lie down and believe what they were told about 'energy fields.'

He could appreciate, better than most, the legal advantages of this treatment, but could not bring himself to go along that route of what he had already criticized in Beverly's and Juliet's treatments as silliness and quackery. Any career move, if he decided on it, must be a respectable one, acceptable also to Trixie who had supported him so well. His relationship with Helen might possibly be renewed by a move from the therapy trade, but he was experiencing a stubborn resistance to being nagged out of a career, even if it survived the inquiry.

He and Beverly managed to be polite to each other after their spat, but their affair was over, a pleasant and instructive interlude for him and a diversion for her while Daniel was away. For this, he was grateful. Trixie had obviously been aware as she was of all the goings-on, and he supposed that, as usual, he would consult the oracle.

She had taken Helen's papers to read, and would not be cheered by them.

Already, Lily had been scathing to Jack about homeopathy and her uncle's Traditional Chinese Medicine. It had gone without saying, at least until he fell out with Beverly, that the curious and diverse treatments for which people offered themselves up at Lavender House, were almost entirely faith-based hokum. He and Jack had made merry in particular about Hopi Candling: the very notion of lit candles being placed in the ears was scary enough, but the dramatic demonstration after treatment of a dollop of brown gunge apparently drawn from the ears was impressive to the patient. In fact, when a candle was opened up after being burnt well away from the ears, it still showed the same residue.

Juliet was defensive about her Reflexology, pointing to her life size chart as if it were proof positive and, true enough, many of her patients declared that they felt much better after treatment.

"Nothing," as Trixie had pointed out right from the start, "like a rest and a long chat for improving well-being. Ask any hairdresser."

Was it too late, Lawrence wondered, to re-train. The ambulance men who attended Bertram had gained his respect. Now that was an admirable calling. Could he cope with messy road accidents, though? Dealing with blood and guts took guts, and he was very much afraid he didn't have any.

His patients that first day were sympathetic to the sad tale of Dr. Hallam's collapse, and probably appreciated his lighter than usual touch on their painful bits and pieces, although he knew from experience that the sound of a loud crack reassured some of them that something was definitely taking place and that they were getting their money's worth.

Although Charlie was pale and often overwhelmingly tired, his response to treatment was reassuring. Liu, guilt-ridden by the aspersions cast on his Chinese Traditional Medicine as an alternative therapy for his brother, was insistent on being responsible for escorting him to and from hospital visits and sitting in on consultations to report the unvarnished truth to Marilyn and Lily who suspected Charlie of underplaying his illness and the prognosis.

Marilyn accompanied him sometimes, but Charlie was keen for her to carry on teaching as normal. They all knew that circumstances were changing and were falling over each other to be mutually supportive.

Jack spent most of his free time at their house, although Lily was persuasive in encouraging him to see Lawrence, especially after 'the incident', as it was being described.

A guided tour of the language schools, organized by Jennifer, was not without an underlying motive. Charlie hoped that he might initiate Jack into the firm, with the aim of handing over to him the overall business management of the schools when the time came that he could no longer cope. Heavy hints from Jennifer at first alarmed Jack, resistant to being catapulted into something for which he had no natural inclination or relevant experience, but she gently insinuated that skilled underlings were the key, and that the post of Director demanded a pleasant presence, good suits and willingness to appear to be involved, rather than knowledge of educational method or even financial acumen. It was taken for granted that he could set Homeopathy aside without regret, and that did appear to be the case. Gradually the prospect became rather appealing, but he wisely did not mention anything to Lily that might be interpreted as ambitious, letting all the overtures come from the Ho family.

Another aim of Charlie's, taken up happily by Marilyn, was to see Jack and Lily married as soon as possible. The bride-to-be had no wishes for a lavish affair, particularly as Jack was divorced. Neither was a believer, so a 'blessing' was out of the question. They both wanted a private civil ceremony followed by a family-only celebration. They would live in Jack's flat after the marriage although, as Charlie pointed out, there was a wing of the house available when wanted. Clearly, Lily's immediate preference was to move out of the family home in order to control their own lives, but neither was naïve enough to reject out of hand the generous offers being made. Although the possibility of their having children was not aired, Charlie would have been totally delighted, Marilyn had her doubts, based on Lily's frequently stated dislike of people under the age of sixteen, and Jack thought they had left it a bit late

A wedding date was proposed for late October, Marilyn praying that Charlie would still be in remission to see his wishes come true.

CHAPTER TWENTY-THREE

Bertram's death certificate stated the cause to be 'Traumatic rupture of the left vertebral artery'. No blame was attached. Veronica was suggesting to one and all that her husband had always been rather clumsy except in fine motor manipulations for which he showed great skill with pins and formaldehyde.

To the surprise of the Lavender House people in attendance at the Methodist Hall for the funeral service, the place was packed. It transpired that Bertram was internationally recognised as an expert entomologist who had written many books and published many papers in learned journals. Fellow enthusiasts spoke of his erudition and dedication, and mourned his death that left a work in progress. Tributes were paid to his widow, collaborator and soulmate.

No mention was made of Angela.

After the funeral, at which Lawrence sat half expecting someone to rise dramatically from his seat, point at him and shout, "Murderer!", Veronica asked whether he would consider helping her to clear Angela's attic, "The scene," and here she smiled, 'of my husband's downfall."

Shocked on more than one level, Lawrence felt that he could hardly refuse, and went to the house the following day, determined to work hard on behalf of his conscience.

There were more shocks in the attic. He carried down eleven large cardboard boxes that Veronica opened on the kitchen table, her face showing neither surprise nor emotion as scores of small pieces of porcelain and silver were revealed. Even Lawrence's untutored eye recognised their value.

"I didn't know she was a collector," he said, guardedly.

"Neither did the police," responded Veronica, crisply. "I'll ask Inspector Bird to check these against stolen property lists, and if that doesn't bear fruit they can go to auction for Peachblossom House."

"A thing I did notice," said Lawrence hesitantly, "is that blue Parker pen. I think it may be Lois Palmer's. She asked us all to look out for it,—she mislaid it at Lavender House a few months ago. I expect Angela picked it up by mistake."

"Don't be foolish, Lawrence. Please take it back to her. Anything else?"

He shook his head. "It was a sickness, Veronica. I'm so sorry. I believe Lois really tried to help her."

"We're lucky she wasn't in Holloway which is what she deserved."

At this point an elderly man, grey-bearded and florid, came in from the garden.

"Oh, Professor Laughton, this is Lawrence, the chiropractor who was so helpful when Bertram collapsed." They shook hands, the professor not bothering to shake the dirt from his. "Bill has volunteered to help me finish the book. Bertram would have liked that. As soon as we're done here the solicitors will do what has still to be done, and we shall return to Fuengirola to pick up where I left off. Fortunately, Bill is footloose."

"Oh, good," said Lawrence, wanting to add that he did so like a happy ending. "What would you like me to do with this stuff?"

"Nothing. I'll 'phone the Inspector and we'll take it from there. You've been so kind, Lawrence. Thank you so much."

"My pleasure," murmured Lawrence, realizing how silly and inappropriate that sounded. He was looking forward to a quiet drink with Jack, who had confided the news of his forthcoming wedding, without quite the amount of enthusiasm Lawrence thought the prospect deserved.

Lawrence wished he had not fallen out with Helen, but could not see how to overcome the pitfalls of having a wife who might be rude in public about the callings of most of his friends and colleagues. An amiable, married foursome with Jack and Lily could have been most pleasurable: regular suppers at each other's houses, visits to matches, the cinema, the theatre and concerts; tennis doubles, Scrabble, perhaps even holidays abroad, certainly weekends away in little rented cottages by the sea. All these would have brought a companionable dimension to add to their wedded bliss.

There would have been no sexual tension as he did not fancy Lily and suspected Jack was not attracted to Helen. Just good friends. But a pipe dream, alas. He was on his own, well clear of Beverly, alone and lonely. Boo-hoo.

He drove home trying to rationalize the effect that the late, unloved Angela had had on their lives. You couldn't describe her as a catalyst because she was herself changed. As in dead.

Later than most, Lawrence was increasingly worried about the randomness of life, and hoped that Trixie might come up as usual with some light pleasantry, probably to do with hairdressing, to get him back on track. But what track? Could he continue as a chiropractor, having done for Dr. Hallam? It was hard to fathom how to counter the encouragement from the cheap seats to pack it in and get a proper job.

He really did need a drink.

Lexie was home, sad at having waved 'au revoir' to Jake after a loved-up, sheep-filled vacation. To finish a dissertation she needed the sanctuary of a quiet room and plenty of coffee for four days before returning to university for her last year.

Kept informed by Boot's regular e-mails, she also wanted to judge for herself the effects of recent events. Although sceptical of the practices at Lavender House, she did not want to see her mother's project going down the drain. Caring nothing for Lois's late husband or for Angela and her father, even her sympathies with Lawrence were tempered by the feeling that his was a tomfool occupation.

There were vets who engaged in alternative treatments which she dismissed as frippery that exploited animal lovers who had more money than sense. Boot had whispered on the 'phone the unsettling details of Ben's filming of the drowning, and she wished he had not. From now on she could not avoid viewing Boot's significant other in a different light. The pale, shy, wide-eyed and harmless young man was now somehow tainted by events.

Ben had invited her, with Trixie, Boot and Lawrence for a meal at his flat. Indecisive about accepting, she supposed it would have been rude to refuse and a break from her computer was welcome. Her paper was almost completed, and there was a limit to the attractions of writing in detail about the incidence of scrapie in Wales.

Predictably, Ben had worked hard to produce a meal of what Lawrence and Lexie regarded as unnecessarily fancy food. Nothing arrived at the table in a recognisable state, but it was all delicious and freely accompanied by good wine. They had not been forewarned that this was a triple celebration.

Boot revealed that Ben had won a prestigious, national photographic competition with a substantial cash prize and had been taken on by the Woolchester Bugle as staff photographer, (the latter not a big deal, in Lexie's opinion.)

Clink went the glasses.

Ben told of Boot's books being displayed in a local art gallery where they were hailed by some supposedly well-known critic as seminal, ground-breaking works that smart collectors should snap up before he was feted by the London cognoscenti.

More, rather incredulous, clinking.

The third announcement, for which Boot moved to hold his mother's hand in case she should faint, was that he planned to move in with Ben at the end of the month.

Clink, clink, clink. Trixie was neither faint nor surprised and, if unhappy, disguised it very well.

They moved to the sofas to carry on toasting each other, Trixie including Lawrence with a cry of, "Here's to the next lovely lady!"

Just why Ben considered this to be a good time to offer to show the film of the Ruby Anniversary party was anyone's guess, but it was assumed by Trixie that this was the jolly, truncated version as seen by the Inspector and passed to the Hos.

It was not. Those not already in the know, watched horrified when it came to the part where Matthew entered the water, grabbed Angela's feet and was seen quite clearly to be holding her head under water before joined by Lois, Jack, Paul and the rest.

Unremarked on, but not necessarily unseen, the shadowy figures of Beverly and Lawrence could be recognised emerging from the summerhouse. Lawrence felt sick, and not only on Angela's behalf.

"Christ Almighty!" he said, as Lexie put her hands over her face, "You filmed it, Ben! For God's sake, you filmed a murder!"

Ben looked surprised. "I thought you knew. Sorry."

When Lawrence tried to stand, his legs did not respond to the messages from his wine-addled brain and he sat down, hard. Lexie was in tears.

"It's not a souvenir, Ben," reprimanded Trixie, sharply. "Delete it. That's just sick. You're treating it like a horror movie. Those were real people, not actors."

Unusually fuddled, Ben seemed bewildered. "I kept it because . . . I don't know why I kept it. I thought I should. It was evidence. You never know." Then, slyly, to Lawrence, "It's lucky nobody was filming your little incident."

Not sure which 'little incident' he was referring to, Lawrence thought it bad enough that the lesser one involving Beverly and the summerhouse was on film. He glared at Ben, who was smiling sweetly.

Trixie rose without falling over and commanded Lawrence to call for a taxi. With the dignity of the slightly tiddly, she carefully enunciated her words.

"It's been a wonderful evening, boys . . . marvellous food and wonderful news. I'm so happy for you both. Now get rid of that bloody thing."

After dropping Lawrence home, and safely but slowly negotiating her many stairs, Trixie kicked off her shoes and began to weep, a sight so unfamiliar to Lexie that she had no idea what to do, but opted for making tea.

"I'm pleased for Boot, if that's what he wants, but Ben is . . . is . . ."

"A voyeur?" suggested Lexie.

"Detached. Unemotional. A bit scary, but I think that's just his pale eyes. Because he's so quiet and polite you think he'll be empathetic, but he's not."

"I think he's fond of Boot," reflected Lexie, sipping her tea. "They look right together. Anyway, they're not getting married, are they? I don't want them stealing my thunder next year. You and Boot will come out to New Zealand, won't you?"

"Wild horses would not restrain us," promised Trixie. "I'm going to bed now and you've a busy day ahead. Come on."

Meanwhile, Boot and Ben filled the dishwasher and discussed, without reaching a conclusion, the pecking order of lies and deception and whether any of it mattered when all was said and done.

Ben locked away the film in his desk drawer, and Boot knew that it would remain unedited.

"Four funerals and a wedding or two," mused Boot. "Somebody ought to make a film out of that. It's mean, don't you think, Mother, that Jack and Lily are having a family only affair? When do I get to wear my pale grey, linen suit and purple shirt? They won't keep for Lexie's nuptials and she'll probably insist on plaid shirts and corduroy trousers: which wouldn't be too bad, actually."

Trixie agreed that a wedding would lift the spirits and decided to start dropping hints to Lily. Jack was also being nobbled by his friends and by Marilyn who, disappointed by their decision, considered him more amenable to suggestion than her daughter. Charlie, of course, favoured another garden spectacular, without the drownings, obviously, but urged gently that the net could be spread to a few close friends and colleagues. Lily caved in, insisting on a maximum of forty to share a wedding breakfast at The Red Sun, with a string quartet, then everybody to leave. No dancing, no singing and not much drinking.

She had only recently been coaxed by Jack into accepting that a glass or two of wine would not speed her road to perdition. He hoped that her puritanical streak would steadily dissipate under his tutelage.

Lavender House was greatly cheered by the invitations, as predicted by Trixie who could also foresee that Jack's new role as a Ho son-in-law would probably quickly lead to his giving up his practice even if Lily stayed on. The consequence from that was the likely exodus of the profitable migraineurs, and with Lawrence growing increasingly flaky, and Juliet already time-limited, she had an underlying feeling of unease.

Whatever doubts, hints and accusations were circulating regarding the validity of many of the therapies, she felt there was no denying the reality of extra-sensory perception operating at Lavender House.

People who should not have had any insight into the latest machinations of the place seemed worryingly well-informed. Instinctively she suspected Beverly to be their reliable source: what Beverly knew, everyone knew. Trixie hoped Ben's film was still classified information

Even Juliet, the fertility goddess, was on the case.

"Some people are criticizing what we do, Bunty, but the bottom line is that our patients return because they feel better, and what's wrong with that?"

Bunty could see nothing wrong with that.

"There's been a lot of research done, Bunty, and it all shows that even gazebos can have positive results."

Bunty thought that one over for a few seconds. She had a soft spot for Juliet who had, she realised, a soft spot of her own.

Nodding kindly, eventually she said, "A garden is a lovesome thing, God wot."

Juliet, puzzled, moved off to treat Inspector Bird's sister who closed her eyes and ears so as not to hear all about the positive effects of breast feeding.

Lexie was back at university, finding time to urge Boot by e-mail to consider VERY URGENTLY whether Ben was the right man for him.

The response was swift and as expected: MYOB. He's a lovely man. Too honest for some people. He's taking Jack and Lily's wedding photographs. Any objections?

His sister temporarily gave up, satisfied that she might have at least sowed a small seed of doubt in his lovesick mind. There was no sign of that while Boot busied himself packing in readiness for the move.

"Do you want me to empty the place?" he asked his mother, fingers crossed.

"I shan't be letting it out just yet, dear. Just take what you need. You won't mind if it's used for a friend to stay over occasionally? Lexie's room's filled up again"

"'Course not. Ben's flat's very nice, as you know, but it is very small, and once we're making real money I hope we'll move. Snag there, though, as he loves the country and I panic when the pavement ends. I'd like Jack's place: I'm impressed by all that video-entrance palaver and maintenance staff about the place."

"When you're both rich and famous you can have both," Trixie consoled him, believing the chances of either to be remote, although Carl had 'phoned to report the need for a reprint of Boot's, 'TREES' which he claimed was going to be the most popular Christmas book of the decade. ('Yeah, right!') had been Lexie's comment. Promisingly though, Ben and Boot were collaborating on a children's book of magic and wizardry with scary photographs, that would make J.K.Rowling fear for her reputation, Boot claimed.

Lois was back at work with a satisfyingly full case-load. All thought, but nobody said, that patients' curiosity played its part. Sympathizing with Lawrence over 'the incident', she volunteered her services should he wish to talk things through. He did not rule it out, convinced that anybody who could so recently have witnessed her husband killing one of her patients, lied about it and bounced back into the therapist's chair without visible sign of emotional scarring, must have very unusual and enviable resilience. She described Helen's actions as 'below the belt', voicing his own feelings.

He thanked her warmly and promised to have a heart to heart discussion at some unstated time in the future.

It took three days for Boot to move his possessions, helped by his mother and, on the last day, by Inspector Bird who had dropped in to check on Trixie. As they packed up more boxes of books while Boot unpacked them at the other end, Dicky shared his good news that he was to be a grandfather in the New Year, his married daughter having obliged.

"I'm jealous," admitted Trixie. "With this fruitless relationship with Boot and Ben, and Lexie's children, if they have any, being in New Zealand, what damn good is that?"

Dicky bit his lip to stop himself from immediately offering a share in his, which was what he had in mind, but decided on a softly, softly approach, knowing she was unlikely to be rushed into anything.

"Shan't see much of mine," he said. "They live in deepest Wales, and I expect Penny will get the lion's share of the visits. Girls gravitate to their mothers even though she won't like the idea of being a grandmother, but there it is, and she'll probably be a good one." He sat back on his haunches and looked up from the piles of books whose authors he had never heard of.

"Are you happy with this move?"

"What do you think?" Trixie quickly reminded herself that he had not seen what she had seen. "Happy enough. Ben's . . .er, pleasant and the two of them seem happy. Anyway, what are the odds for any couples?"

"Let's get these boxes over there to them, wish them luck and come back for a drink. If you don't mind?"

"I don't mind," said Trixie and kissed him lightly on the brow. "I don't mind at all."

CHAPTER TWENTY-FOUR

September mellowed without disaster into a warm October. Marilyn and Jennifer appointed themselves style consultants to a Lily who had unintentionally slimmed down through worry. Jack approved, but was wise enough not to mention it for fear she would interpret any comments as implied criticism of how she was before.

A jacket and long skirt in heavy, cream satin were chosen; no hat or headdress but a spray of cream orchids to hold. Jack bought a replacement cream linen suit and on the day they made, all agreed, a handsome pair.

As they stood on the Register Office steps Ben busied himself with the official photographs in his usual quietly efficient way, and continued to do so at Charlie's restaurant where the staff cheered heartily when the wedding party arrived. They served course after course of delicious Chinese dishes while the string quartet, including Denzil's widow Audrey, played light classics.

Firmly, Lily had stipulated two-minute speeches and toasts, but Charlie managed a little longer to praise his beautiful, good and clever daughter and her charming, handsome groom, a welcome addition to the family.

Short, sweet and tasteful, according to Beverly, disappointed that there was no trickling on into evening celebrations. Some guests, feeling too sober, moved on to the Wig and Pen, others drifted home.

Jack and Lily planned a Christmas in the sun as a belated honeymoon, but went back to Jack's white flower-filled flat. Manfully he hid his twinges of regret about lost space as Lily's belongings began their invasion. The prospect of accepting the invitation to move to the Ho's west wing with its enviable elbow room, became increasingly attractive.

A similar sense of loss was being experienced by Ben, whose dismay at the size of Boot's wardrobe alone led to their first disagreement, quickly followed by one regarding books and enough shelf space for beauty maintenance products.

When Boot drove to Lavender House huffily to return two boxes, Trixie elicited from him that there had been little or no discussion of the practicalities of the move. Both men were obsessively tidy, which was fortunate, but each was equally inclined to regard each other's possessions as disposable, which was not. Although by modern standards Ben's place was spacious, it did not compare with the one at Lavender House. Also Boot was unused to the sound of neighbours, which he found unnerving.

Ben's late uncle and aunt had left him the flat, luckily not burdened with mortgage repayments. Talk of council tax, food and heating bills, the television licence and the cost of broadband came as a terrible shock to Boot when he realised there was an expectation for him to contribute more than his charming presence and delightful wit.

Cushioned by a small allowance that he received on reaching twenty-one, thanks to his late father, his mother had picked up all his bills during and since his truncated time at university. Life was now real, earnest and cramped.

Trixie foresaw trouble but did not intend encouraging him to move back, with or without Ben. Well aware that she was responsible for his being spoiled, she tried to harden her heart at last and exercise tough love.

"Sort it, Boot. If you can't manage on your unearned income, you'll have to make some in the traditional way. Your royalties aren't going to keep you in cashmere just yet. You need a job."

"You're a hard woman," said Boot, only half joking. "What, though? I'm a good-for-nothing, a dilettante. What can I do? Ben's doing quite well now with his 'Bugle' salary and weddings most weekends. Nobody wants a writer."

"Take anything, Felix. Wash dishes, sweep the streets. There's no shame attached. Regard it as collecting literary material. Fill your notebook."

Once she used 'Felix' he knew she meant it, and was not going to encourage his notion of being a writer 'kept' for his contribution to artistic life.

"I don't suppose you've any vacancies for any more funny therapies?"

"There are always vacancies for funny therapies but the funny therapists need qualifications of sorts. I can't employ you here. What do you fancy doing? Lois's is the easiest option if you ask me: no overheads, no messy oily treatments, no physical contact with the less than beautiful. You'd manage that—you've got a sympathetic face. You could write up your case notes like Oliver Sacks, changing names of course, and make a fortune. Then there's television."

"Excellent. Where do I train?"

"Ask Lois. Or you could create your own, I suppose. Instant therapy. Steal bits from other people then present

The Callender Method. Let the punters talk themselves dry and then put the onus on them to heal themselves. That works. I've watched it."

"By George, I think you've got it!"

Boot drove away to have a chat with his partner, in which he would explain that if they were both to be working, household chores must be shared as equally as the expenses.

He had no expectation that Ben would do anything other than laugh, but he embraced the idea wholeheartedly. By late evening they visualized the Callender Method as a world wide franchise, operated either from their large country estate or their Regency town house. Relenting, Ben proposed more shelving for Boot's books to return.

He also made another surprising offer.

Both Trixie and Bunty were in Reception when Ben arrived bringing proofs of the wedding photographs for approval, which they received. In them, Lily again appeared magically to be quite lovely, with her dark hair artfully arranged over one shoulder, skilful make-up, thanks to Beverly, and the beautifully fitted cream suit drawing praise from even the most critical.

Ben's other mission was to have 'a quiet word' with Trixie who did not like the sound of that. She invited him up to her flat where he outlined a cunning plan. He wanted to enrol with Lois for a course of therapy, immediately raising Trixie's suspicions, which he allayed by explaining his aim was to absorb the methodology before passing it on to Boot, who would then advertise himself as a counsellor in this unregistered profession, working from home.

Flabbergasted that Boot had taken her flippant suggestions seriously, Trixie asked,

"What will be your excuse for seeking treatment?"

Ben tapped the side of his nose, irritatingly. "Highly confidential, Mrs. C. We all have our little worries."

"We most certainly do, Ben. Well, fine, if you're sure you want to tread that rather precarious path. Fix it with Bunty. I expect there are vacancies. You're talking about a course, presumably. That doesn't come cheap, Ben. No discounts for family friends, I'm afraid. The therapists set their own fees."

"Naturally. We're regarding it as an investment. Traditional courses would cost thousands rather than hundreds."

Trixie was tempted to say that in the case of Lois's training that was hardly true, but she nodded. It crossed her mind that now he was to all intents and purpose her son-in-law, she ought to invite him to call her Mother, but instead suggested that he call her Trixie like everybody else, which he acknowledged with a sweet smile.

This was, she believed, a terrible idea. What were the boys thinking? The other therapists were likely to laugh their socks off at Ben needing therapy after a few weeks of living with Boot. She could imagine the ribald comments. She trusted that Lois would again ignore any ethical code she was supposed to follow, and confide in her.

Of course, she did.

Ben was, apparently, abandoned by his father who walked out on his aggrieved mother who also could not relate to her son. He was bullied at school and painfully shy. He needed advice on the adjustments needed in embarking on a relationship he hoped would last for ever. There were problems regarding the quantity of Boot's books and clothes and pictures, and some bickering about money and what they should watch on TV. There were arguments about who should cook and load the dishwasher.

Lois assured him that all of these issues were common to couples when they embarked on a life together and gave him a few tips from the RELATE handbook on consideration for each other.

It occurred to Trixie that Ben might be raising these difficulties suspecting that Lois might not be adhering strictly to the rules of confidentiality, to make her aware of Boot's shortcomings, but she decided it was not important and that if Ben was in fact receiving the right help for the wrong reasons it was all to the good. If Boot could learn from these sessions second hand, and put them into practice, there was nothing to worry about. After the first few visits she lost interest.

Eight appointments passed with Ben arriving promptly, pale and polite to report on his week's progress. On the ninth, Ben shared with Lois his big, dark worry.

Having decided to work through minor issues before confronting this, he confessed there was an all-enveloping, guilt-laden burden to unload on her.

Lois perked up. Homosexuality?

No, of course not. Who worried about that, these days.

Commitment? He was content to commit to Boot, the love of his life.

Financial concerns? In a way. Money was tight, but that was not it.

"What then, Ben? You can confide in me."

He looked her straight in the eye.

"I witnessed a murder and did nothing about it."

Lois's head spun. "Whose?" she whispered.

"Angela Smith's."

"Angela drowned accidentally. You know that, Ben. Everybody knows it. You weren't involved and mustn't feel guilty about an accident that had nothing to do with you."

"I saw it all. I saw your husband pull her in and hold her under. It was murder."

Lois's mouth opened and closed three times before a sound came out.

"That's rubbish, Ben dear. Your eyes deceived you. I was on the spot and can tell you there was a struggle and she drowned accidentally, as did Matthew. You must put it out of your mind. I can help you do that. You poor thing, have you been worrying all this time over something that didn't happen? It's a figment of your imagination, Ben, probably brought on by quite unrelated stress. I'm so glad you came to me. You can relax and forget it, Ben. We all have these dreadful dreams at some time, but we have to get back in touch with reality. Focus on your lovely life with Boot and . . ."

"I filmed it."

"You did what?" The soothing tone suddenly became very sharp round the edges.

"I don't believe that. You weren't even around when it happened. I happen to know that Boot left early with a migraine."

"He did. I didn't."

"Anyway, that's immaterial. It was an accident. Everybody who saw it knew it was an accident. I witnessed it and so did Jack and so did Paul."

Lois tried to stare him out, fixing him with her sharp blue eyes, but his pale ones merely enlarged and stared back, unfazed.

"Matthew went in before Angela and pulled her in by the ankles, Lois. You know that's so. However much you dream and wish it weren't so, those are the facts. They may have been altered in your mind by stress, as you've kindly explained to me, but anyone who sees my film will know the truth. I've done wrong by keeping quiet about it, and it's on my conscience now."

Dear God, here we go again, thought Lois.

"Even if we assumed for a moment that you think you're telling the truth, what would it take to ease your conscience, Ben?"

"You agree I have a good case for blackmail?"

"Of course I don't. You have no case at all. Whatever the facts you could cause pain and distress to me and my little boy and our families. I'm surprised you want that. But who'll believe you?"

"Anyone who sees my film."

"Have you shown it to anyone?" Ben's face remained blank. "I'd like to see it. Show it to me. You can come to my house, on your own. 'Phone and tell me when you're coming. After eight: I have to get my son to bed. I'm not having him disturbed."

"That's fair, Lois. I'll give you a ring. Don't worry. Just relax."

"Now sod off," she hissed and, as he was going through the door, "Little prick!"

He heard, poked his head round the door and said, "It's academic as far as you're concerned, but I'm told it's considerably above average size, as a matter of fact."

"Good session?" asked Bunty automatically.

"Very helpful, thank you," said Ben, and went out smiling.

The last time Lois confided in Trixie the outcome was worse than anything she might have imagined. Without doubt Ben would have shown the film to Boot and probably his mother. Who else? Jack and all the Hos? That Inspector who was so attentive to Trixie? There was no security anywhere. She clutched at a straw. If half of Woolchester were aware of the contents of the film and nobody had mentioned it, possibly nobody cared enough about Angela Smith to raise doubts about the story. Matthew was popular with a lot of people who would be prepared to be sympathetic about aberrant, drunken behaviour rather than believe he was not the hero they wanted him to be. She admitted to herself that this was all unlikely, but the whole nightmare had been unlikely.

She could try to bluff it out, if challenged: blame panic and poor light for what she could now say she only thought she saw. She could allege the film was a fake. Everybody knows the camera always lies. Where had that little creep been to get any pictures anyway? Lois had a week to fret and to plot. If he really did have incriminating evidence, she could buy him off as a last resort, but if the thing was common knowledge she was sunk and might as well go to the Police now before they came to her. Another alternative was to wrestle the damned thing out of Ben's hand and destroy it. She was bigger and probably stronger than the blackmailing, slimy little runt and could easily see him off.

Gradually, she formulated an alternative plan. Several of Matthew's friends had taken to visiting her to make sure she was 'managing,' and offering help if needed.

"Just say the word," they said. Mostly they were members of his rugby club, big, burly and kindhearted. Suppose she were to say the words,

"I'm being blackmailed by a little, gay photographer who wants to ruin Matthew's reputation and make me out to be a fraud. Would you mind just frightening him off?"

Would they refuse? She would owe them, but they were unlikely to collect favours. They were Matthew's loyal mates. Lois considered her options.

CHAPTER TWENTY-FIVE

Boot posed, pen raised delicately, for Ben's entertainment.

"Tell me in your own words, and your own time: How did you feel when your stepfather raped you/ your house burned down killing all your family and a basket of puppies/ you lost all your money/ you discovered you had terminal cancer/ you found out you were not only adopted but gay as a May morning/ that you had failed all your exams and were about to be sent down? How did you feel about that at the time? How do you feel about it now? What do you think yourself? What do you think you can do about it? Think of two options. Which do you think is the better one? Why do you think that? How does that make you feel? Now let's list our five goals. How do you feel about them? Have you got a snowball's chance in hell of achieving even one of them? How do you feel about that? Have you practised achieving any of them? How did that make you feel when you failed? How does it make you feel now? That will be hundreds and hundreds and hundreds of pounds, please. What do you feel about that?"

Ben paid attention before laughing and Boot went on,

"I know it's money for old rope, but it's given me some ideas of my own. I shall offer the writing treatment. They can spend the first ten minutes or so writing down their problems, which will probably cure them anyway, then we'll start on the 'And how do you feel about that?' mullarkey. I could get into this in a serious way, Ben."

"It's daft, I know," replied Ben, "and I started this for all the wrong reasons, but it was actually quite helpful."

"You have problems?"

"Well, nothing major. Day to day stuff. You know."

"I know what mine are. I don't know what yours are."

"You know quite well what mine are: adjusting to a shared life. It's not a problem, exactly, just minor bread and butter stuff."

"And how do you feel about that?"

"Shut up, Boot."

He did not mention his revelation to Lois regarding the film because he had not made up his mind what to do. It was only when learning that Lois had benefited from a hefty life insurance claim that the notion of relieving her of £1,000 of it seemed initially appealing. He regarded himself as a deliverer of retribution until the moment when he saw the look in her eye, which was a considerable deterrent. Even knowing that he had witnessed the drowning did not make her falter for a second. Plainly she was his match where deviance was concerned, and now he realised that she had a backbone of steel, which he lacked. Also he knew that Boot would not be at all happy about this mercenary show of initiative. He regretted starting what seemed now to be a doomed venture, and guessed that she would persuade him to destroy the footage. If she started in on being a widow with an orphan child, he knew he was sunk.

It did not occur to Trixie or to Lawrence that Ben might have ignored her instruction to get rid of the offending film. Boot knew it was in the drawer, but did not suspect his loved one of being capable of blackmail and took the nonsense of Ben's enlisting in therapy at face value for what he deemed feasibly cheap tuition. Trixie kept the secret close to her ample chest, almost believing that Boot might become an established writer/therapist.

Beverly and Juliet thought it sweet of Ben to enlist with Lois, believing it to be a genuinely generous financial boost for the young widow, a theory they passed on to the others who did not question it, considering the nervous, pale and shy young man to be a suitable case for treatment.

Robert Lister responded without hesitation to a call from Lois, who sounded anxious and in need of a friendly ear, at the very least. Divorced and unattached, it was always a mystery to him that his old friend, the late Matthew, had attracted such a lovely woman as Lois whom he regarded as extremely pretty, amusing and clever. Aware that the couple had been through what was described as 'a rough patch' a few years earlier, he had supported Matthew but hovered hopefully in case of a serious split, which did not happen. He was hovering again and this was the first time he had been offered an opportunity to show her that he was willing to be a true friend. Robert hoped this was not a cry for financial help, as he was himself a bit strapped for cash, but he understood from other friends that Lois had been left mortgage-free and with a substantial insurance pay-out.

When he heard the story of the film, edited by Lois slightly in her own favour, Robert was astonished, but understood immediately that Matthew's reputation should not be tarnished. Think of poor little Oliver! Lois was not in any way the guilty party, quite the reverse. Nothing would bring back the Smith woman who, by all accounts, was as mad as a hatter, or Matthew, so it was unfair that she should be harassed by some little, jumped-up gay snapper who plainly needed to be taught a lesson. Robert quickly outlined a plan to frighten the little bugger.

Lois's stepmother was always eager to have Oliver to stay overnight, and he loved all the extra cuddles and spoiling with hot chocolate with cream and flakes on top. She was glad that Lois was granting herself a night off to spend with a friend. The poor girl deserved a break. It was too soon to consider a new relationship, but Matthew, though a nice enough man, had never seemed quite good enough, not Lois's intellectual equal nor even a good financial provider, until he died, of course.

Bunty was trying to soothe Trixie's unusually frayed nerves as they sat in the flat sipping vodka. Already Jack had given notice that, due to Charlie's deteriorating health, he had promised to take over the business side of managing the language schools, He acknowledged that he would be greatly supported by Jennifer in this, but would reluctantly be forced to give up his practice at Christmas. He and Lily were moving into the west wing at the Ho's house, for the sake of convenience. Trixie recognised his reluctance but it was obvious that the lucky devil had fallen into a honey pot.

That morning Celia, in her role as spokeswoman for the migraineurs, had told her that they all felt that sadly, with Jack leaving, they would not wish to continue making the journey to Lavender House, wonderfully therapeutic as the treatments had all been. The women arrived with a large wooden crate, a belated wedding gift for Jack and Lily. When in York, Elizabeth had spotted an old apothecary jar in an auction sale catalogue that she believed Jack would love to add to the two she had previously bought him. She suggested they club together to bid for it and here it was. Lily was not totally smitten by the gesture, but accommodated it in her surgery, 'as a lovely reminder of Elizabeth and Jack's fan club', she remarked acidly to Trixie.

On Friday morning, Beverly had delivered a bombshell. During a home visit, Daniel had persuaded her that their standard of living would be so much better in Germany and they could enjoy an exciting, fresh start together. There would be no financial need for her to work, but if she wanted to he thought there were openings for her to have her own very profitable Therapy Clinic. Out of the Lavender House window went not only homeopathy, but Reiki, Indian Head Massage, Cranio-sacral therapy, hot stone treatments, candling and an inexhaustible supply of gossip.

Juliet and her embryo would be leaving soon, and Lawrence was muttering darkly about a career change. Lily was unlikely to stay much longer, thought Trixie, which left the lovely, dependable Jason, and Lois, who attracted trouble to a quite remarkable degree. There would be five empty rooms.

"That kinesiologist who was interested haggled so much about the rent that I turned him down, like a fool," said Trixie. "What shall I do Bunty? I could probably let out the rooms to beauty therapists who are ten a penny, but that wasn't what I intended for the place. It's so disappointing. I might as well have stayed in hairdressing. I turned Elizabeth down flat when she offered to buy. I expect she's lost interest now with the credit crunch and all. What a mess."

"Don't panic, sweetie. Nobody's actually left yet. It's such a lovely place I think they'll be queueing round the block to join the group, and if they're not we'll take crash courses at the Tech in Bowlsby and have two of the rooms ourselves and practise hot towel therapy with weird oriental incantations. As you know very well people will pay anything for a chat and a nice lie down especially something with a funny name and a strong scent."

"I'm sorry to admit you may be right, although you do make it sound like a massage parlour. Of course it may come to that. Another vodka?"

They settled down more cheerfully to watch TV. When Bunty realised that driving home might not be a good idea, she accepted the offer of Lexie's room, and by midnight the women were sound asleep.

It was common for Ben to have evening engagements for The Bugle. Many were charity presentations of cheques, or sports awards or society dinners, all of which he claimed were stultifying dull and in which Boot took no interest at all, offering sympathy that Ben was forced out to work. When Ben said that he was going out to take some family photographs, not for the newspaper, and should be home by ten, Boot was happy enough to spend time on his own re-arranging his books yet again.

It was when he was temporarily using Ben's desk to sort out some papers, that he noticed that the key was in the drawer where the disks had been placed.

On an impulse he made an executive decision to destroy the thing, as instructed by his mother. Puzzled by its absence, he vainly searched all likely places. Unwilling to contact Ben when he was working, he checked the desk diary, which was blank for that evening, contrary to the usual practice of leaving an address. Usually he walked, if possible, and occasionally asked for a lift back. Boot assumed that he had forgotten, put away his papers tidily, sat and watched TV feeling rather like a cartoon wife, waiting with rolling pin for an explanation of deviant behaviour.

At ten he made coffee and called Ben's mobile, which was switched off. Ten-thirty came and went, time ticked on to eleven, with Boot trying the mobile every ten minutes or so. Eleven-thirty, twelve. Boot looked again for the disk. At twelve-thirty he 'phoned Trixie who was not pleased.

"How should I know, Boot? Does he go clubbing? Cruising? Doesn't he tell you where he's going?"

"Yes, that's my point. You know we don't go clubbing. We're home bodies. He said he wouldn't be late. If it was people I knew he'd have said. It was just work. He took his camera."

Then he told her about the missing disk.

"Surely to goodness he's not showing it to someone else?"

"Why on earth would he do that? I'll leave it until one o'clock then if he's not back or hasn't 'phoned I'll call the police, but it's going to sound ridiculous, isn't it, coming from me?"

Trixie agreed that the police might be merely amused by Boot reporting Ben as a missing person when he was only a couple of hours late getting home. They might well compare this to their own domestic lives. On the other hand, Ben was a vulnerable-looking young man probably walking home carrying a camera bag. She decided she would risk Dicky Bird's annoyance at being disturbed at this hour, and hoped he would not take the official line.

He was awake, reading in bed, and listened attentively as their concerns were outlined. He told Trixie to get dressed and wait for him so that they could go to Boot's together, leaving Bunty to receive possible messages.

They talked through the matter for the ten minutes it took, and found Boot looking green and ill with anxiety.

It was out of character for Ben not to have said where he was going, and for him to be late home

"That's it? He's late?"

"He's never late, Dicky. He walked. Said he wanted some fresh air."

"To clear his head? You hadn't had a row?"

"No!" cried Boot. "We were fine. He said it was a job. Family portraits. I don't ask where."

"It's a bit difficult for me to put out a red alert for a grown man who's a bit late home. No diary entry? You've 'phoned, of course."

"It's been switched off all the time." Boot looked at his mother who looked away.

Dicky intercepted the look and sighed, crossly.

"I don't mind at all being plucked from my nice warm bed at midnight when friends are in need of assistance," he said. "But if I'm to be allowed only half a story, then I'd prefer to go back there. I was coming up to the solving of a fictional murder, which is the kind I like, so either tell me, one of you, what the hell's going on or change your choice of policeman."

Trixie was near to tears, but assumed responsibility since Boot looked as if he might faint. "I'm sorry, Dicky. This story gets worse and you won't like it. You saw the film that Ben took at the Ho's party. Well, he did go on filming and kept the original copy with footage of the actual drowning. You can see Matthew going in first, dragging Angela in and, well, it's all there. I've seen it and so have Lawrence and Lexie. I told him to destroy it, but he hasn't and now it's missing from his desk."

Dicky digested that, frozen-faced. "Before we cut to the chase, what have Lawrence and Lexie got to do with it?"

"Nothing," said Boot, softly, "They happened to be at our place when Ben decided to show it. I honestly thought he'd edited it and wanted to show the party."

"Did you now," said Dicky, not actually calling him a liar. "I don't want to spend time now arguing about this, but I shall do so later I assure you. The obvious place if it's in Ben's hands is at Lois Palmer's for a blackmail attempt."

"He wouldn't!" said Boot robustly finding his voice. "He wouldn't do such a thing."

"I wouldn't have expected him to, but something appears to have happened. I'll 'phone Lois."

"Before you do that, you should know he's been seeing her professionally," said Trixie.

Dickie's eyebrows shot up as Trixie went on, "He had a few issues he wanted to talk through."

The warning look at Boot to keep quiet about the therapy-stealing initiative did not pass unnoticed but Dicky did not comment. He felt suddenly overwhelmingly tired and disappointed.

Lois answered the 'phone sounding breathless and received Dicky's apologies for such a late call politely and with appropriate anxiety.

No, she said, she had not seen Ben and would have been surprised to see him. She had been home all evening. Oliver was at her stepmother's. She had intended going round to a friend's house, but was tired and went to bed at around eleven. What was wrong?

"Nothing as far as we know, but he failed to return home at the expected time and Boot's worried. I'm ringing round all possibilities: Trixie said you'd been treating him, so I wondered whether he might have dropped in on the offchance, you know?"

"I don't invite clients home. I don't know him, really, apart from when he took our photographs at Lavender House."

"I apologise again for disturbing you so late. Thank you, Lois."

"Let me know when you find him," said Lois, now genuinely concerned. "He probably sheltered somewhere from the rain. It's been bucketing down."

"Very possibly. Sorry to have bothered you. 'Bye."

"I wonder," he said to the others, "how she knew he didn't drive to his appointment. I don't expect she knew his liking for walking. I didn't mention he was on foot. I'm reporting him missing."

When Robert gently patted her back and said, "Leave it to me," in a confident voice, Lois trusted him to sort things out. Matthew had been inclined to let her do any sorting out that needed doing, and it was a comforting feeling to hand responsibility over to a big, strong, well-disposed man. To hell with feminism, she thought. There are times when a clunking fist, metaphorically speaking, is the answer.

When Ben arrived promptly at eight she greeted him politely, took his wet, black jacket and rucksack as he told her how the rain began soon after he started out, but that he had found it refreshing after a day indoors. She invited him into her lounge where he put the film on the coffee table, refused her offer of a glass of wine but asked for orange juice. Lois went into the kitchen where Robert, lurking quietly, topped up the tumbler of juice with an industrial dose of vodka, to her silent unease. Ben said that it tasted very nice. Having by then abandoned the notion of extorting money from her, a feeling reinforced by the photograph of Matthew, Lois and Oliver on the mantelpiece, he was regretting the whole enterprise that had been prompted mostly by annoyance at Lois's chipper attitude and easy lies. He wanted to tell her that knowledge was power, but that on this occasion he chose not to exercise it and that she should regard herself as lucky, which the film would show. He sipped his drink but, alarmed, spilt some of it when Robert entered from the kitchen and sat heavily beside him.

"How do you do," said Robert politely. "I'm Robert, a close friend of Matthew."

"This was meant for Lois's eyes only," said Ben bravely.

"Well, Mr. French, she asked me to share the experience. Funny, these days, that when everybody's got camera 'phones, nobody else considered filming the death throes of a young couple. This won't be easy for Lois, so I'm offering moral support. You understand the word 'moral', Mr. French?"

"Look, let's forget it," said Ben. "I'll get rid of it, I promise. I didn't approve of those lies being told, that's all."

"Ah, I see. Mr. Moral Guardian calling us all to account, is it. We'll watch the film, make our own judgement then we'll get rid of it. You weren't, by any chance, considering blackmailing Lois, a widow with a young son?"

"Of course not! I wanted her to know the truth was on record."

"Let's see it then. Lois would you rather not?"

She shook her head. "I'll see it. I lived through it." Robert was filled with admiration.

Lois held a handkerchief to her eyes as the scene played out.

"Happy now?" asked Robert, and removed the film. "I can't think in what way that has improved the situation for any of us. Lois's life has been shattered already and you just wanted to rub her face in it, you sanctimonious little poofter. You okay, Lois? I'll drive Mr. French home now."

"No!" cried Ben, thoroughly scared now, and dizzy when he stood up. "I'll walk home. Leave me alone. You've got the film."

But they gave him his coat and rucksack and Robert steered him out of the door and walked him down the drive. Lois watched as Ben was shoved into the passenger seat of Robert's car and driven away. She hoped Robert wouldn't hurt him. Obviously the little creep was frightened, and Robert had the film, so that should be the end of that.

CHAPTER TWENTY-SIX

Central locking scuppered Ben's first thought of jumping from the car and executing a triple roll while instead he sat trembling so much that his jacket was rustling embarrassingly.

"Fasten your seat belt," ordered Robert, which struck Ben as ludicrously caring, given the circumstances. He found it was true that the mind raced manically in scary situations, supposed that it was too much to hope for that Robert might actually be about to take him home, and assessed the likelihood of several deeply unpleasant alternatives. It was soon plain that he was not going straight home when they reached the end of Lois's road and Robert signalled a right turn.

Managing only a whisper, Ben started, "I live . . ." but was cut across curtly by Robert's, "I know where you live, Ben. You live round the corner from my friend Paul, the saxophone player who gave you a lift home after the accident. Don't you ever take your car anywhere? I know petrol's dear, but it must make your life inconvenient. You remember Paul?"

Ben remembered reading somewhere that it was important in hostage situations, which might be the case here, to befriend one's captors, of establishing common ground.

"He's an excellent player," he said. "Do you play an instrument?"

Robert nodded. "Drums, keyboard, bass guitar. Bit rusty now, but before I got married I used to play with Paul's band, The Big Bad Boys. Do you play anything?"

Heartened, with the trembling easing slightly and his bowels feeling less deliquescent, Ben admitted that he did not, but enjoyed all kinds of music, especially jazz.

"Where are we going, Robert? I'd like to get home. I can easily walk from here."

"We're just taking a little detour. No need to walk when I've got a nice, warm, comfy car."

He drove to the outskirts of Woolchester, past the Hos' house, which was a small relief to Ben who had considered the possibility of being thrown into their pool as retribution, and on into the rural hinterland, dark and unfamiliar. He tried to concentrate on landmarks and had managed to memorize the number plates of the only two cars to overtake them. When Robert drew into the roadside and parked he began to sweat: no buildings in sight, no traffic, no help at hand or, apparently, for miles.

"Take your coat off," Robert instructed.

Ben was familiar with 'Deliverance,' and quaked. "What for?"

"'Yours not to reason why, yours but to do or die,'—take it off."

He waited patiently while Ben wriggled out of his jacket, stopped him from retrieving his mobile from a pocket, then got out of the car and tossed the coat into the hedge. Seizing a chance, Ben slid over to the driver's seat but was smartly pushed back into the passenger seat by the fast-moving Robert.

"Nice try, Ben, but don't do it again." He drove a further mile, stopped again and demanded Ben's shoes and socks, which he threw out of the window before driving on. It was now raining heavily, making it difficult to read the few signs there were, but Ben did make out 'BOWLBY SIX MILES'. Robert turned left at the next corner, drove fast through a hamlet of six unlit cottages and repeated the process of parking, bullying Ben out of an item of clothing and casting it out of the window. Out went his rucksack, then on for a few more miles during which Ben was reduced to a panic-stricken silence, which he broke only when his camera was chucked into the road before they came to the edge of a copse.

By this time, near to tears, Ben was wearing only his shorts.

"You've had your fun, Robert. That was an expensive camera and my livelihood ruined. Drive me home, please."

"No, Ben, I don't think so. I'm told you'd rather walk than ride, so off you go, son. I'm a bit lost myself, but I think you need to turn right at the next junction, about five miles on."

"I need my 'phone."

"Haven't seen it, Ben. Out you go."

Ben stood in the pouring rain and watched as the car disappeared into the blackness, trying to calculate whether he should turn back in the hope of retrieving some clothes and his 'phone, which idea he dismissed as absurd, or carry on to try to find some human habitation. Boot surely should have done something by now,—'phoned friends to come looking for him in their cars. He thought angrily of his camera, destroyed by that unfeeling great oaf. For no reason that he could explain, it was always referred to as Clarence, in the same way that some people give names to their cars, a practice derided by Boot. Now shaking from cold as well as fear, with the rain whipping across his face, Ben thought this was the nearest to hell he had ever been. In all the driving round there had been no more than five cars. This was an area where folk went to bed before eleven unless there was an unusual cause for celebration in which case they might allow themselves to stay up until midnight.

Despairing, Ben feared it was a mirage when headlights appeared hazy and yellow in the distance, but he made out the approaching car with unspeakable relief, stood in the middle of the road, waved with both arms and yelled, "Stop! Oh, please, stop!"

The driver did not see him until the last moment, braked hard, skidded on the wet road then clipped Ben's side, sending him spinning into the air until he landed with a thud and the car careered off the road into a clump of bushes.

The elderly driver, on his way home from the British Legion Club a few miles away, and slightly anaesthetized, was shocked but amazingly able to climb from the car, unaware that there was blood trickling down his face from a cut on his head. He checked to see who or what he had hit, went back into the car for his 'phone and reported that a naked man, drunk he supposed, had run in front of his car and was possibly dead, certainly unconscious. Fortunately the old man was local and was able to describe exactly where he was.

Ben's brief period of euphoria had been overwhelmed by a deafening thunderclap and enveloping blackness.

As promised, Robert rang Lois when he reached home, assured her that he had not laid a finger on Ben but had dropped him off somewhere that ensured he'd have a bit of a walk in the rain. He stressed that she must deny having seen either of them and that he would be in touch soon. Lois did not feel either as reassured or as pleased by this as she would have wished and spent a sleepless night.

Assembling a party to sweep-search a non-specific area in the lashing rain in the early hours sounded like an impossible aim, but news spread quickly adding bands of waterproof and wellie-clad citizens who did not even know Ben, to the organized police groups.

At Lavender House, Bunty was put in charge of volunteer communications, a complicated procedure that she tackled efficiently and enthusiastically. Dicky Bird did not want to make too apparent his suspicions as to where Ben had been visiting, but he subtly directed other officers to fan out from that area.

The call from the hospital in Bowlby which had earlier been approached for any helpful information, came at one-thirty. It proved quite difficult to abandon the search, with some of the many volunteers still beating bushes in the dark at three o'clock in spite of Bunty's best efforts to call them in. There were caustic comments from certain members of the force who had advised against doing anything until the next morning, and educated guesses that Inspector Bird knew things that he was not yet sharing. When it became more generally known that Ben had been knocked down by a car, miles from his home and was, more excitingly, near naked when found, the enterprise gained more credibility and the ensuing rumours were regarded as sufficient reward for getting soaking wet in the dark, and Dicky Bird was vindicated.

Boot, Dicky and Trixie went immediately to the Accident and Emergency Unit at Bowlby General where they learned that Ben was already in theatre. Certainly he had fractured a hip and several ribs, but there was as yet unspecified damage to his head, and some internal injuries. At this stage no-one would offer a prognosis, but they were told it would be hours before anyone could see him, to Boot's very obvious distress. Some comfort was offered by a sister who said Ben had been conscious briefly on arrival before being sedated and had asked repeatedly for Clarence. "Is that you?" she asked Boot kindly, and did not blink when told that Clarence was his camera. She encountered stranger things than that on a nightly basis.

Inspector Bird was allowed to speak briefly to the car driver, Mr. Herbison, whose head was swathed in bandages, and who had already been breathalysed and found to be over the limit. He was chirpy and seemed to be enjoying the attention, his version of events growing in narrative detail throughout the next twenty-four hours. There was no Mrs. Herbison, and he regarded the overnight stay as a welcome diversion from going home to an empty cottage. Ben in his underpants in the pouring rain, shouting for help, became an aggressive, stark naked drunk brandishing a bottle, swearing and threatening to kill the old man. An ambulance man had noted the smell of alcohol on Ben's breath which gave the story some credibility, except that no bottle was found at the scene.

As items of clothing, Ben's camera and rucksack were picked up throughout the night and their positions logged, a pattern became to emerge. He had been, so it seemed to Dicky, abducted, assaulted, stripped and abandoned. By whom and for what purpose posed a big question. There were suggestions that it might have been a homophobic attack, a likely proposition according to several officers, who needed persuading that Ben was not in the habit of cruising either that or any other area, but was a respected employee of The Bugle. It was unfortunate that the editor had to confirm Boot's story that Ben was not out on the paper's behalf. His destination and purpose, apart from allegedly taking pictures of an unknown family, remained a mystery. His camera was reasonably intact, but empty, which signified a lot to Inspector Bird and raised suspicions among his colleagues who were assuming a gay connection, possibly for blackmail. Dicky feared Ben's reputation was about to be irreparably damaged. Although furious with him for what he regarded as inexcusable behaviour, almost certainly he would be blamed for something which was untrue and totally out of character. He did not doubt for a moment that Ben had visited Lois. It was a matter now of pinning her down to tell the truth, a concept that she seemed unable to grasp. The mystery was not deep, but it might involve interviewing fifteen or more rugby players. It was four a.m. but Dicky did not care. He went off to interview Lois again.

Boot refused to budge from the hospital waiting room, but Trixie decided to go home for a short rest, promising to be back by eight, by which time there should be news of Ben's condition. Having raised with one of the nurses the question of how they knew it was Ben when he was brought in unconscious and naked and they would not allow Boot even a glimpse to confirm that fact, he was told that one of the ambulance drivers recognised him from when he photographed his daughter's wedding, which the nurse found a confirmation of the smallness of the world and brought tea for Boot and gently patted his shoulder.

Dicky Bird parked quietly in the road outside Lois's house before he 'phoned her to warn of his visit, watching as the bedroom light went on.

"I'm sorry to disturb you again, Lois, but I thought you should know that Ben has been found."

"Oh, thank goodness," she said with genuine relief.

"Actually, it's not good news. Can I come in? I'm outside now." He saw her peek through the curtains and waited for only a few minutes until she appeared at the door, her white face rigid with anxiety. He closed the car door softly, not wishing to alert neighbours, and she let him in, indicating the kitchen where she started to make coffee.

"He's in Bowlby General, seriously injured. He was knocked down by a car some miles from Woolchester."

"Oh, Lord, I'm so sorry. How did it happen? Was it a hit-and run?" Her immediate and alarming suspicion was of Robert deliberately mowing him down.

"No. The driver's in hospital as well with head injuries. Some poor old fellow skidded into him, apparently. The thing is, Lois, that Ben was wandering about in the middle of the road wearing only his underpants."

Lois was lost for words for only a few seconds. "Are you asking me whether I thought he might be disturbed, having a breakdown or something? You know he'd been coming to me for therapy?"

"I did know that," replied Dicky, "but I wasn't going to ask you that. You knew he was on foot?"

"You mentioned it before. What . . . . had he been mugged or something?"

"Something, certainly. His clothes and belongings were scattered over quite a distance. It's the kind of thing you hear of when stag parties get out of hand and they think it's highly comical to handcuff the naked bridegroom-to-be to a lamp-post in Hull. Hardly the case here though. Any suggestions?"

Lois passed over a mug of coffee and made a good show of trying to be helpful.

"I can't imagine anyone wanting to do that sort of thing to Ben. Where was he exactly? Have you spoken to anybody else? Why ever didn't he contact Boot?"

"His 'phone was stolen along with everything else. You assumed he was on foot when we spoke earlier. Why was that?"

"Did I? Well, I knew he usually walked wherever possible. He always walked to Lavender House rather than drive. Cared about his carbon footprint, I daresay. I naturally assumed he wasn't going too far from his home, but I didn't know, obviously."

Dicky nodded. "I'd like to talk to you about the filming of Angela and Matthew's deaths. Sorry, Lois, but we've got to put our cards on the table. I've seen the film, and I believe you have, too. We're lucky it hasn't been on YouTube. I understand why you'd find it offensive and would want to get hold of it and want to have something to say to Ben about it. A warning, perhaps?"

Lois had half-hidden her face behind her coffee mug, her eyes wide and scared. She took a sip then put it down carefully, leaving, so Dicky thought, too long a pause before she said, "I have absolutely no idea what you're talking about. What film?"

"I suspect Ben came here last night to do a deal."

"No, he didn't. What sort of deal? I've not seen him or done any deal."

Dicky blatantly ignored her denials.

"I need to know from you who else was here last night, which loyal friend is protecting you and may have got you into very deep trouble. The car accident was exactly that, in my opinion, but somebody, maybe more than one, stripped and robbed Ben and abandoned him miles from anywhere where he was likely to die from exposure. It was dark, cold and lashing down with rain. Serious charges will be brought and if he dies, which is very possible, it could be seen as murder or manslaughter at the very least. Now, was it someone from Matthew's rugby club or the gym club or one of his work colleagues or an old friend of yours?"

Aware that his voice had gradually increased in volume, Dicky stopped when he saw that Lois looked as if she might faint. She rallied, though, like the trouper she was, reminding him horribly of Angela Smith, her late doppelganger.

"I've been here all night on my own. I know nothing of any film. I have no idea what you're on about. I'm very, very sorry about poor Ben but it's nothing, NOTHING to do with me." Her chin came up for the coup de grace. "Perhaps instead of wasting time here you should question some of his gay friends."

Really, thought Dicky, you had to admire the woman's determination. He smiled at her, which caught her by surprise.

"Perhaps I should. Thank you, Lois. If you think of anything, give me a call. Sorry again for interrupting your beauty sleep. Good morning."

She watched as he drove away, went to the kitchen and made herself a fresh mug of coffee. In a few minutes she would shower, dress and prepare for work, believing it important that she should show up as usual and hear in the role of interested observer, what was being said by the Lavender House people.

First, though, she 'phoned Robert and quite spoiled his day.

CHAPTER TWENTY-SEVEN

At six in the morning, still in theatre, Ben suffered a massive, fatal cerebral haemorrhage. One of the surgeons broke the news to Boot as gently as he could, himself angry and disappointed at losing a young life. Boot was initially too shocked to be able to speak at all and was put in the charge of the kindly nurse who had watched him and brought tea through the night. She telephoned Trixie who soon arrived with Bunty.

Calls were made to Inspector Bird and to Ben's parents who were not, it turned out, estranged from each other and Ben, but pleasant, retired schoolteachers who had always been supportive morally and financially, loved him dearly and were devastated by this dreadful death. They set out immediately from their home in Devon.

The role of bearer of bad tidings and general disseminator of information was again filled by Bunty, described by Trixie as an absolute treasure. Fortunately all therapists were present, Lois showing no sign of having been grilled at dawn by the Inspector.

There was immense sympathy for Boot and unsurprising unease that there did indeed seem to be a bit of a jinx on those who 'passed through the portals' of Lavender House, as Juliet expressed it. She was glad that she'd soon be away from the place. Clients studied with renewed interest the portraits on the wall with their Ben French signature, and expressed their sorrow at a lost talent.

Details dribbled out to be broadcast on the local news in as sensational a way as ever happened in the small town, although as someone remarked, that made two grisly tragedies in six months. All this in an area where people expected to die in their beds after a respectably conducted, long life.

The 'Woolchester Bugle' devoted a page to the story, with photographs of Ben receiving his recent award.

BEN FRENCH (1985-2008)

The talented young photographer Ben French who joined our staff after national recognition as a most promising newcomer, died on October 24th in tragic and mysterious circumstances. He was knocked down by an elderly driver, who remains in hospital with head injuries said not to be life-threatening, at the edge of Bowlby Copse. The accident occurred late at night in the pouring rain when visibility was poor. Ben was reported to have been wandering unclothed in the middle of the road. He suffered severe head injuries, broken ribs and pelvis and internal damage. Sadly he died from a brain haemorrhage while undergoing surgery at Bowlby Hospital. We are told that, had he survived, he would have been left with brain damage.

Inspector Richard Bird who instigated a search when informed that Ben had not arrived home as anticipated after an unknown photographic assignment, not for The Bugle, has put forward several theories currently being pursued. It is possible Ben accepted a lift and was then assaulted, stripped, robbed and abandoned. His clothes were scattered over a long stretch of road, suggesting there was a vehicle involved.

Ben told his partner that it was a family photo appointment which was assumed to be in the neighbourhood since he chose to walk. No-one has yet come forward to confirm this, nor to report a non-attendance. A homophobic attack cannot be ruled out as there have been several such in Woolchester over the last year.

Ben and his partner Felix Callender were collaborating on a children's book to be published before Christmas. Mr. Callender is said to be both devastated and perplexed that such a quiet, gentle and unassuming young man should have met such a fate, with which we wholeheartedly agree and are offering a £5,000 reward for information leading to an arrest.

Ben's parents, Mr. and Mrs. Lionel French have asked us to thank the good people of Woolchester who tried so hard in wretched circumstances to find their son. They say they have been overwhelmed by the kindness received and hope for an early resolution of this disturbing tragedy.

Inspector Bird decided to have a word with Jason Rugg who was familiar with most of the local football and rugby hearties, mostly through their troubled tendons and strained groins. He wanted to know who were the friends of the late Matthew Palmer.

"They must gossip," he encouraged, "What have you heard over the horse liniment?"

"Nothing relevant. I can mention a few former mates of his, but this isn't a hairdresser's. We talk about sport and politics and suchlike manly topics. Bit of sex, naturally, but never anything personal. All I do know is there was the annual rugby club dinner on the night of the accident, so they're all accounted for, including me, as it happens. You could check on the absentees."

Dicky felt like kissing him, but refrained, and made his way to interview the secretary of Woolchester Rugby Club. He was a short, stocky man bearing a few facial scars. He was immediately on the defensive when asked about attendance at the dinner and made it plain that he did not like being quizzed. There were only six refuseniks of whom three were on holiday, one was undergoing knee surgery, one whose wife had gone into labour and Robert Lister who had developed a stomach bug and sent an apology on the day. The secretary asked, crossly, what was up? Dicky told him that the police had been informed of a rumour circulating that a rugby club member had been involved in an assault. It was to everybody's advantage, said Dicky, to eliminate as many people as possible, preferably all of them.

"That Ben French thing?"

"That Ben French thing, precisely. Please keep this under your hat. It's only a rumour and I've lots of other fish to fry."

"I can't think of anyone who'd do a thing like that. They're a decent bunch—family men with respectable jobs. When I heard about it I reckoned it sounded a personal matter. Gay, wasn't he?"

Dicky agreed that was the case, adding that Ben's private life was also perfectly respectable as far as he knew.

"I'll keep my eyes and ears open," promised the secretary, "but I honestly think it is just a rumour and a nasty one at that. I'd lay good money none of our chaps are involved. Better off looking for a bunch of local hoodies on a fun night out."

"I'm inclined to agree," lied Dicky amiably and left to have a little chat with Robert Lister, the last man standing.

Robert was home and pale enough to substantiate his claim of being housebound with a stomach bug at the critical times and affronted at being singled out.

"I never knew the chap. What would be my point? I've never hurt anybody, well, not off the rugby pitch. We're not the hooligans people think we are. You're barking up the wrong tree, Inspector."

"Your name was mentioned," said Dicky sweetly, "and we're bound to follow things up. Did you go out at all that day?"

He's going to look at the car, thought Robert. He nodded, "I drove to the minimart for some bread and a bottle of milk. The rest of the day was spent mostly in the bathroom."

"There's a lot of it about," sympathized Dicky. "You were a close friend of Matthew Palmer?"

Robert's allegedly delicate digestive system somersaulted painfully. "Yes, a rugby friend. I wouldn't say we were close. That was a terrible thing. Shook all of us. Why do you ask?"

"His widow, Lois, had been treating Ben French. She's a therapist, you know. She must be feeling really upset."

"I imagine so."

"Well, I won't keep you. You still look a bit groggy. If you hear anything, or think of anything that might help us, give me a buzz."

Promising that he would and surprised that the Inspector had not asked to see his car, Robert was glad he had not yet put it through the carwash, as a bright and shiny motor might have raised more suspicions than a few mud splashes. Already he had cleaned inside. He wondered, he really wondered how far he could trust Lois not to implicate him if the Inspector started putting more pressure on her. His headache and upset stomach were now quite genuine.

The call to compare notes again with Lois added to his unease as he recognised an icy edge in her voice. True enough he had got carried away with the humiliation theme, and might have gone too far. Well, obviously he did, but on whose behalf? He wasn't the one who knocked him over, after all. He had a nasty feeling that he was going to be forced into taking responsibility for something that was of no personal advantage to him. He tried to remember that phrase about hanging together, but needed to throw up again.

It said much for the characters of Ben's parents that they felt enough sympathy for old Mr. Herbison to visit him with a pair of new pyjamas, some toiletries and a bottle of Lucozade. The police mentioned that he might be prosecuted for driving without due care and attention, but they hoped not.

They believed the events leading up to the accident were too ill-defined to lay too much blame on the old man, particularly bearing in mind the inclement weather.

He was touched by their kindness and concern and when thanking them, and assuring them that he would soon be discharged from hospital, he mentioned that nobody yet had asked him whether he had noticed any vehicles driving towards him as he travelled from the British Legion club, guessing that they probably thought him too befuddled by concussion, which he was not. It was unusual to see anything on that road at night, so he had taken special note of the black Citroen Picasso, a car he rather fancied himself. Mr. French passed on this information.

After a short pause for reflection, Dicky Bird 'phoned Robert to ask him for the registration number of his car.

"A Citroen Picasso, I believe?" he asked, pleased to be able to frighten the man without having asked to see the car in question, and raising for Robert the unwelcome spectre of a witness. The Inspector thanked him and put down the 'phone.

One of many unpleasant aspects of dealing with sudden and suspicious deaths, he thought, was the embarrassment of enquiring about financial arrangements in a way that did not immediately pose the question, 'Did you kill him for his money?' an insinuation that never went down well. A difficult position had arisen for Boot, having so recently moved in with Ben, finding that the flat and all Ben's worldly goods had been left to him, all properly witnessed, signed and sealed.

Mr. and Mrs. French were grateful to be able to stay with Boot to co-operate in the many arrangements to be made. He had unhesitatingly told them he could not accept the legacy and offered them the flat and Ben's other possessions, an offer turned down immediately. Pointing out that Ben had received the flat from an aunt and that they had no need for it or the money it might raise, and that money had never been a priority of theirs, they added that they derived happiness from the fact that Ben had reciprocally loved Boot. They selected some photographs and asked whether they might have Ben's camcorder as it would be useful when they took their annual break escorting a group of underprivileged children on an adventure holiday in Wales.

When Boot, impressed, related to his mother this demonstration of their generosity, sweetness and goodness, she could not help but feel she was being compared unfavourably with their selfless lifestyle. Lexie, too, who had rushed down to offer solace was also feeling rejected. The Frenches were currently urging Boot to join them in Devon for a long period of tranquil recovery, an offer which he did finally turn down.

He agreed to deliver the eulogy at Ben's funeral. Yet another woodland burial was agreed, and the service was well-attended. It was an admirable effort in which he fashionably quoted Larkin, Auden and Dylan Thomas, but added a moving testimonial of his own, spoken in a strong, clear, unwavering voice that surprised everyone. Ben's parents especially liked, "It was not a life cut short, but a good and beautiful life completed."

There were those in the congregation who might have argued with that had the occasion been thrown open for questions, but the funeral passed without any unpleasantness.

The pathologist had declared himself certain that all of Ben's injuries were consistent with having been hit by Mr. Herbison's car, which proved a small comfort. How he came to be standing near-naked in the path of the car remained under investigation.

CHAPTER TWENTY-EIGHT

When Dickie called Trixie a few days later to invite her to Sunday lunch to be followed, weather permitting, by a nice, long walk in the country she accepted gladly. She was less happy about his follow-up statement that he was going to subject her to a long speech of significance to them both. He was, he said, at a crossroads. If this was to be, as she hoped, a marriage proposal, she was not too encouraged by his tone of uncertainty. Only a positive approach would meet with her acceptance as she felt she would prefer occasional socializing to an angst-ridden marriage.

As it happened that was not what he was fretting about. The Super had called him in to press for a reason why he had not yet made an arrest in the French case. He was aware that friends and acquaintances of his were involved and the Super asked to be assured that Dicky was maintaining impartiality. It did not take long for Dicky to admit he was experiencing some difficulty in giving that assurance, and to ask to be taken off the case. He recommended the sterling work already done by DC Shirley Pickering in advancement of the investigation. While relieved at receiving this push, disclosure of everything he alone knew was a tricky issue still to be wrestled with. In truth the case should have been cut and dried by now. He was conscious of the less than encouraging nod the Super had given him which had been accompanied by a hard, critical stare and the sensation of words as yet unspoken that might at any time crash round his ears. He was not trusted, and for very good reason.

It truly was his intention to propose to Trixie on Sunday, but she might not regard him as much of a catch, all things considered. His considerations included broad aspects of the meaning of life, and whether having joined the force all those years ago to extract the truth from villains, who were then brought to justice, the whole thing was a big, shoddy sham.

Disclosure of all he knew was a tricky issue when undeniably the case should have been solved by now. Still there was doubt in his mind as to whether it was Angela Smith or Lois Palmer who was the initial spark that led to this apparently never-ending conflagration. He had worked in less salubrious areas where a couple of dysfunctional families created decades of mayhem from petty vandalism to murder via GBH. That these Woolchester misfortunes appeared to be emanating from a sweetly-scented clinic filled with nice, benevolent people and their friends was odd, to say the least. He nurtured a hope that Lois might give notice that she was moving to the Hebrides, but knew that Trixie disliked the notion that her practitioners were abandoning ship.

He began counting the liars. Ben lied about the film and had received a terrible comeuppance. Lois had lied about the drownings. She and Boot and Trixie and Lawrence and he had covered up knowledge of the film. All liars. Almost certainly Robert Lister had seen, or been told about, the film, abducted, assaulted, and abandoned Ben to please Lois. Dicky at the time had found it suspicious that it was

Angela Smith standing behind the poor actor fellow who 'accidentally' fell to his death, and that the events that led to the death of Angela's father happened in the presence of the upright young chiropractor, Trixie's protégé, Lawrence.

He remembered a line of Robert Louis Stevenson, 'The cruellest lies are often told in silence.' Ain't that the truth, he thought.

Dicky did not believe in the theory or practice of homeopathy or that there were symbols in the chakras or that ear candling was all it claimed or that cranio-sacral therapy was a bona-fide treatment for anything at all or that kinesiology was worth diddly squat or that Lois's therapy/counselling qualification would warrant investigation. He was swimming in a sea of lies, omissions and hypocrisy and requests for faith in placebos perpetrated and perpetuated by people who were not evil, but, on the contrary, quite well-meaning, and he was adding to the tide by his reluctance to speak out because he loved one of the participants enough to ask her to marry him. If everybody suddenly started to tell the truth, half the population of Woolchester would be banged up on charges of corrupting the course of justice.

There were no guardian angels, no Father Christmas, no Easter bunny, even the tooth fairy turned out to be your mum. It had been a lie when he told Trixie she looked lovely in that purple outfit, a colour he hated; a little, white lie to oil the wheels of civilized behaviour. Where was the line to be drawn? The only person at all likely to end up in jail was the unlikeable, stupid, bullying Robert, who would deserve it but had had no personal axe to grind nd probably only wanted to get into bed with Lois, who was a lying, devious schemer, slippery as an eel and unlikely to receive justice because she could lie her way out of a chained sack.

Dicky wanted to lie down and dream his troubles away, but sleep was elusive.

'Beauty is truth: truth beauty . . .' What utter rot, he mumbled.

Of course, when in Trixie's presence much later, the long speech he had threatened shrank mercifully to something much smaller. After their pleasant lunch the weather put paid to the idea of a long, healthy country walk, to mutual relief. Keeping his disillusioned views to himself regarding reflexology and the tooth fairy, he told Trixie that he had decided to retire in the Spring and rather wondered whether she could find it in her kind heart to join him.

Pressed to clarify exactly what that proposal meant—a moving-in for him or her and on what basis? Must she retire too? Dicky was generously prepared to let Trixie make all those difficult decisions which he declared would make him happy whatever and wherever the permutations were. He would be made happiest by a proper marriage. The question of retirement was her choice alone, understanding as he did her love for Lavender House, and he knew, too, that she had to see Boot settled and receive Lexie's approval.

Trixie, controlling her excitement, but pink around her neck, nodded.

"Okay," she said slowly. "Yes, please, to the marriage proposal. I'd love to be Mrs. Dicky Bird. I don't think I can give up on Lavender House just yet. I'd like to get it back on track—just a few months without deaths or disasters so that I could decide when it's going well. In fact I am only the landlady, but as you know I'm regarded as a sort of mother hen and the chicks have been a bit troublesome lately. We can keep both flats for the time being, can't we?"

She received a warm hug along with the suggestion that they take a morning to go in search of an engagement ring, an idea that appealed to her at once.

Not altogether recovered from his philosophical meanderings, Dicky knew that at some stage there would have to be a painful discussion about how much truth to disclose. But not today.

When Trixie hesitantly broke the news to Boot who was being treated with eggshell delicacy in the wake of his bereavement, he sounded genuinely pleased and immediately offered his services as pageboy. His mother quietly believed that Boot had in fact been shocked by Ben's behaviour and that the relationship had already begun to decline before the tragedy. He was being quite brisk in disposing of Ben's goods, and installing his own from the Lavender House flat. Lexie, due to return to university, reported that he was not overwhelmed by grief, as feared, and could safely be left. She was only cautiously congratulatory about her mother's engagement, but made the suggestion of a double wedding in New Zealand in the Spring, which idea seemed popular apart from having to consider Dicky's daughter who would by then have a baby and might not wish to travel.

"Don't upset her," cautioned Trixie, forcing herself to acknowledge the responsibility of being a step-parent and soon-to-be step-grandmother. An additional celebration in England seemed the easiest solution.

When Dicky took a call from the rugby club secretary he did not immediately reveal that he was off that particular case and was busy investigating a burglary at a High Street jeweller's, but listened as the man made clear he was not the one responsible for naming names now circulating among members. They've arrived at their own conclusions and narrowed it down to Lister, he said, but nobody believes he would do such a thing. It was unfortunate that all his mates were at the dinner because they'd all tried an 'I'm Spartacus' approach to help the man until they realized the police were seriously considering him as a suspect. It was Robert himself, of course, who confided in a friend that the police were badgering him. There was no point in offering alibis that so plainly wouldn't hold water, but the secretary hoped the guilty man would soon be found so that Lister could be left in peace.

"Absolutely," said Dicky. "Actually, I'm off the case now so I can't really comment on progress, but keep your fingers crossed."

When Robert, against strict instructions, telephoned Lois at home, she was furious.

"Are you out of your mind? I suppose you're making this call in the Wig and Pen in the middle of a group of interested bystanders. How do you know we're not being bugged?"

"Now you're being paranoid. Of course we're not being bugged. There's no connection between us. I'm in the office on my own as I have been for a long time now. I'm an estate agent, remember? All I wanted to say was that we must firmly deny as often as necessary that we met at your house and that we'd better not meet up at all until all this has blown over."

"I can assure you we shan't be meeting up at all. Ever. Why should we?"

"There is the little matter of my seeing a film of Matthew bladdered and guilty as hell, but forget it. We didn't meet. We shan't meet again. I shall say I don't know you, and that's the truth."

Robert put down the receiver.

So did little Oliver, sitting on his mother's bed with a crayoning book. Usually when the 'phone rang he listened in if he was near the extension. He wasn't allowed to touch his mother's mobile, because that was for mummy's work. Sometimes it was Nana, making arrangements that he liked to know about, but mostly it was boring stuff that he didn't bother with. The gist of this last conversation had largely escaped although a couple of phrases sounded interesting. Mostly he was surprised by his mother's cross voice. One of the things he liked about her was that she always sounded gentle and kind. Also she hugged him and read to him and always smelt nice. She was very busy making money to buy his toys, so Nana looked after him mostly. He wondered who that man was but decided not to ask in case he got into trouble for listening. There was one question, though.

"What does 'bladdered' mean, Mummy?" he asked at tea-time.

Vaguely Lois recalled Robert using the word and put down her cup. "Where did you hear that? It's not very nice. It means drunk."

Oliver had inherited his mother's ability to react swiftly and to his own advantage.

"I heard it on the telly at Nana's," the little fellow lied. "I shan't say it if it's rude."

"Good boy," said Lois, "Would you like to watch a DVD before you have your bath?"

She must remember to ask a few questions about his viewing habits.

When Trixie received a letter from Elizabeth at the beginning of December she was initially surprised, then irritated by the woman's persistence. Written on impressively headed paper, there was an uncrunched offer for Lavender

House that stopped her from throwing it into the basket immediately. She was forced to sit down with Boot, Dicky and Bunty, who had become a valued, clear-headed advocate. Their reactions and opinions were sought as she explained that things were not going to plan.

Lois was hanging on apparently untroubled by her personal traumas, a credit, according to Boot, to her self-counselling.

Jason, an acknowledged treasure, reliable, capable and discreet was being encouraged by Hightown Gym to work full time for them, financially a better proposition.

Lawrence, practising hands-off chiropractic, had fewer patients and was considering teacher training college.

Lily was regarded as unlikely to be a long-term tenant as Jack had decided to leave at Christmas. Juliet would soon be gone, and Beverly was packing for her move to join Daniel in Germany.

Boot had no hesitation in suggesting widening the scope of the place if there was a dearth of the kind of therapists his mother preferred. After joking, "Here comes the Massage Parlour!" Bunty was more understanding. Having resisted attempts by Trixie to pay her for what had developed into a near full-time post on Reception, she insisted on volunteer status on the grounds that earned income would only confuse the tax man. Ten years into widowhood, she enjoyed the atmosphere and occasional dramas of Lavender House and was willing to work for nothing more than regular refreshment, especially at the end of the day when she enjoyed a vodka and tonic in the company of her old friend, Trixie. News of the engagement had taken her by surprise and she had to cover her sense of dismay at the prospect of losing their close relationship. She would not rule out staying on under new management and had to concede that Elizabeth's offer was so remarkable that it would be difficult for Trixie to resist, but she was nervous of the woman's motives, especially since she knew Jack was moving on, which eradicated a possible but puzzling revenge scenario.

They all nodded sagely. Dicky, wisely, remained quiet.

Eventually they came up with a positive maybe: Trixie should not decide until Christmas was over, by which time things might be more settled.

Boot's embryonic Callender Therapy Method was scuppered as he appreciated that he had no real wish to counsel or advise anybody. He had the book to finish and, thanks to the late Ben, some cash in the bank to see him through for a while without bothering his mama.

It was Lawrence who was of most concern to Trixie, with his loss of confidence and his fiancée he was rudderless, unsure about a career change, although he hoped Helen might be tempted back if he decided to become a teacher. Encouragement came from Lily and Jack to take the plunge, with the added inducement of colleges being full of bright young women, less critical than Helen, willing to help the few years pass quickly and pleasantly and unlikely to be deterred by his label of 'mature student,'

All of these troubling decisions were put to the back of her mind as Trixie, elegant in a new, cream coat with her nails polished to perfection for the occasion, was collected on Monday morning by her fiancé to look for a ring—nothing ostentatious she assured a relieved Dicky, and no objection to a second-hand one, a condition she said she could easily relate to.

Left in charge and feeling tearful out of love and happiness for her friend, Bunty had to gather her wits when a brief-case carrying stranger appeared at Reception. No, he said, mildly affronted, he was not a sales representative. He had heard that there might be a surgery becoming available soon, and he wondered whether he might have a word with Mrs. Callender to discuss his taking on the lease, a prospect that appealed immediately to Bunty, attracted by the small, olive-skinned, brown-eyed man, fifty-ish, white shirt, good suit, pleasant voice, nice smile, good teeth. What, as she later asked Trixie, was not to like?

She invited him to join her for coffee behind the desk, as she was on duty, explained that the owner was out on Important Business but that she could outline the financial implications for him and show him Juliet's room as soon as her client left.

His name, he said, was John Pilgrim and he was well used to being asked whether he had made progress, which he felt he had for he held a doctorate and was a Reiki Master.

The title impressed Bunty, who was aware that Reiki was listed among Beverly's long list of therapies on offer, but had not pursued its meaning and had no idea that practitioners could be sufficiently advanced to merit the title of Master, which sounded very grand. Her short enquiry elicited a long response during which she became more lost in his soulful brown eyes than in the content of his explanation.

In the space of an hour Bunty, sceptical non-participant in processes claiming to be more therapeutic than her daily vodka and tonic with Trixie, was entranced as Dr. Pilgrim talked her through the theories and practice of Kinesiology.

She supposed she should mention that a former enquiry from a Kinesiologist had come to nought because of resistance to what he considered too high a rent.

Dr. Pilgrim considered the rent to be reasonable for the facilities and the special ambience of the place, and had no intention of haggling. He revealed, as they sipped more coffee, that he was a widower with a married son living in California, from whence he himself had recently arrived, homesick for grey skies and English accents. He added that, whatever the outcome, if Mrs. Callender did not like the look or the sound of him, he hoped Bunty, if she were free, might be tempted to join him for dinner the following evening at the Wig and Pen where he was staying. He looked at her pretty, porcelain features and big, blue eyes with undisguised admiration that made her (so she later related to Trixie) come all over peculiar.

"Sounds like we're stuck with him then," smiled Trixie, back from the shopping trip and displaying a large opal and diamond ring that was examined closely and admired by Lily and Lois. Juliet felt obliged to mention that some people regarded opals as very unlucky stones but she urged Trixie not to worry too much about it.

Up in the flat, toasting her engaged friends in vodka and tonic, Bunty patiently told at considerable length how she had listened to Dr. Pilgrim explaining how Qi could be harnessed in Applied Kinesiology by Goodhart's diagnostic method using muscle testing. There was information about Prana and Universal Life Energy.

Unhelpfully Dicky, who had been listening more attentively than Trixie, chipped in with a comment about the ideomotor effect being well known. Unconscious and involuntary muscle movements can demonstrably be initiated by autosuggestion, he said.

But Bunty was already in love and insisted that she was now a believer.

"The woman's lost her senses," said Trixie kindly, "and if she wants to believe it, who are we to confuse her with the facts."

The following morning, after an amiable interview, Trixie was happy to welcome him even after hearing, in response to her query as to how he had heard in California of a vacant room in Woolchester, that there was an Elizabeth connection. Dr. Pilgrim told how they had met at a business convention in Los Angeles and heard from Elizabeth of the attractions and potential of Lavender House among many others she wished to add to her enviably expanding empire, that he confessed he would like to emulate. He had not known of the offer to buy, but was not surprised. Elizabeth was filling her life profitably, he confided, having come into vast amounts of money to invest to compensate for her husband's long absences and lack of a cosy domestic life. He had to admit that she did not seem unhappy.

"The dear man," Trixie related later to Dicky, "has signed up and wishes to take on any other rooms as soon as they become vacant. He intends to run training courses using the USUI system,—don't ask me, dear—for the National Federation of Spiritual Healers' Certificate which, if you'll believe me, is a qualification recognised by University College Hospital, London."

Blimey," said Dicky. "You have no reservations regarding receiving tainted gold?"

"None whatsoever, dear. I don't have to believe anything at all. I am merely a simple landlady."

"Oh, good," replied Dicky. "I'd hate to think that that by owning Lavender House you were associated with anything at all shady."

"Perish the thought," said Trixie, aware of, but immune to, irony.

CHAPTER TWENTY-NINE

By the autumn of 2009 **LAVENDER HOUSE** had become **PILGRIM HOUSE**, the name tastefully done in gold on black over the front door.

It was dedicated mostly to training people with enough disposable income to pay Dr. Pilgrim's exorbitant fees to be inducted into the arts and craft of Kinesiology.

Trixie still owned the building but followed her solicitor's initial advice to merely bank the money and maintain the building.

Dr. Pilgrim, (who rarely said, 'Call me John), channelled enough cosmic energy into Bunty to persuade her to become his wife. They rented the top floor and live there happily, confident that good vibrations are beamed from below.

After the double marriages in New Zealand, a joyous occasion as all agreed, Trixie moved in with Dicky, but they bought a little cottage in St. Ives as a regular retreat.

Boot's and Ben's children's book was a minor sensation, regarded as darkly significant with undertones of violence and malevolence, loved by the critics. Those who read the reviews bought the book but then hid it from their children. Currently Boot, who now understandably prefers to be known as Felix, is cautiously corresponding with Adam, an art teacher he met in New Zealand. Lexie encourages this relationship, having vetted the man and declared him wholesome.

Jason Rugg succumbed to the blandishments of Hightown Gym and the urging of his wife, and left to receive more money but to work longer hours. He regarded Dr. Pilgrim, quite irrationally, with some suspicion and was content to leave, but misses the smell of patchouli in the morning.

Soon after Lawrence was accepted for teacher training, he and Helen were reconciled. She moved into his flat and has offered to pay the mortgage and bills while he is a student. She was secretly impressed by and grateful for certain skills Lawrence had acquired during their rift, but was too polite to ask how and where and would certainly not have written a letter of appreciation to Beverly had she known.

Juliet and Simon are totally bewitched by their baby daughter, Felicity, and speak of nothing else. It is unlikely that she will practise Reflexology again unless money becomes very tight as she has achieved her destiny of becoming a Full Time Mother.

The biggest and sweetest surprise, and the event that it is claimed has so far kept Charlie in remission, was the birth of his twin grandsons in July. Charles Ho Kent and Louis Ho Kent are surrounded by love and the attention of many kind people. Lily has also surrendered to full-time motherhood and wants to extend her mother's experimental herb garden when the twins are a little older. Jack has adapted to earning a high salary for doing nothing very much, and is learning Mandarin.

Lois is hanging on in there as a counsellor/therapist, many of her clients being the Reiki students. Robert Lister moved to Spain where he is said to have opened a bar, address unknown. He and Lois never spoke again.

There are a few people who were associated with Lavender House and have inside knowledge, who believe that Lois is a reincarnation of Angela Smith, an impression reinforced by the physical likeness that sometimes gives people a start when they see her out of the corner of their eyes. Unfortunately this perpetuates a suspicion of a malevolent or, at best, mischievous spirit about the place that no amount of therapeutic practice will overcome, and only the removal of Lois Palmer will cure.

But, then, as Trixie says, some people will believe anything.